LETHAL MEDICINE

Tennant squinted unhappily. “Pathology indicates that large amounts of a heart drug called Lanoxin have been found mixed with sugar, yogurt, and instant coffee samples from the victim’s apartment. His only prescription was for something called Rythmol. How the Lanoxin got in his food is at issue now.”

“I don’t get it. So what are you saying?”

The detectives grunted, their eyebrows rising. “Ms. Morelli,” said Tennant, “the scenario we’re working with is that someone introduced high dosages of powdered Lanoxin into the gentleman’s food over an extended period of time. Our problem right now is that you and Ms. Woo have just engaged in highly suspect activity by gaining illegal access to the property of someone we consider a murder victim.”

“Someone put Lanoxin in his food to poison him?”

“Yes, ma’am, that’d be right. To poison him.”

Other Professor Teodora Morelli Mysteries by
Linda French
from Avon Twilight

TALKING RAIN
COFFEE TO DIE FOR

Steeped in Murder

A PROFESSOR TEODORA MORELLI MYSTERY

LINDA FRENCH

This is a work of fiction. Names, characters, places, and incidents either are the product of the author's imagination or are used fictitiously. Any resemblance to actual events, locales, organizations, or persons, living or dead, is entirely coincidental and beyond the intent of either the author or the publisher.

AVON BOOKS, INC.
1350 Avenue of the Americas
New York, New York 10019

Map by Tim Hollenbeck
Inside cover author photo by Don Anderson
Published by arrangement with the author
Library of Congress Catalog Card Number: 99-94466
ISBN: 0-380-79576-0
www.avonbooks.com/twilight

First Avon Twilight Printing: December 1999

Printed in the U.S.A.

WCD 10 9 8 7 6 5 4 3 2 1

To the history department
and to
Etta Egeland of San Juan Island, Washington

I have realized as I grow older that history, in the end, has more imagination than oneself.

Gabriel Garcia Márquez, *The New York Times*, 1991

NORTHWEST PUGET SOUND

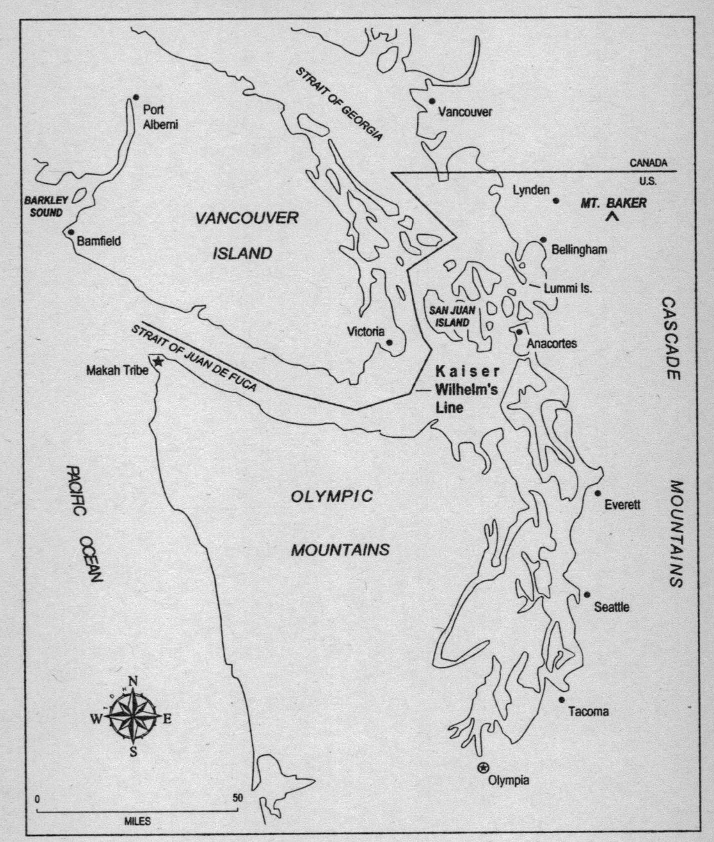

1

Teddy Morelli extended her hand, waiting for the worst. Junior faculty—untenured junior faculty—did not get invited to fund-raisers for heavy hitters without a reason.

Beside her stood Rainwater State University president Walter Rhodes—The Roadster, but not to his face. He turned to the two gleaming Californians across from Teddy and beamed. "Herb and Sally, I'd like you to meet Professor Teodora Morelli of our history department. Teodora is our Pacific Northwest specialist. And Dr. Morelli"—he cleared his throat—"I almost feel like I'm making history here. I'm very privileged to introduce my dear friends Herb and Sally Patchett."

"Sally *Pickett*-Patchett," corrected Sally.

"Sally *Pickett*-Patchett," he repeated, touching the small of her back. "Which is, of course, why we're out here this lovely Sunday evening." Rhodes gestured across the boat deck to the shimmering orange sea, the outsized snowy mountain chalked on purple sky. "We thought Sally needed to get out on the water and see things the way her ancestor did back then. Got around by boat, didn't they, Professor Morelli?"

So there it was: Teddy's job for the evening. She sighed with relief. All that would be required was a cozy chat in the saloon, telling this well-coiffed brunette,

Daughter of the Pioneers, how courageously her nineteenth century ancestors had fished out all the salmon, cut down all the trees.

Teddy nabbed a goat cheese canapé from a passing student waiter and turned back to Sally, smiling her company best. "Did your ancestors live out here in the islands or back in Bellingham?"

Sally frowned, somehow offended by the question. Instantly President Rhodes picked up the ball. "Oh, you didn't catch that, did you, Professor Morelli?" He moved in close for effect. "What do you know about . . . General George E. Pickett?"

"Well, my goodness." Teddy nodded deferentially to Sally. That Pickett. The Southern general who led the most disastrous charge in American history. The man who lost the Civil War. "Then you must be out here learning about his early service on the frontier."

Sally bowed her head modestly. "Actually, we know quite a bit about it already. My great-great-grandmother wrote some articles for *McClure's Magazine* in 1908. We have them in an album." Sally's succulent Virginia-ese was rich enough to anchor television news back in Richmond. The Pickett-Patchetts' spiffy new nautical togs were the only thing from California, it appeared.

"*McClure's*." Teddy nodded. The 1908 articles by Pickett's widow had almost single-handedly created the myth of the heroic and doomed Confederacy—the Southern version of the war still in use today. "Well," Teddy said, "you mustn't be too hard on old George Pickett. He hasn't exactly been given the best press." Not to mention he was a borderline incompetent.

"Oh, I know better than to listen to all that." Sally's *ts* were tipped with treacle. "In fact, the man who wrote *Pickett's Charge* thinks that Grandpa George was the greatest man in American history."

"Well." Teddy bobbled her head, as if truly considering the thought. "I don't kn—"

"He says, right off the bat, since the Civil War was

the greatest event in American history and Gettysburg was the climax of the war *and*"—she took a breath—"Pickett's Charge was the climax of Gettysburg, Grandpa George is the most important man in American history."

Teddy kept nodding. "Interesting."

Handsome, blond Herb Patchett slipped an arm around his wife. "Don't get old Sal all stoked up about George Pickett. She can be a real fireball."

Teddy glanced up at the sun-kissed Californian. Herb Patchett had the most amazing head of hair for a middle-aged man she had ever seen. Still blond as a beach boy's, the hair was wavy and gorgeous, gleaming with champagne highlights in the sunset. Herb had important hair, executive hair. No wonder tall, lanky President Rhodes was keeping his balding pate under a driving cap.

"Well," asked Teddy, "when we motored around San Juan Island, could you see any of Pickett's Camp from water level?"

"No." Sally pouted.

President Rhodes sniffed. "Actually we were searching for you to help flesh out the story. Excuse me. I'm going to close that door."

They watched as he strode over to the saloon sliding door and got caught up with the mountain-climbing crowd, a new group of donors Rhodes was cultivating from his own contacts.

Realizing he'd be a while, Teddy said, "Sorry I wasn't around to help. I've been up in the observation lounge, and my department chairman just now told me to come down and introduce myself." With the door closed, the saloon immediately became stuffy. Teddy unzipped her red canvas jacket. "But don't worry. There're plenty of Pickett sites back in Bellingham. And with your credentials, you can probably even get the women who run the Pickett House to give you a private tour. Have you been to the house yet?" She stuffed her watch cap in her pocket. "It's where Pickett and his Indian wife lived before he went out to the islands. In fact, little Jimmie Pickett was born in the Pickett House."

"Who?" Sally's face blanched.

"Jimmie Pickett. He was Pickett's son by his Indian wife."

Herb Patchett choked on his ice. Sally's skin turned the color of low-fat milk.

"No," Sally said flatly. "Grandpa George never, ever had an Indian wife. That half-breed boy that lived with him was the son of a great chief. The chief *gave* Grandpa that boy because he had so much respect for him. I can show you in Grandma Sally's *McClure's* articles."

Teddy kept her mouth firmly shut.

"Well." President Rhodes rejoined the group. Someone had playfully turned his driving cap backward. "I'm so glad you two are hitting it off. " He raised an eyebrow to Sally. "Have you sprung it on her yet?"

Teddy looked from face to face. "Sprung what?"

Sally Pickett-Patchett looked askance at Rhodes. "You ask her. It's too complicated."

President Rhodes scowled through the saloon windows at bottle green Lummi Island gathering secrets in the dusk. "I can't ask her," he said. "She'll feel compelled."

"Oh, that's right. You're like her boss, aren't you?"

Stiffness swept up Teddy's back. She waited, fighting panic. Everyone smiled awkwardly, and Sally finally began. "Well, you see, we were hoping you could help explain something for us."

"Sure."

"Good. Because it seems fashionable these days to psychoanalyze George Pickett and say how stupid he was and how weak. But he wasn't stupid, he knew languages—you can see that in his papers. Now, I know I can't do anything about the people who are trying to make their reputations by trashing him for Gettysburg, but I also know that in both the Mexican War and out here he distinguished himself totally. Great-great-grandma Sally Pickett says tha—"

"You're calling her Sally . . ."

"La*Salle* Pickett, Sally for short—I'm named after her. Anyway, Grandma Sally says in *McClure's* that out here in Washington Territory, Grandpa George held off forty thousand Indians during the Indian Wars, then turned around and single-handedly kept peace with the British when *some* people wanted to go to war over these islands. Now, I think that's important, don't you?"

Rather muddled, but not too terribly. "Well, that's a little inflated about the Indian threat, but George Pickett was certainly a big player in the Pig War with the British. We love the Pig War out here, maybe the most charming war in American history."

"It's about a pig, isn't it?"

Teddy blinked. "Yes."

"Did both sides want it?"

"No, actually what happened was that both American and Hudson's Bay settlers were living on San Juan Island—its ownership was in dispute—and an English pig from the Hudson's Bay farm was shot while routing in an American potato patch. Hudson's Bay demanded a hundred dollars in compensation, the American farmer wouldn't pay, so gunboats were called in on both sides. Happily, cooler heads prevailed, and everyone decided they should set up both English and American military camps until it was determined who the islands belonged to. War is hell. Twelve years of parties, dances, horse races."

"How did they finally decide?"

"They asked Kaiser Wilhelm of Germany to be arbitrator. He assigned the San Juan Islands to America in 1873."

Sally made a sweeping motion with her hand. "Are they all called the San Juan Islands, together?"

"Yes."

"And the biggest one is also called San Juan Island?"

"Confusing, isn't it?"

"Oh, I understand. And I think the whole thing is absolutely fascinating. About the Pig War and all."

Teddy nodded in agreement. "It's one of my favorite episodes."

"Good. Good. Then that'll make it easy. What we'd like for you to do is write a book about it, if you don't mind. It won't be that hard. Grandpa George's letters from Camp Pickett are all in the National Archives."

Teddy poured Perrier down her chin.

"I can help research, if you like," said Sally. "We'll certainly pay your expenses."

Teddy turned to President Rhodes, eyes desperate. Rhodes, in turn, rattled his empty glass. "Excuse me, I need to freshen my drink."

Ex-beachboy Herb Patchett leaned toward Teddy. His rippling locks caught the light, gleaming like fresh beer. "Sal's cousin is editor of the *Chesterfield County Historical Review* in Richmond. He can help you get published."

Finally Teddy found her voice. "I'm sorry, I already have a writing project, and some contract work—with Indian burial caves." She looked back and forth between the Pickett-Patchetts. "The caves are really interesting. We're trying to date the burials from the age of the trade goods inside."

The Pickett-Patchetts feigned interest.

"It's really quite intriguing, you know. Some caves were used over and over again."

The Pickett-Patchetts admired the approaching harbor lights.

"Good evening, passengers. This is your skipper, Nels Christensen. I'd like to thank you for cruising with us this evening on the *Island Dream*. We'll be back in port in approximately fifteen minutes, at which time we will disembark from the starboard side—which is the right side of the boat as you face forward. Please check the lounges for your belongings, and we hope you'll join us again on Puget Sound Charters."

Passengers began streaming down the steep stairs from the upper decks. President Rhodes rushed off to look for the fund-raising director to see if he was actually finished hustling money for the evening. Down the stairs came tubby, gray Ira Dedmarsh, chairman of the history department.

"We'll be in touch," said Sally Pickett-Patchett. She put out her hand. "Maybe you can even go with us to the island this weekend. I'd love to take an in-depth tour."

"I don't . . . mayb—" Teddy exhaled. "Good night."

"Good night."

Herb Patchett popped a final canapé in his mouth, licked his fingers, and shook her hand. "I want you to know we really appreciate this."

"Yes."

The Pickett-Patchetts walked over to the monied side of the room, where donors to the Umbrella Club were being plied with bottles of thirty-year-old Portuguese sherry (faculty needn't apply). Beside her Dr. Dedmarsh plucked a miniature blue corn quiche off a passing platter and tossed it into his mouth.

"Everything tastes so good out here on the water. I haven't enjoyed food this much in months."

"Dr. Dedmarsh . . ."

"Oh, Teddy, I forgot." He unzipped his jacket, relaxed and happy from his time in the wind. "I turned in your request for bookshelves, slipped it into next trimester's maintenance."

She was supposed to say thank you. "Dr. Dedmarsh! Those people you told me to meet . . ."

The wry lines at Dr. Dedmarsh's gray eyes smiled in the kindest way. "Teddy?" Even in boating togs, Dr. Dedmarsh looked worn-out and bookish, shabby as a blackboard eraser. Ira Dedmarsh was the kind of person who, when he talked of his boyhood on the blighted

Montana potato farm, made you feel the yearning of a book-fed child for the genteel life.

Without touching him, she urged him across the room—still separated from the Pickett-Patchetts by a dense wall of bodies. "Dr. Dedmarsh, they want me to write a book!"

"No, no, an article." He furrowed his brow. "All President Rhodes said was an article."

"You didn't—" She turned, mastering her anger; she had no business talking to him like that.

"Oh, Teddy, I've done something wrong, haven't I?" His wispy gray hair stood straight up from being under his hat. "I'm so sorry. When I talked to Walter Rhodes, all he asked was if his guests could meet with our Northwest historian. He indicated they might have a lead for a possible article."

Across the saloon the donors were being cordoned off with a blue velvet rope. The Pickett-Patchetts were handed fish forks and something in oyster shells. Bow-tied student waiters poured cognac into snifters and moved with trays through the crowd.

"Dr. Dedmarsh, I can't do it. I'm already working on something else. And besides, those people want me to eulogize George Pickett."

"I'm not quite familiar. . . ." Dedmarsh raised his woolly eyebrows. They vaulted in the center like cumulonimbus.

"George Pickett was this C-minus-type military commander who was stationed out on San Juan Island. He fought with his superiors, had a terrible time with desertions, and was totally, maddeningly, passive. This is his great-great-granddaughter, and she wants me to write a book about him."

"I see."

"Can I just tell them I'm too busy?"

"Of course, certainly," said Dedmarsh. "No one could ever force you to research something you weren't committed to. Although let me check about the Pickett

Scholars Program before you tell them no."

"The what?"

"I believe that's what they're calling it—3.4 million dollars was the figure I heard."

Teddy's eyes turned to portholes. "You mean . . . they'll donate money if I write a book?"

"No, no, no, Teddy, never think of it like that. It would never be *quid pro quo*."

The boat cut an artful turn around the granite riprap of the inner harbor, and instantly the wind died. The donors were being urged to sample giant walnuts baked in rosemary, Macedonian olives pickled in wine.

"Dr. Dedmarsh." She faced him squarely. "I can't do this—ever. It would look like a hack job on my tenure file!"

"Teddy! A job like this could never affect your bid for tenure." Dedmarsh straightened his back. "I wouldn't let that happen."

"Thank you." She exhaled. His pencil-gray eyes were the exact color of her fourth-grade hamster. His pasty skin was nearly the same shade—he really needed to get out more. Teddy smiled. "I think I could politely explain to the Patchetts why I can't do it. But what do I say to President Rhodes?"

"No, dear. Don't talk to anyone yet. I'm sure the Pickett Scholars thing is in a tender stage of negotiation. Let me chat with Rhodes in the morning." He prodded gently, "And you're sure there's nothing you could do on George Pickett? He's not worth an article, a mention . . . ?"

"Anything I could write honestly would not make Mrs. Patchett happy."

He nodded. "I'll talk to Rhodes."

"Thank you, Dr. Dedmarsh."

"My fault in the first place. I should have inquired a bit more aggressively about what they wanted a Northwest historian for."

"I appreciate your bailing me out, sir."

"My fault in the first place."

The marina parking lot was in view, and he dipped into his pocket for his car keys. "Do you need a ride home?"

"No, thank you, I have my car." Teddy smiled. "I have to drop by the office and pick up my grade book. I want to get the midterms back tomorrow morning, while I still have their attention."

"Well, don't work too late tonight, Professor." He kissed the last word with irony.

They watched the skipper graze the dock with his bumpers and the deckhands wrap shorelines. Passengers off-loaded onto the floating concrete pads, and Teddy made her goodbyes, dashing up the aluminum ramp to the marina parking lot.

Hopping into her little beige station wagon, she rolled through town along the waterfront. The late April evening had almost settled in for the night—pink turning to violet—and the snow-covered mass of Mount Baker was gray, ready to shut down the show.

"Komo Kulshan," she said out loud—reputedly the mountain's Lummi Indian name. The Great White Watcher is what it meant, and it was as good a way as any to think of the somber, snow-covered peak looming behind the foothills.

Pulling into the faculty lot, she trotted up the stairs to the history department. The hallway was as quiet as the Capuchin catacombs. Teddy unlocked her office door—and walked in, astonished.

A crate nine feet tall stood in the center of the tiny room. *Espedito* was stenciled in several places.

"Expedite?" she asked the air.

No one answered.

2

Teddy climbed up on her desk to examine the crate. It was from Italy—Ortisei—and was addressed to Ira Dedmarsh's wife, Irene, care of the history department. But what was it doing in her office?

Her nostrils flared at the scent of mothballs and footsteps sounded in the hall. She waited.

"Good evening, Teddy."

"Nigel, what are you doing here on Sunday night?"

Tiny Nigel Czerny peeled his reading glasses off his high, shining forehead and struck an artful pose in the doorway. It was Nigel's tweeds that stank of mothballs. No one had the heart to tell him. "My neighbor started her hedge trimmer at noon, so I came here to get some peace." He gestured to the crate. "I see you've found your statue."

Teddy hopped off her desk and tried to peek through the slats. "Is that what it is?"

"Our Lady of Guadalupe, I'm told."

"What's she doing in *my* office?"

"Quiet, dear, people are working. Simply: when she arrived Friday afternoon, there was no place else to put her. The deliverymen wanted to drop it in the center of Reception, but the typists screamed bloody murder. Then someone remembered all the room in here"—he waved his arms at the pocked plaster where her bookshelves should have been—"so Esther gave them a key, and they rolled it in. Although it's quite a tight fit, isn't it?"

"Nigel, this was your idea."

He shrugged. "I think you're being short-sighted, dear. Look at it as fate. Old man Patterson rips out the bookshelves so he can sleep in his Barcalounger, which allows you, in turn, a personal visitation from the Virgin Mary."

"Nigel, I hate you."

"No, you don't. You have a deep, unrecognized affection for me that you'll realize late in life."

"When are they taking this out?"

Voluptuously Nigel ran his finger across the spines of her Oxford history series. "Relax. Irene Dedmarsh knows it's here. I'm sure she's made arrangements. And speaking of takeout, I'm just about to go for sushi. Want to join me?"

"Can't." She held between them her black leatherette grade book, the single most important document in her working life. "Got to go home and finish my midterms."

"We can go after."

She met his gaze directly. " 'After,' I'm going to bed. I've been out on the water all afternoon. I'm exhausted."

Angrily Nigel worked his jaw, then pivoted, calling back over his shoulder. "Clever of you to say no. I was going to make you pay for your own food."

"Oh, Nigel." She slithered around the statue and went home to work.

Next morning at 8:54 the crate was still there. Ignoring the Virgin, Teddy hung her coat on the door hook, pulled her notes from her book satchel, and bounded down the stairs to the classrooms.

At 9:01 she distributed the corrected midterms, taking time to offer hope and suggestions, then opened her Pacific Northwest lecture by asking how many students from Everett had heard of the 1916 Everett Massacre.

One shy girl raised her hand and said, "I know something really bad happened, but nobody will ever say what it was." And with that provocative introduction, Teddy held them captive for the rest of the fifty-minute hour with the story of why—to this day—Seattle holds the town of Everett in such contempt: how the Everett sawmill workers were beaten savagely for trying to lobby for higher wages, how the Sunday boatload of Seattle labor activists steamed into the Everett dock to help and were met by an alcohol-fueled posse led by the sheriff.

"Turn back," called the sheriff from the dock.

"We won't!" came the cry from the boat.

A shot was fired—either from the dock or boat, then many shots. When it was all over, seven were dead, fifty wounded, and several Seattle activists tried and convicted. She spared them no details, telling how the simple-minded sheriff was taking his orders from the Everett gentry and how the whole pathetic conflagration was fueled by alcohol, rhetoric, and fear. As they soberly left the classroom, Teddy sighed in relief: Wednesday's dreary lecture on labor ideology would now be a piece of cake.

At 9:54 she dashed across the hall to another classroom and chalked an outline for Utopianism I: Thomas More, moving quickly through Fourier in France, across the Atlantic to Edward Bellamy, and ending, at 10:48, with the suggestion that they ride their bicycles out to the ruins of Equality Colony, south of town.

Brain-dead, she trudged upstairs to find an outsized navy backpack propped next to her office door. It was not a student daypack at all; it was worn, gadgeted, and strapped to an aluminum frame the size of a stepladder. The pack had seen some hard outdoor use, and whoever owned it was probably living out of it. Teddy stepped around the pack and fished in her pocket for keys.

Out from the stairwell popped a vigorous, wild-haired

old man carrying a latte. He was weathered and keen-eyed, wearing a battered Aussie hat and high-laced hiking boots. The thick skin of his cheeks was as shiny as red crockery.

"Teodora! You're here!"

"Uncle Aldo?"

Aldo was her deceased father's older brother, who had dropped out of eighth grade to help his widowed mother raise the younger siblings. And between Uncle Aldo in the shipyards, and Nonna in her bakery, they had succeeded famously. The two younger boys managed to finish high school, join the navy, then attend University of Washington in engineering. Their baby sister Emilia, the star of the family, started out in church choirs, won a performance scholarship in voice, and went on to an opera career in Stuttgart and Munich. Emilia was now retired to a town outside London with her English husband.

So now it was Aldo's turn. After his beloved Beatrice had died six years ago of cancer, Aldo announced his project of walking the entire length of Puget Sound—from Olympia to the Canadian border—with the intention of giving up smoking. When he was finished walking, he said, he would no longer crave nicotine.

The trek went famously at first. Aldo was fed, fussed over, and interviewed by every suburban newspaper whose turf he tramped through. But then he got to the big city of Seattle and things began to bog down. Cosmopolitan Seattleites cared not one whit that a crazy man was trekking their shoreline. And finally, when he got up to Everett, the old fraud was exposed for what he was. The *Everett Herald* caught Aldo hitching rides with railroad repair crews, avoiding whole peninsulas altogether. Chastened by the exposure, Aldo vowed to play straight for the rest of the journey. Last thing Teddy had heard he was sleeping on the beaches near Marysville, stymied by the problem of how to cross the marshes of the Stillaguamish Slough.

"Uncle Aldo." She kissed his cheek. "I though you were lost in the Slough."

Aldo beamed. "No, Teodora, my invention! They haven't sent my patent yet. I invented the first overall waders glued to an inner tube. Teodora," he whispered, "*I walked on water.*"

"Jesus waders."

"Hush, Teodora."

"Well, Aldo, that's wonderful. And you only have about thirty more miles, don't you?" She unlocked her door and opened it onto the nine-foot crate.

"Teodora!" Aldo leaped back. "What's that?"

"Our Lady of Guadalupe, I'm told."

He nodded knowingly. "I hear she's good. I use Our Lady of Lourdes, though. She was excellent with my new false teeth."

"Come inside, Aldo. There's a bit of room in the corner."

Aldo clutched his latte. "No, no, I can't stay. I'm just waiting for my tent to dry. I have to get back to the arboretum before anybody finds it."

"You slept in the arboretum? Why didn't you come to my house?"

"Teodora, I don't sleep inside anymore, not in places with electricity. I only came by to tell you about my other new discovery. You're the professor, you'll know what to do with it."

"What discovery?"

Aldo smiled cryptically. "Well, that's what they all want to know, isn't it? The secret of the whole Pacific Northwest—the answer to the mud slides on Chuckanut Drive, the Spanish fort south of town."

"The what?"

"Shhh. Not so loud." He peeked down the hall. "But I don't really want to talk about it until after I pick up my photographs. They're getting developed now. I just came by to tell you I'm here"—he backed away to the staircase—"and that I'll catch up with you later. After I do my errands."

"Wait! Where will I find you?"

"Don't worry. I'll find you." He raised one arm in goodbye and disappeared down the stairs.

Exhaling deeply, Teddy dropped her keys on the desk and wandered down the hall to ask about the statue. In the head secretary's office she found Esther Erickson simultaneously talking on the phone, directing a work-study student, and closing a file drawer with her hip. Teddy leaned against the doorjamb, waiting.

Esther plunked down the receiver. "Morelli, your statue."

"It's not my statue."

"Exactly." Esther Erickson was a very tall, fifty-nine-year-old spinster—if that's what you called a Norwegian woman who wouldn't marry her boyfriend of fourteen years because he was a Swede. Actually, it was Esther's father who couldn't abide the Swedes. Sweden had laid down and played dead for Hitler in World War II, leaving Norway to take the brunt of the German wrath. But everyone in both Lutheran congregations agreed that Esther and Ole would probably marry after Old Man Erickson croaked, which didn't look to be any time soon.

"What did Irene Dedmarsh say?" asked Teddy.

"I don't know. I just left her a message Friday." Esther kept her hands moving.

Teddy gestured next door to Dr. Dedmarsh's closed office door. "Should I ask him?"

"No! Irene's the one who'll make arrangements."

"He's late today," said Teddy.

Esther's steel-blue eyes peered over her glasses. "We'll just have to straighten him out when he comes in, won't we?"

Teddy wandered back down the hall and slithered past the statue to her desk. Punching in the Dedmarsh's home number, she waited.

"Hello, this is Irene Dedmarsh." She sounded as if she hated the sound of her own name.

"Mrs. Dedmarsh? I don't mean to bother you, but this is Teddy Morelli in the history department . . . you might not remember me."

"Of course, dear." Irene relaxed. "You're the cute little brunette."

"Thank you." Teddy straightened her back, pretending that she had not heard the words "cute" and "little." "Mrs. Dedmarsh, I'm calling to find out when you think Our Lady of Guadalupe might be taken out of my office."

"Your office? You poor dear! I'm sorry, I thought they put it in the storeroom."

"Oh, so that's what happened. There's a dead Xerox machine in the middle of the storeroom. They couldn't fit it in there."

"Teddy, dear, I want to take care of this, really, but I can't talk now. I'm just about to walk out of the door for my volunteer work," said Irene. "And my problem is that Ira has our truck."

Teddy urged, "Well, if Dr. Dedmarsh has your truck, maybe I can get him to haul it home this afternoon."

Irene paused. "Then I guess you haven't heard. Ira and I are divorcing. We've been separated for the last two months. He's living in town."

Like a falling redwood, it hit her on the head. "I'm so sorry, I had no idea."

"Thank you, dear, but don't worry. Other than the financial side, it actually feels good."

"It's always sad to hear th—"

"Yes, exactly. And I'll see what I can do about getting someone to pick up the statue. May I call you back?"

"Certainly, no hurry." Liar. "Thank you, Mrs. Dedmarsh." Teddy hung up the phone and slithered out past the statue, ambling down the hall with her new secret. She tucked her hands in her pockets and slouched in

Esther's doorway, watching the secretary work. "Mrs. Dedmarsh told me about the divorce."

Esther considered. "Happens."

"Is *he* coming in today?" Teddy nodded to Dr. Dedmarsh's still-closed door.

Esther looked up, a sturdy giant suddenly vulnerable. "I've called twice. He's not answering the phone." Behind her glasses her eyes were as fragile as robins' eggs.

"Esther, do you think something's wrong?"

Brightly she said, "Probably not. But he's been complaining about his medication. He went to see the doctor Friday."

"I didn't know he was on medication. He looked fine last night." No, he didn't, he looked awful, now that she thought about it.

"Heart attacks," said Esther. "Run in the family."

Teddy pulled her hands from her pockets. "Do you think somebody should go check on him. Mrs. Dedmarsh said he's living in town—"

"Absolutely not," Esther interrupted. "He doesn't want anybody to know where he lives."

"Where *does* he live?"

"The BOBs."

"The BOBs?"

The BOBs was a terrible dive: 808 High Street, BOB being the student rendering of the giant numbers painted on the side. The BOBs was one of those stucco apartment buildings from the forties that sprouted like mushrooms around older college campuses. The BOBs was known for its odd cooking smells, peeling plaster, and dead couches on the curb every June.

Esther shrugged. "He had to get something fast. He wanted to be in walking distance."

Teddy glanced at her watch. "Look, I don't have anything else until committee at two o'clock. Why don't I trot on down there with some soup. I've done this kind of thing before with my mother through church. I won't even notice how things look."

"Yes, you will, I promise."

Teddy went back to her office and pocketed her keys and wallet. Bounding down the stairs, she dashed over to the student union and bought a Styrofoam beaker of lentil soup at the vegan snack bar. She wandered down the hill to the student ghetto, descending mossy stairs hidden in right-of-ways and crossing playfields that even at this hour were filled with Frisbee players and their dogs. From the safety of the sidewalk she examined the notorious Skunkworks, where parties were raided every weekend, then crossed the street to brush her fingertips on the rough stucco of beloved old First Pres Church with its storybook stained glass and homey old-growth woodwork.

Across the alley at the BOBs, she stepped around an overturned dinette chair in the middle of the sidewalk. On the grass was a dead Econ book that had flown down from the second floor. She entered the foyer, letting her eyes adjust to the light; the place smelled like cigarettes from the 1960s. Down a half-flight of stairs was a wall of cheap aluminum mailboxes. Teddy went down and squinted at the boxes in the dim light. "Dedmarsh" was written on masking tape on number 107.

Climbing two half-flights to the first floor, she found 107 at the end, directly across the hall from a fanatical Christian who had papered the walls around his door with loony messages of apocalypse and human flight.

BOEING=DEATH:
Even now there are many ANTICHRISTS,
whereby we know it is the last time.
1 John ii 18

She leaned her head against the door of 107 and heard a droning inside, an alarm. She banged on the door. "Dr. Dedmarsh? Hello?" She banged again. No answer. Dashing across the hall, she banged on the Christian's door. "Hello? Is anybody home?"

BOEING=ANTICHRIST:
Simon Magus, first ANTICHRIST,
met death in his proud attempt to fly.
(Pusey, *Min. Proph.*, 1860)

With growing fear, she dashed down the hall and took the stairs two at a time. In the half-basement was a swinging sign: *Manager.* The office door was open, but no one was inside. To the left a doorway was hung with strings of blue plastic beads. A TV set blared beyond. Teddy knocked on the door, peering through the hanging beads into a living room decorated with bizarre metal weapons. In the corner a female store mannequin wore a complete set of antique Japanese armor—incredible stuff. Two fat men sat at the dinette table polishing brand-new Nazi-style helmets.

"Yeah?"

Teddy stepped past the beads. "I think something's wrong at Dr. Dedmarsh's." Her eyes rested on a pair of ornately tooled brass knuckles with vicious protrusions on the knuckle rings. And the men weren't cleaning the helmets; they were applying black shoe polish.

"Sorry, no can do." The heavier of the two men stared Teddy straight in the eye. "I can't even open the door unless something's wrong. City ordinance." The man wore a peroxided buzz cut. On his forearm was tattooed a blurry blue Chinese dragon, "Scotto" written underneath. Ash from his cigarette fell on the table, and he brushed it to the tiled floor.

"I just told you," she said. "I think something *is* wrong."

Scotto kept rubbing the helmet a few more seconds, then put down his rag and helmet slowly, just to indicate that he could not be swayed by amateurs. Grunting like a weightlifter, he lifted himself off the chair and ambled out into the office. He squatted in front of the open safe and pulled out a pegboard from the top shelf, unhooking a key.

"Please hurry."

Meticulously he fitted the pegboard back into the safe and slammed the door, making a great show of locking it. Teddy glanced at him a moment, then dashed out to the hall so he could keep his stupid little secret: the safe door was broken. She scurried toward the stairs, and Scotto called, "No, this way," walking to the rear of the building. He led her to a fire exit and up a narrow flight of steps. Several times he leaned over to pick up trash, mooning her with his huge posterior. Each time she had to step back and look away, chastised for her urgency.

At apartment 107 Scotto cocked his ear to the drone inside. "Umm." He knocked. "Dedmarsh?" He waited. "Dedmarsh?"

Unlocking the door, he blocked her path with his bulk. "You can't come in. City ordinance." He slipped inside, shutting the door in her face. In a moment she opened it and poked her nose in. "Is he okay?"

The living room was furnished with saggy brown couches. Freshly slapped on the walls—still smelling of paint resins—was the most appalling shade of taxicab yellow. On a rickety end table stood the only graceful thing in the room, an elaborately carved tea caddy with dozens of little drawers. Dedmarsh was a China scholar—an old China hand, as he put it; he must have bought the tea chest in Taiwan on one of his research trips.

"Is he okay?" Teddy called.

She stepped into the living room just as Scotto came from the back. Bad news was written on his face. "Better not go in there." He reached for the phone.

Teddy ran to the bedroom: empty, the bed unmade. She dashed to the bathroom and stopped in the doorway. She gasped for air. Dr. Dedmarsh lay on the floor, naked as a beached whale. He was wedged on his side between the toilet and the bathtub, his face hidden by the toilet bowl. She hadn't realized he had so much flesh.

She peeked over the toilet to see his face. His eyes

were open—pale gray rings around wide black pupils. Then she saw he wasn't naked at all. He had on jockey shorts, a dingy gray color from being washed with dark clothes. Vomit was in the toilet, congealed like scrambled eggs.

It was wrong to be here.

3

"Miss?"

Teddy turned, staring gravely at the dragon on Scotto's forearm. "It runs in the family," she said. "Heart attacks."

"He's dead." Scotto urged her out of the room.

Wandering into the bedroom, she looked at Dr. Dedmarsh's dingy sheets. All he had for blankets was a stiff, new electric one. She unplugged it and dragged it into the bathroom, covering him as best she could. Then she went back and perched on the bed.

Alertly, she sat with her hands in her lap; Scotto was nowhere to be seen. Here it was Monday morning, and she was keeping vigil over Dr. Dedmarsh's body. How had this happened?

In a few minutes a large truck roared out on the street. She leaped up to peek out the window. It was a fire engine; a medic van followed. Neither had its siren running. Soon there was clatter in the hallway and fuzzy radio static from the portables. A fully turned-out fireman poked his head through the bedroom doorway. His rubberized jacket was the same tawny canvas as the Morelli children's pup tent.

"He's in the bathroom," Teddy said. The fireman nodded and disappeared, taking with him his personal cloud of static. Three medics came in; she pointed them to the bathroom and listened to their murmur through the door. Then they popped their heads back through the doorway.

"Are you a relative?" one asked.

"A friend." She watched their discreetly smirking eyes wonder how the fat gray man could have a "friend" like her. She hated them all. She ran to the corner and waited.

A policeman came and took her name, asking delicate questions about the exact relationship between Dr. and Mrs. Dedmarsh. After a while he walked away to commune with his portable.

A gurney came in from the hallway, Scotto tugging urgently, to get this mess out of his building. But for some reason, no one wanted to move the body. She gave out phone numbers for everybody—the history department, Mrs. Dedmarsh—and even had to explain that she herself would be reachable over the weekend only via cell phone at the remote Indian burial caves off the coast of Vancouver Island.

Things finally began to move. The gurney clattered in the bathroom, and Teddy peeked in just as they were dragging Dr. Dedmarsh's corpse onto the flattened bed. Someone looked up. "It's okay if you leave now." Which meant that she should go.

Without a word, Teddy bolted down the stairs and out the door. When finally aware of her surroundings again, she was up on campus, sweaty and panting; it was the end of lunch hour. She wove through throngs around the espresso stands and past the violin student with his hopeful open case. Scurrying over to Humanities, she bounded up the stairs.

A caucus of historians was in the hall. They fell silent, staring as she approached. Almost in unison, they slipped their hands in their tweed pockets, waiting.

Teddy walked up slowly, tucking her hands in her pockets, too.

Finally Esther said, "Why didn't you call me?"

Teddy flapped her jacket fronts like wings. "I'm sorry. I didn't think I could use the phone."

The assembly looked on, and finally Nigel stepped forward. "Your private life is your own, dear, but we need to make sure that no one else knows you've been going down there. Poli Sci will have a field day with this."

She gasped, then went into seminar defense. "Nigel, you're making assumptions with pencil snot for evidence."

"What I'm *trying* to do is keep rumors to a minimum. It's called damage control."

"Nigel, there won't be any rumors unless you start them. Esther, please tell him."

But nobody was looking at her anymore. She turned.

President Rhodes and Dean Handy of Arts and Sciences were standing at the top of the stairs, waiting for heavyset Dean Handy to catch his breath. Dean Handy was a regular up here in the department, but the last time—the only time—President Rhodes had ever been on the second floor of Humanities was two years ago on his first official visit as president.

"Ladies," he nodded. "Gentlemen." A tall, wiry mountain climber, Rhodes calmly waited for pot-bellied Dean Handy to collect himself and take charge of the proceedings. The dean mopped sweat and surveyed the task.

Dean Arvil Handy was a fifty-five-year-old former boy chorister who, despite his extra weight, would still not have looked out of place in the back row. He had chubby cheeks, fading blond hair, and bright blue eyes that immediately sought the power brokers in any situation.

Turning to Esther, he tucked away his handkerchief. "Do we have a room?"

"Down the hall," she said. She led the procession to the seminar room, and as the academics tramped down the corridor, students stiffened against the walls as if terrified of catching some loathsome disease. The historians filed into the room. The senior faculty took their

God-given places at the seminar table while junior members stood against the wall. Teddy joined them. Dean Handy and President Rhodes—the only men in the room whose jackets matched their pants—instantly turned what had always been the foot of the table into the head by standing in front of it. Nigel's naphtha fumigated the proceedings.

"Are we ready to start?" President Rhodes poked his hands into the pants pockets of his gray pin-striped suit.

"By now you all have heard about the untimely death of your colleague Ira Dedmarsh. I have talked to Mrs. Dedmarsh on the phone and expressed condolences on behalf of the college. As you know, Ira and I shared the academic field of Traditional China, and, like you, I consider this a great personal as well as professional loss." He was already rehearsing the eulogy.

"I know you all have your own ways of coping with tragedy, but the fact remains that we are compelled to carry on, each of us, with our professional duties. And while Esther assures me she can keep the paperwork moving, your being able to find someone to finish out the last six weeks of Dr. Dedmarsh's classes will be a bit more problematic. I even considered taking them myself"—he raised his eyebrows ironically—"but was assured by my staff that if I left the office unsupervised for that long, they would never let me back. So—" He turned to Arvil Handy, who was leaning against the wall.

"Dean Handy has already advised me about how he plans to deal with this emergency, and I have every confidence that you and he will be making good decisions about your future as a department in the coming weeks and months. Having said that, I now turn you over to Dean Handy. Arvil?"

"Thank you, Dr. Rhodes." Handy stepped forward unbuttoning the single closed button on his navy jacket. "I would like to join President Rhodes in offering my condolences for the loss of a great scholar and a good friend. I've known Ira Dedmarsh for twelve years, and I know he was a friend and mentor to everyone in this department."

From the corner of her eye, Teddy watched Nigel Czerny bristle at the thought: Dr. Dedmarsh had trained at Iowa, in the cow-ridden state Nigel still tried to pretend he wasn't from.

"As you know," said the dean, "Dr. Dedmarsh was an able administrator, one of the best department chairs I've had the privilege of working with. Filling his shoes will be no easy task." He shifted his weight. "We won't be rushing into any long-term decision right now—I will need to consult with you all individually first—but the fact is, History needs an interim chair immediately so that we can move forward with the accreditation work in progress and, equally pressing, find a substitute for Dr. Dedmarsh's classes. After consulting with President Rhodes and several of your senior members, I have appointed Nigel Czerny your *pro tem* chair. As you know, Professor Czerny has proved himself an able and facile administrator, working diligently on such bodies as the Faculty Affairs Council, the Faculty Senate, and most recently as Faculty Parking Representative."

"Hear, Hear," said Tim Lainey, who loved his new, cheap parking spot.

Nigel beamed as if he'd swallowed a flashlight.

Dean Handy continued, "Like you, I have every confidence in Dr. Czerny's ability and I'm sure you will assist him during this difficult time. In addition, I will be available for consultation during this period, taking any suggestions you might have about the permanent administrative solution for your very distinguished department." He raised his chin. "Are there any questions?"

Unbelievably—for a group of professional Socratics—there were none. Tucking their hands in their pockets, the historians broke into clusters of two and threes, murmuring as they walked away, closing the oak slabs behind them. Alone, Teddy stumbled down the hall to her office door and fumbled with the keys.

"Professor Morelli?"

She looked up to see President Rhodes. His balding head and pin-striped suit made him look even taller and thinner than he was. Under his arm he carried a file folder thick with red-edged papers she recognized as "Eyes Only" personnel documents. She had never seen so many in one stack before. "Professor Morelli, I had forgotten you would be here. May I talk to you a minute?"

She shrugged, exhausted.

"This morning, before the day turned so incredibly ugly, I spoke with Herb and Sally Patchett. I know this is a bad time to bring this up, but the Pickett-Patchetts are still very interested in San Juan Island, hoping to tour Camp Pickett with you. Herb went ahead and booked rooms for the three of you this weekend, since the tourist season is starting to get underway. He was going to confirm with you later today." He read her face. "I hope that'll work out for you"—his voice rose in a question—"and that this turns out to be a viable research project?"

Mortified, Teddy shook her head. "Dr. Rhodes, first of all, I can't go this weekend. I'm flying out to Vancouver Island to help a friend date burial caves. And secondly, even if I were interested in George Pickett as a research subject, I couldn't write a word of what Mrs. Patchett wants. She and I don't even agree on the most basic facts of General Pickett's life."

Rhodes was nodding vigorously. "Yes, exactly. She showed me her great-great-grandmother's magazine articles. They're pure drivel. But I think you underestimate your own potential as an educator."

"My—?"

"Dr. Morelli, without putting too fine a point on it, Herb Patchett has been very successful in condominium development in La Jolla and is interested in relocating up here. The Pickett-Patchetts will be bringing immense resources with them." He let that settle in. "We feel very fortunate that they've taken an interest in our institution, and we're trying to make them feel as welcome at Rainwater State as possible. I consider it a stroke of great good luck that Mrs. Patchett has a family connection with the area, and we're hoping that you can take the time to help her understand what it is, and what it is *not*."

"Mrs. Patch—"

"Bear with me, Professor. What I mean to say is, because the Pickett-Patchetts are accustomed to dealing with experts in every field, it's going to take someone with your level of expertise to convince Mrs. Patchett that if new historical treatment is given her ancestor, it needs to be authentic and realistic to be of any lasting value." He shifted his weight with a new idea: "In short, we're hoping you'll be the one to step up to the plate for truth and beauty."

"Dr. Rhodes, I can't. I'm already going to have contract work on my *vita*—this stuff I'm doing with the burial caves—and Dr. Dedmarsh said he thought that while one was okay, I shouldn't get in the habit of it. Any more than that just wouldn't look good on a tenure file."

"You're not ten—?" Rhodes's eyes narrowed keenly, and he looked away to shift the stack of documents under his arm. "Well, Professor. Well. We all realize you have your own professional interests, but over in Old Main we always say that service to the university is one of the greatest attributes we value in our faculty, tenured and *un*tenured."

She stared, stunned. He wouldn't really do that, would he? He couldn't! It violated tenuring procedure so badly the American Association of University Professors would burn him at the stake. Fury rushed to her cheeks. How dare he! Dr. Dedmarsh would—But Dr. Dedmarsh was dead.

Rhodes sniffed innocently. "Well, Professor? The Pickett-Patchetts are very busy people. I know they want to be home by next week."

Flatly she countered, "I already told you, I can't go this weekend."

"Then we'd have to give them an alternative time, wouldn't we?" He waited.

"Dr. Rhodes, look at it this way: what do you suppose will happen when I go out to the islands and end up insulting Mrs. Patchett? Besides the university losing 3.4 million dollars," she gestured ironically at the stack of documents under his arm, "will you also put a black mark on my file and lose your Northwest historian, too?"

"Dr. Morelli! Of course not. I'm hurt you'd think in those terms. And I promise, you can't possibly insult Mrs. Patchett. She wouldn't know if you tried. I've already given her a pep talk about what to expect from you, and she indicates she's entirely open to truthful scholarship—wouldn't have it any other way. And as for your part, all we ask is that you do the best, most diplomatic job under the circumstances. Herb Patchett is a valued friend of the university."

Teddy postured, mimicking the imagined conversation: "I'm sorry, Mrs. Patchett, I hate to break it to you, but your ancestor was a crashing mediocrity."

"Ha-ha. Very good, Professor." He wasn't laughing. "But you're much too good an educator to say that, aren't you? You'll have her figure it out on her own." He changed his tack, his eyes suddenly pleading. "Professor, you don't know how much I hate asking you this, but we really do need your cooperation. We're in a very difficult spot, and as I said, only an expert like you has the kind of credibility the Patchetts will respect. Please, Professor . . ."

Teddy looked away, sighing. "Well, if you're certain I don't have to go into the project with the intent of pleasing Mrs. Patchett, I'll be glad to show them the George Pickett information, see if we can't explain to her why she doesn't want a hack job done on her great-great-whatever-he-is-grandfather."

"Yes, yes! Fine! Splendid!" he gushed. "Then I can tell them right away? You'll put off your trip to the burial caves till some other time."

She dug her hands into her pockets. "No, I can't do that. A friend at University of Victoria has had me penciled in for a long time. What I could do, though, is go over to the islands with the Pickett-Patchetts after my seminar Wednesday afternoon, and we could stay overnight—I'm off Tuesdays and Thursdays this term." Teddy pivoted. "No, wait, I know: could you ask the Pickett-Patchetts to meet me at the state archives Wednesday at 3:15 and say we'll leave from there? If Mrs. Patchett wants authentic information on General Pickett, we might as well hit her with all our big guns right up front."

"Ha-ha. I trust you won't be too hard on Mrs. Patchett."

Coyly Teddy poised with her key in the lock. "I'll just do my truth and beauty thing. How she takes it is up to her." She closed the door behind her, her heart thumping in her chest. She was in way over her head. The Pickett-Patchetts were a setup for disaster. And the only man who could help her was down at the morgue.

Scrunching sideways around the crate, she pulled out the bagel and cheese from her book satchel and tried to eat. Her mouth wasn't making saliva; the bagel tasted like wallboard. She stepped out in the hall and saw two members of the department dash into their offices. A pariah. She went back in and worked.

At two o'clock she slipped out for her committee work: the Cold Beverage Contract Committee, whose job it was to determine whether the campus cola contract for the next ten years should go to Topsie Cola, which was offering 3.5 million dollars over that period—or to Koolie Cola, which only offered 2.2 mill in cash but was also interested in building a new weight room, provided it could put tasteful brass eye-level Koolie Cola logos on all the fitness machines.

When her fellow committee members saw that she wasn't going to spill her guts about the history department heart attack, they settled down to discuss whether Koolie Cola would want their tasteful brass plaques at eye level for the average student—a female—or at eye level for the average American male. With Dr. Dedmarsh settled like a tight cap over her brain, Teddy watched herself ably perform—concentrating, reading, responding—almost ashamed of the callousness she had been trained to.

Bursting outside after the meeting, she saw that the air was now golden and that students were dribbling soccer balls toward the intramural fields. It was respectably late enough to go home. She packed her book satchel and drove out to her condominium on the north shore of Lake Whatcom.

Dropping her things in the study, she walked to the back of the house to see if the lake was calm enough for a swim. Out on her patio was the gargantuan navy backpack. She slid back the glass door.

"Uncle Aldo?"

He was nowhere to be seen.

She stepped onto the thick grass and scanned the perfect emerald lawns. The children's play yard was empty. No one was on the dock.

Out of the woods came wild-haired Uncle Aldo, carrying a handful of weeds. His face was gravely serious until he spotted her on the grass. "Teodora, you're home!" He held up his weeds, shaking them angrily. "Look what they've done to these greens."

"What?"

He came close. "See this black center line? Never eat them like this. It means they've been sprayed with weed-killer."

"Uncle Aldo, those are dandelions."

He raised his chin. "This is also *radicchiella.* You pay fifteen dollars a pound for this at The Market." He threw his tainted greens over her woodpile. "Your grandmother grew wonderful *radicchiella.*" His eyes stalked the groomed lawns for forage.

"Have you eaten today?" she asked.

"I can take care of myself."

"I know you can." She urged him inside. "But I have leftover chili, or I can make you a grilled cheese sandwich."

He jerked his head, alert. "Only a sandwich sounds nice. Maybe a bowl of chili, too. I don't need much. I can wait out here."

"Nonsense. Come on in."

Aldo squinted through the glass, glaring at the microwave and the frosted-glass chandelier. "I'm not comfortable in buildings anymore. Electricity."

"I know, but you can stand by the window. Come on."

Bug-eyed, Aldo took a step inside and looked around. Teddy opened the refrigerator, and he jumped back, panting. "There's a lot of current in here!" Resolutely, he sat in a chair and watched her move about the room. "Do you think electricity affects the food?"

"Not that I'm aware of."

"You can feel the heaviness if you haven't been around it for a while—the gravity moving in the walls. I don't think it's good for you."

"Uncle Aldo, I have to tell you what happened today. After I met you, I went down to see the chairman of my department, and he was dead from a heart attack. I'm the one who found him."

"Teodora! The poor man. How old was he?"

"Fifty-eight."

"I'm seventy-three." Then he added, "May he rest in peace."

"Uncle Aldo, I really liked him, and he was helping me with my academic career. I'm going to be lost without him."

"Oh, Teodora." Uncle Aldo's brown eyes softened. "Then you have to be good to yourself, you've had a bad thing happen. I was good to myself after Beatrice. That's why my heart stayed strong." He thumped his chest. "Your father, though, sometimes I feel it was my fault, those boys worked too hard." He added wistfully, "We all worked too hard."

"How long will you be here, Uncle Aldo?"

"Teodora, I live here now. I've been in Whatcom County for three months."

She spun around. "You're kidding! And you haven't told me! Where are you staying?"

"I can't tell you. If everybody shows up there, the Arawaks will stop coming."

"The who?"

He lowered his voice conspiratorially, "Shhh. That's what I was telling you this morning. I found their secret in the library. I've been studying them for months."

Teddy slid a bowl of chili into the microwave and covered it with a salad plate. "Uncle Aldo, who are the Arawaks?"

"You people call them bigfoot or Sasquatch. I happen to know Bigfoots are Arawaks, the black tribe of Cubans that Hernando Cortés left here in 1539. That's what I was telling you, about the mudslides on Chuckanut Drive. Teodora, you can take my discovery and write a book. I don't care—I give it to you."

She punched three minutes into the microwave. Madness. "Uncle Aldo, you'll have to slow down here. This is a bit hard to follow."

"No, no. It's simple." Aldo sat at the table. "You see, I'm living in a boathouse on Chuckanut Drive. The owner's a widow, she talks too much, she likes me. Anyway, in February there was a mudslide. She said last February there was also a mudslide. So I said, what's going on here? And then I starting doing research, hiking in to the library every day. And that's where I found that *both* mudslides happened at the full moon *and* at the lowest minus tide of the year. So I said to myself, this is curious, I wonder why? So I hiked up into the hills where the slide came down, and I saw it." Aldo's eyes were feverish. "Teodora, the rocks and mud hadn't just fallen. *They'd been pushed!*"

Teddy gasped. "By whom?"

"Well, that's the question, isn't it? So I went back to the library and started reading all about the West Coast, all I could find. And one day I was looking at old Spanish journals and books about the conquistadors."

"And?"

"I found a record of the whole tribe and how they got here." His eyes glanced out to the book-lined living room. "You have it!" He dashed across the room and pulled down William Prescott's *History of the Conquest of Mexico.* "This is the book I found at the library." He flipped pages and frowned. "No, this is a little different from the one at the library. I can't find my page. I'll look in the index. It's next to the page about Captain Ulloa."

Teddy laid a place mat on the table, set the too-hot chili bowl on a plate, and bracketed the bowl with sandwich halves. Pulling back the chair, she waited. Aldo ignored the food, skimming pages and murmuring to himself. "Okay! Here it is. This paragraph." He handed her the book and sat down to eat.

Teddy took the book and read:

> Hernando Cortés was joined by a little squadron which he had fitted out from his own port of Tehuantepec—a port, which, in the sixteenth century, promised to hold the place now occupied by Acapulco. The vessels were provided with every thing requisite for planting a colony in the newly discovered region, and transported four hundred Spaniards, and *three hundred negro slaves,* which Cortés had assembled for that purpose. This was his intention when he crossed the Gulf.

Teddy looked up. "And what is this supposed to mean, exactly?"

Aldo munched happily on his sandwich. "It means, if you read the part before it and after it, that Cortés took an expedition of seven hundred people to Bellingham."

"Hernando Cortés was in Bellingham?"

"Yes." Aldo swallowed. "And do you see the part about the Negro slaves in italics?"

"Yes."

"Well, if you read the whole book, you find the Negro slaves are never mentioned again. They simply disappear from history." He bit off sandwich. "So the question is, what happened to the black people?" He used his napkin, then walked out to his backpack on the patio. "Now," he called, "flip to the illustrations in the back of the book. Look at the third one."

Teddy flipped to the back. "Uncle Aldo, I don't think anyone's ever documented that Hernando Cortés sailed this far north." The book illustrations were black-and-white reproductions of watercolors made by sixteenth-century artists who went along on voyages of discovery. The third one was of Spanish soldiers and distinctly dark-skinned men in loincloths erecting a scaffolding and walls.

"Well?" Teddy glanced at the caption. "All this says is that it was sketched by Miguel Herrera, during the expedition of somebody named Captain Ulloa: *'hecho por las goletas de Urbino Ulloa.'* It doesn't say where this is. Or who Ulloa was."

"Ulloa was an officer for Hernando Cortés. Now I want you to look at something." Aldo dumped an envelope of newly developed photographs on the table and spread them out. Selecting one—a panoramic shot of Bellingham taken from a boat—he laid it directly above the Herrera illustration and stood back. The glossy new photo showed the city of Bellingham; the old black-and-white book illustration showed the building of a sixteenth-century Spanish fort.

"What am I supposed to see?" she asked.

"Compare the backgrounds."

Bingo. Both pictures had matching mountainous backdrops, the distinctive jagged peak of Mount Baker at the left, two smaller peaks called The Sisters on the right.

"You see, Teodora? You see? Cortés built a fort in Bellingham."

Teddy looked at the pictures again. Okay, he had a point. But in its details, the Spanish illustration did not quite follow the contours of the photographed mountains, either due to artistic license, or because these were two entirely different mountain ranges. She rubbed her forehead. "So, Uncle Aldo, what are you telling me here?"

"I'm telling you that Hernando Cortés built a fort at the south end of Bellingham, then some kind of trouble soon developed—probably with the local Indians—and that Cortés abandoned the three hundred Negro slaves while he and the white people fled in their ships. I'm also telling you that the descendents of those Negro slaves, originally the Arawak tribe from Cuba, are still secretly living in the Chuckanut Hills and that they are the people who close down Chuckanut Drive with mudslides during minus tides so that they can get to their ancestral clamming beds." Aldo's brown eyes glowed triumphantly. "Teodora, the Arawak tribe of Cuba is the elusive Sasquatch of the Northwest. This is the answer the world's been waiting for."

Teddy stepped back. "Uncle Aldo, this is a lot to absorb."

"I know," he nodded. "It overwhelmed me, too, when I first realized what was going on." He picked up Prescott's *Conquest of Mexico*. "The best thing to do, though, is read the book a little each night. That way you can get used to it, the whole story." Reverently, he handed her the Prescott. "It will change your life."

"Thank you, Uncle Aldo, I'll look into it." She glanced at the lake, a perfect mirror in the chilled rose evening. "Uncle Aldo, I'm going to put on a wetsuit and go swim for a while. I have to get ready for my triathlons this summer."

Aldo chewed happily. "Exercise is good for young girls."

"Old girls, too." Teddy pulled her black neoprene wetsuit out of the hall closet and went upstairs to change. Coming down barefoot with her zipper already done, she tugged on her cap and tucked in her hair. "I'll be about forty-five minutes. Please make yourself at home."

Uncle Aldo spooned up chili. "Oh, no. I'll be gone by the time you get back. Marjorie doesn't know where I am."

"Marjorie is your widow friend on Chuckanut Drive?"

"Marjorie Ramey. They were the Ramey Concrete Company. Aren't you going to put something on your feet?"

Teddy wriggled her toes. "I lost my deck shoes at a picnic last summer." She pushed back the sliding glass. "Just leave this unlocked when you go. I'll be a while, I've got a lot of things to think about."

"Goodbye, Teodora. I'll be in touch." He blew her a kiss.

Teddy trotted down the icy lawn and out to the end of the dock. Diving into the shockingly cold water, she turned on her back and exhaled several times to stop her racing heart. Then she flopped over to a crawl stroke. Dr. Dedmarsh's flaccid gray body surfaced as soon as she put her face in the water. She thought of his dingy jockey shorts; all he would have needed was hot water and bleach. She sucked in air and exhaled, heading for the center of the lake. After a while there was no more jockey shorts, no more Dr. Dedmarsh, only the khaki TV screen of her vision, her two black arms intruding. She poked her head up and saw she was nearly halfway across and that dusk was hunkering down in coves and creek mouths.

Aiming her face at the faraway emerald lawn, she

swam hard, kicking deeply to make work. Finally she came to undulating grass, her fingers touching scummy pebbles. She stood and walked the last few feet, pulling off her goggles to trudge up the lawn. For some reason her condo lights were on, and there were people inside.

Teddy stepped dripping onto the patio. In the living room Aldo waited with two burly men wearing sports jackets and loafers. She slid back the glass. One man was Asian, but almost identical to the second, a Caucasian, in build and posture. They were teammates of some kind—entirely physical animals.

"Uncle Aldo, could you get me a towel, please?"

"Certainly, Teodora." Aldo disappeared.

"Hi." Teddy and the men stared at one another.

"Ms. Morelli? I'm Detective Tennant and this is Detective Bao. We're with the Bellingham Police Department, investigating the death of Ira Dedmarsh. We understand that you found the body this morning."

"Investigating? What for? He had a heart attack." She looked back and forth between the two. "Didn't he?"

4

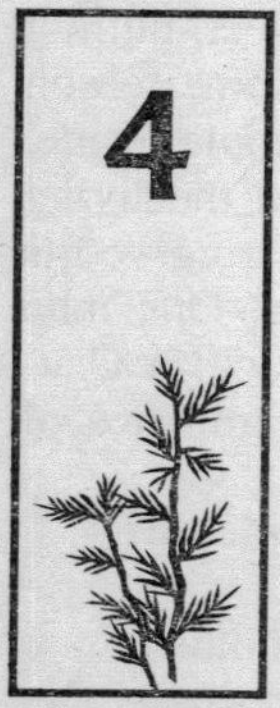

Uncle Aldo came back with a towel.

"Thank you." Teddy laid the towel on the carpet and stepped onto it, water sluicing down her legs. The detectives gawked at her black rubber suit, watching each movement of her limbs. But she wasn't about to take the wetsuit off. "I don't understand," she said. "Heart attacks run in his family. What's to investigate?"

"Oh, no problem." Detective Tennant crossed his arms. "It's just an unattended death. There're still a few blanks on the report." Tennant was in remarkable physical condition. His tee-shirt stretched across his chest, and his neck muscles exploded out of the cotton neckline like tree roots. "How long have you known about Mr. Dedmarsh's family history?"

Teddy shrugged. "I suppose for a long time, but it never really registered until this morning. The secretary told me."

"And this morning, when you found him, you let yourself in with your key?"

"My key?" She looked back and forth between the detectives.

Tennant nodded at Aldo. "Your uncle says you were quite close to the victim."

Stricken, Teddy glanced at Aldo. "I—I liked Dr. Dedmarsh very much, but we weren't intimate or anything."

Detective Tennant nodded sympathetically. "And this lack of intimacy, this was causing problems?"

Teddy opened her mouth, and choked. The towel and her carpet were both soaking wet. "You don't understand. Dr. Dedmarsh was married."

Detective Tennant nodded. He knew that; he also knew *how* married.

"I mean, he was my mentor. I had a lot of respect for him. Look, do you mind if I change clothes? I'm making a mess on the rug."

"No problem."

Dripping water up the stairs, she closed the bathroom door and peeled the wetsuit off in front of the mirror. How had they gotten it so terribly wrong? She draped the wetsuit over the shower bar and changed into fuzzy sweats.

Back downstairs she found Aldo holding up Prescott's *History of the Conquest of Mexico* and explaining how the moon's gravity in a minus tide is just enough to help the Arawaks precipitate a mudslide. Detective Bao had been assigned the job of listening to Aldo, and he stood smiling and nodding, thick arms folded across his chest.

Teddy pulled out all her clean dishtowels and dropped them on the carpet by the door. Stepping on them to sponge the rug, she raised her chin bravely at Detective Tennant. "Now explain to me what needs investigating."

"Oh, nothing special. Little things. We didn't get your exact title on the report this morning."

"Assistant Professor of History." She had told someone that at least three times.

"Also, we need to know the last time you had dinner in the Dedmarsh apartment and how often you helped him with his medication."

Teddy shook her head. "I never saw his apartment until this morning, and I didn't even know he was on medication." She sighed. "You really do have this all wrong. I wasn't that close to Dr. Dedmarsh. I didn't know that much about him."

Tennant nodded the whole time, ignoring her. Opening his palm, he read something he had scribbled there. "And what do you know about the drug Rythmol?"

She shook her head.

"How about"—he read again—"Lanoxin?"

She shook her head again. "Was he taking these?"

Detective Tennant stared at her a few seconds, then turned to Detective Bao. "Tom?"

Detective Bao barely moved his head.

Tennant tried again. "Is there anything else you'd like to tell us about your relationship with Dr. Dedmarsh?"

"Only that there wasn't one."

"You said that." He turned to Bao, and they read each other's eyes a few seconds, then Tennant said, "Well, I guess that's all for now."

The two men shuffled slowly to the front door, glancing in every open doorway they passed. In the foyer Detective Tennant reached for his wallet and slipped out a business card. "Thank you for your cooperation, Ms. Morelli. If you can think of anything else you'd like to tell us, please call me anytime, day or night."

"You're kidding." She smiled.

"No." Solemnly he turned to go. "I'm not."

Out in the cul-de-sac, neighborhood children had caucused on bikes, waiting to see who would come claim the dark sedan with police lights mounted on the back deck. All her neighbors were outside, too, casually gardening in their front yards.

"Hello, Teddy!"

"Hello, Mrs. Boudin." Teddy waved.

As the policemen settled in the car, the cyclists dispersed, wheeling off in all directions. Teddy watched the sedan drive away, then calmly rearranged flower pots on the porch to indicate her lack of concern.

When she got back to the living room, Aldo was on the phone, his reading glasses perched on his nose. He scribbled on her blue phone pad, asking someone pointed questions. Teddy leaned against a sofa arm, waiting for him to finish. Finally Aldo hung up.

"Who's that, Aldo?"

"The pharmer at the all-night pharmacy. They're the same as the daytime pharmers, aren't they?"

"Yes, I think so. Aldo, I have to talk to you."

"Of course, Teodora. What is it?" He peered earnestly over his reading glasses.

"Uncle Aldo, you've got to stop telling people about the Arawaks. I know they're important to you, but when other people hear it, they think you're a little crazy, okay?"

Aldo regarded his notes on the blue pad, then said, "Teodora, listen to me. I told the policemen Arawaks on purpose. When you were out swimming, they played a trick on me; they made me say that you liked Dr. Dedmarsh, and that made me mad. So all I could think to tell them was about the Arawaks. That way, they think I'm *buffo*, they don't pay attention to me. Those are dangerous men, Teodora. I want you to keep away from them."

Teddy dropped onto the sofa. "I still don't understand what they wanted."

Aldo ripped a paper off the notepad. "What they wanted to know is why a Rythmol man was taking Lanoxin. Or a Lanoxin man taking Rythmol. I don't know which one."

Teddy's eyes grew wide. "Aldo, how do you know this?"

He waved the blue sheet. "Teodora, this is all my friends—their Viagra, their heart pills, their blood pressure. This is why I left Seattle to walk up the state. I don't want to listen to old men yak, yak, yak all day long. Remember Albino Siecheri? He had the Lanoxin to make his heart stronger, and then they gave him something else for rhythm. After that, he was in the hospital so much for blood poisoning, they almost killed him three times. Finally, when his insurance ran out, they left him alone. He's dead now." Aldo pointed to the phone pad. "What's this word. I can't say it."

"That says"—Teddy peeked over his shoulder—"digioxin toxicity."

Aldo nodded. "That's what the pharmer called it. He said these two drugs, you have to be very careful. Rythmol makes the Lanoxin increase ninety percent. If you take the Rythmol and Lanoxin at the same time, you have to get blood tests not to get digox—what you just said." Aldo looked out at the black night and sighed. "It's too late to get back to the boathouse. Poor Marjorie. Do your neighbors mind if I sleep in the woods?"

"Yes! Very much." She pointed to the stairs. "You can sleep in my spare bedroom."

"I already told you, I don't sleep inside anymore."

"Then how do you sleep in the boathouse?"

"Marjorie let me take out the wires. There was only one."

"Why don't you set up your tent on my patio. Is it the kind with tension rods?"

Aldo's brown eyes gleamed. "Oh, yes. It's a beautiful little tent."

"Good." She slid off the sofa arm. "And in the morning you can take a hot shower, and we'll make lattes."

"Teodora, you twisted my arm." Aldo slid back the glass and began unloading his pack; immense amounts of green nylon came springing out. Teddy watched him slide the tension rods into the slim pockets of the tent, then went into her office to work.

At ten o'clock she came out and saw the tent was dark and quiet. She went upstairs and changed into pajamas. In front of the bathroom mirror, brushing her teeth, she could hear Aldo down below, secretly huffing one of his sister Emilia's arias—he thought he was alone. Without realizing it, Teddy walked downstairs again, toothpaste in her mouth. She spit into the kitchen sink and slid back the glass door.

"Uncle Aldo, why did the police come *here* to ask about heart medication? What would that have to do with filling in blanks on their report?"

Aldo pushed back the tent flap. For a second he considered putting in his teeth. "Don't take it personally, Teodora, I imagine they asked everybody. His wife, you know?"

"No, I don't know." Politely Teddy looked at the lake, away from his caved-in mouth. "What do they think? Just because we're women, we'll mess up his pills? Dr. Dedmarsh was perfectly capable of taking his own medication."

Aldo rolled his head, weighing his thoughts. "Teodora, you're not going to like this, but if the police are investigating, they believe Dr. Dedmarsh was poisoned with too much heart medication. And if they came here, they want to know if you did it."

"No, they don't."

"Good, that's fine. It was nothing." Aldo closed the tent flap. "It was just my opinion."

She might have slept a little between first light and the alarm, she couldn't tell. Downstairs in the morning, she found the espresso machine partially disassembled and Aldo missing from his tent. She microwaved oatmeal, and as she ate, a shadow darkened the patio. Aldo triumphantly held up a giant chanterelle mushroom. Wiping his feet over and over on the mat, he finally slid back the glass. "Teodora, what a wonderful place! Your woods are full of nettles and mushrooms. I bet there are fish in the lake."

"Yes," she admitted.

"It just came to me." Aldo gestured to the blue hills down the lake. "If I were an Arawak, I would probably also want to live on Stewart Mountain. I'm going down there today to look for sign. I won't be back until tonight."

"You're coming back here?"

Aldo nodded. "It's good camping here. Hot water for showers, and I'll fix your latte machine."

"It wasn't broken."

His eyes swept over the landscape. "Don't make dinner tonight. I'm going to fix cream of nettle soup and a wild mushroom omelet. Do you get Oprah?"

Oatmeal stuck in her throat. "Yes."

"Good. After you leave, I'll work on the latte machine, then shower and hike down to Stewart Mountain and be back in time for Oprah. I can walk the beach here, can't I?"

"No. It's all private property."

"Too bad. We'll teach them to share."

Teddy scraped up the rest of her oatmeal and ran upstairs, dressing quickly for school. Handing a house key to Aldo, she bussed him on the cheek. "Call me from jail."

"Teodora, I'm a cautious man!"

She drove to campus and parked in the faculty lot, dashing eagerly up to the department. Tuesdays and Thursdays were writing days this semester. Dedmarsh had helped her arrange her schedule so that she had no classes.

She unlocked her office door. The statue was still there. She trotted down the hall and found a note on Esther's door: *Old Main*—which meant that Esther was over in central administration straightening out the dimwits. Teddy walked three doors down to Nigel's. His door read, *Find me in 203.* Dr. Dedmarsh's office. She went over and knocked.

"Come in." Nigel was at Dr. Dedmarsh's desk, staring into the computer screen. "Oh, Teddy, I'm glad you're here, I wanted to talk to you. Damn him. I can't get into his files. We were supposed to use our last names as passwords just for this reason."

Teddy leaned against the desk."Ask Esther, she'll know his password. Nigel, I need to get the statue out of my office."

"Guess what." He pivoted the chair. "The police came to see me."

"They came to see me, too."

"So you know about his cardiologist."

"No. What about him?"

Nigel pointed to Dedmarsh's open appointment book. "Ira went in to the cardiologist last week, and they ran some blood work."

"He *had* been looking terrible."

"Yes, he had, hadn't he? Well, evidently they found outrageous levels of some drug he'd been ingesting by mistake. The cardiologist called him Monday morning—too late, as it turns out—to tell Dedmarsh to immediately check himself into the hospital, and now the cardiologist is making a huge stink to the police—that's the reason they're investigating. The man will be in huge trouble if the death looks iatrogenic—"

"I don't know that word."

"Doctor-caused."

"Oh, then that explains it." Teddy sat on the edge of the desk. "My uncle thought the police interviewed me to see if I *poisoned* Dedmarsh."

"Oh, how funny." The computer screen blinked to screensaver. "The detectives who came to see me were much too bored for that to be the case. My impression was that all they needed was an explanation of why Dedmarsh was ingesting Lana-cox-in, or whatever it is, without prescription. Evidently he'd been taking it for several weeks." Nigel rolled the computer mouse, and the screen flicked onto a little blue window, where the cursor impatiently waited for a password. "Oh, guess what, I've hooked a live one for us. And dirt cheap, too. But young people have no choice, do they?"

"I'm not following, Nigel. Does this mean you've found someone to take Dr. Dedmarsh's classes?"

Nigel bobbed his head like a wobble doll. "Yes, indeed. She's from Seattle. Her name is Jocelyn Woo—

Muffy in parentheses. She's so excited by the prospect of her first job, she's coming up today."

"Muffy Woo?"

Nigel swiped a faxed sheet off the desk. "Finishing her dissertation in Traditional China, tentative diploma date December. I think she needs to change her dissertation title, though. It seems more arrogant than erudite." He passed Teddy the fax.

"*Sizhi-lu zhi Renleixue: Anthropology of the Silk Road*," Teddy read. "What's the matter with that?"

"Well, no one can read the Chinese part."

There was a colon between the two parts. "Nigel, *lu* is Chinese for 'road.' So I imagine *Sizhi-lu zhi Renleixue* is exactly what it says: Anthropology of the Silk Road."

"Well." He snatched the fax. "One expects perfect clarity from the hired help. And Miss Woo must be made to understand that if she's coming from the first-ranked department in the state to the second-ranked, she will find it only a matter of size, not quality. The only difference is that our department doesn't allow *prima donnas*."

"Nigel, grow up."

"But my problem, Teddy, is that I have to find her a place to live for six weeks, which is why I wanted to talk to you."

"Me?"

Nigel shrugged. "It's April 27. I can't imagine her finding anything this late in the term. And you have an extra bedroom."

"Nigel, no."

"Teddy, she's not earning enough for a damage deposit. I'm—"

"Well, pay her more!"

"I can't. I just now took a third of the money and hired a grad student to finish off the microfiche cataloging."

"What microfiche?" She gasped. "*Your* microfiche. Nigel, how could you?"

Viciously, he whispered, "Hush! I need the microfiche done so I can demonstrate that I'm entirely ready to work on Catherine de Medici next year. Otherwise—no sabbatical."

"Oh, Nigel."

Nigel looked away, embarrassed. "You won't tell anybody, it's not your nature."

"Oh, Nigel."

"Will you take Muffy Woo for me? I can make it worth your while."

"Nigel, stop it! It's not your money. Somebody's going to find out. I'll take Muffy Woo for you, but you have to stop trying to buy your friends. No, wait! I know what I want. I want Our Lady of Guadalupe out of my office."

"Deal!" Nigel leaped up. "And so cheap, too. May I tell Muffy you'll take her tonight? She was going to get a motel."

Teddy thought of Aldo and his cream of nettle soup. With a happy feeling, she rehearsed telling him goodbye. "Tonight would be fine."

"Oh, Teddy, thank you." Nigel reached for her hands, and she instantly tucked them in her pockets. "That's okay, Nigel, you're entirely welcome." She ambled down the hall to start her day of writing.

Her phone light was blinking. She punched the button.

"Dr. Morelli? This is Hillary Younkin at the Archives. A woman named Mrs. Patchett is here wanting to check out General Pickett materials. I tried to explain that we're not a library, but she says she's working on a project with you and President Rhodes told her she could take anything she wanted. I don't know if he actually told her that, but the problem is we're a federal reposit—"

Teddy pulled out the campus directory and looked up the number for Archives. "This is Teddy Morelli. May I speak to Hillary, please?"

Instantly Hillary was on the line. "Dr. Morelli," she

pleaded, "I tried to call President Rhodes, but Penny says he's at a fund-raiser. I don't think I can hold this woman off much longer."

Teddy looked at her watch. "Tell Mrs. Patchett I'll be right down and not to touch anything, otherwise she'll miss the most important Pickett documents."

Hillary exhaled. "Thank you. I'll tell her."

Teddy ran down to the parking lot and made the two-minute drive over to Archives. As she signed in, she could see Sally Pickett-Patchett through the plate-glass windows of the research room. Sally sat at the huge table, clutching a small object, while Hillary hovered over her, trying to take it away. They both spotted Teddy and stopped fighting, waiting for her to come in and take sides.

Teddy stood at the door waiting to be buzzed in, smiling at them both through the glass. Finally the door opened. "Hello, Mrs. Patchett. Hi, Hillary. What's up?"

Sally Pickett-Patchett held up an antique photograph of a mustached young Indian man in a dark suit. The photo was sepia-tinted, backed with antique cardboard, in a plastic document bag.

Teddy smiled. "You've found Jimmie Pickett."

Sally clutched the picture possessively. "And as I was telling this helper, if that actually *was* his name, it's because Grandpa adopted him." Sally glared up at Hillary. "And we could probably find out a lot more about him if she'd let me pry off the cardboard and see if there's writing on the back."

Hillary hovered over the picture. "And I explained to Mrs. Patchett that this is a very fragile piece and if there had been information anywhere on the photo, the archives would have noted it during accessioning."

Scattered on the table were the hanging files on General George Pickett—browning newspaper articles and brittle pictures mixed together.

"You know," said Teddy, "I don't think we need that photo at all." She grabbed Sally's hand and pulled her toward the bookcase wall. "If we're going to get our work done on George Pickett, we have a much bigger mystery to solve."

Sally viewed the wall of massive leather-bound volumes. "What's that?"

Hillary snatched the photo and left the room.

"Well." Teddy scanned the bookshelves. "First of all, I have to tell you about one of our most distinguished local families. Their name was Eldridge."

"You're kidding!" said Sally in surprise. "So that's where he got it!"

"Got what?"

"Oh, that's so exciting!" Sally's eyes danced delightedly at this piece of knowledge. "After the Civil War broke out, when Grandpa George was still out here in the Union army, he had to resign secretly and sneak back to Virginia to join the Confederacy. Since Yankees were on the lookout for Southern military men doing just that, Grandpa George traveled in street clothes under the name of Edward Eldridge. I had no idea Edward Eldridge was a real person."

"That was clever. I didn't know he did that." Teddy nodded. "And since your grandpa was in Bellingham for at least two years, I'm sure he knew the whole Eldridge family quite well. We have an Eldridge Avenue here in town." Teddy dragged down from the shelf the elephantine Whatcom County Deed Book of 1888. "But look, I want to show you something." She turned to the back to look up "Pickett" in the hand-crafted index. Finding a Pickett entry, she turned the huge folio pages to page 325. "Look at this and help me with some detective work. See if you can tell me what's happening."

Sally put on her reading glasses.

" '*Number 3298. LaSalle Pickett et al. to James T. Pickett.*' Who is James—? Oh, that's that Jimmie boy you were talking about. '*This indenture made this twenty-third day of July in the year of Our Lord, One Thousand Eight Hundred and Eighty-Eight by and be-*

tween LaSalle Pickett (widow of Geo. E. Pickett deceased) and Geo. E. Pickett (son of the said Geo. E. Pickett deceased) of Washington D.C. The said LaSalle Pickett & Geo. E. Pickett being the only heirs at law of the said Geo. E. Pickett (deceased) of the first part and James T. Pickett of Portland, in the state of Oregon, party of the second part.

" '*Witnesseth, that the said parties of the first part, for and in consideration of the sum of Five Dollars in lawful money of the United States paid by the party of the second part . . . do by these presents grant, bargain, sell, alien, quit claim and convey unto the said James T. Pickett all our right title and interest in and to the following described parcel of real estate situated in the Town of Whatcom, County of Whatcom, Washington Territory'*—Whatcom, where's that?"

"That's what the west side of Bellingham was called in 1888."

"So they sold him some land."

"Five dollars. They practically gave it away."

"Well, isn't that sweet?" said Sally. "Is it valuable now?"

"No, it's just a decaying old commercial building on a corner lot."

"Good. I mean, fine. Everyone says that Grandma Sally was always doing nice things."

"The interesting part to me," said Teddy, "is the next page."

Sally tumbled the huge folio page over to 326. "Where?"

"The next entry, number 3299."

Sally read:

" '*Number 3299. Affidavit of James T. Pickett. Territory of Washington, County of Whatcom} So James T. Pickett being first duly sworn on oath saith that he is a son of George E. Pickett'*—Oh my!—'*that said George E. Pickett died on, or about July A.D. 1873. That he left surviving him as his sole heirs at law his wife*

Sallie E. Pickett, and his two sons George E. Pickett and this affiant, and no other children, or other heirs.' Well, of course he would say that! Being the son of a great white chief would have been very prestigious."

Teddy pointed the bottom line of the entry. "I guess the curious part is the name of the person who took the affidavit. And if you'll look, you'll see this was recorded the same morning as the land transfer."

Sally scrutinized the signature and the dates. " *'Hugh Eldridge, Auditor of Whatcom County.'* So he's one of your Eldridges, isn't he?"

"Edward's son, I assume."

Sally fidgeted with the page. "So you're saying right after the land sale, Hugh Eldridge let this Indian boy swear he was George Pickett's son?"

"That's how I read it."

"No, no, that can't be right. Because in the entry above, it says that Grandma LaSalle and George Junior are the only heirs."

Teddy rubbed grime off her hands. "Confusing, isn't it? I guess the question is, why would Hugh Eldridge record these two conflicting documents back to back on the same morning? I hope you can come up with an idea, because I just don't know what to make of it." Teddy looked at the wall clock. "Are you going to be here long?"

"All day. Herb is out looking at beachfront."

"Well, if you'll excuse me, this is my writing day. I should get back to work."

Sally looked up. "But *this* is your work now. We've got to put this information in my book. I wasn't going to have the biography go past grandpa's death, but this is so interesting. Oh, Miss?" She looked around for Hillary. "May I have all the information you have on Hugh Eldridge?" She looked back to Teddy. "That's a good place to start, isn't it?"

Teddy stared her straight in the eye. "I really do have to go."

"Oh, well, see you later. We're really excited about going out to the islands with you. Herb says he wants to buy one." Sally wiggled her nose.

Teddy checked herself out of the Archives and drove back to the department. It was eleven o'clock. She had already lost her best writing hours. She stumbled down the hall and remembered that the statue was in her office. Dr. Dedmarsh's door was still open. She went down the hall and walked in, dropping into a orange plastic student chair.

"Nigel. I'm having a problem. You have to help."

"Just a minute. The computer center told me how to override his password. When Miss Woo walks in, we are going to hit her immediately with his lecture notes, his class lists, his syllabuses. I'm not given to intimidation, but Miss Jocelyn Woo is going to be blown away with the professionalism of this department."

"Nigel, listen to me. I've got an impossible situation on my hands. I had just told Dr. Dedmarsh about it before he died, and he said he'd take care of it."

"I told you I'd take care of it." He pecked the keyboard.

"Not the statue. This is something else. The problem is that some very important college donors want me to write a book about their ancestor. He's this mediocre military man who played a big part in the Pig War out on San Juan Island."

"George Pickett."

"Oh, good. You've heard of him."

Nigel lowered his head. "If you recall, we visited Camp Pickett on San Juan Island together. Can't you just throw something together for them?"

"Nigel, this woman wants a hagiography. But anything honest about Pickett would just be too awful in print. I mean, what do I say? 'Mrs. Patchett, your great-great-grandfather was too dumb to read law with his uncle in Illinois and he was last in his class at West Point.' As far as I can tell, the best thing you can say about George Pickett in the Pig War was that he did very little damage because he was so maddeningly lethargic."

"There is a mystery about his passivity, isn't there?" Nigel firmly pressed three computer keys at the same time, then turned to face Teddy. "But, dear girl, you must look this Pickett woman squarely in the eye and tell her it's not in her family interest to have an honest biography put out. You must tell her exactly what you've told me: General George Pickett will not look good in print, that there is a *reason* he was last in his class at West Point. Just say that."

He turned back to his computer. "What's happened? Where're my files?" He punched keys. "Oh, damn, I've erased all of Dedmarsh's files. Oh, damn! Oh, damn! No, I haven't, they're in Recycle." He clicked the mouse. "Yes, I have! Teddy, I've erased his files. Oh, damn, what am I going to do?" He ran into the hall. "Esther, come quickly."

Teddy stared at the computer screen. Recycle was empty. She popped the other window: *Files not found.*

Nigel and Esther came through the door. "Teddy, stop! Don't touch anything. Esther, call the computer center. We've got to get this fixed."

Esther picked up the campus directory. "Czerny, I told you to call Irene Dedmarsh. Now you've really screwed up."

"Esther," he said firmly, "I need your collaboration in problem-solving. It's important that we present a professional departmental appearance to people like Miss Woo."

"Did someone call me?"

They all looked up. In the doorway was the most adorable young Asian woman, exactly Teddy's size. She was wearing a heavy red silk shirtwaist gorgeously printed with the Royal Stewart plaid. On her feet were an expensive pair of strappy red *high*, high heels.

Teddy stared in humility and awe—she herself would break a leg in shoes like those.

5

Nigel lunged forward. "How do you do? I'm Nigel Czerny. I talked to you on the phone." He took her hand and shook and shook and shook.

Muffy's nose wrinkled at his mothball smell. "I'm so glad to meet you." She looked around, and Nigel said, "Miss Woo, this is Administrative Assistant Esther Erickson and Professor Teddy Morelli, with whom you'll be staying for the next few weeks."

"Thank you! Teddy, is it?"

Teddy put out a hand. "Yes. Glad to meet you."

Muffy stirred a zephyr scented like the Hermés Shop on the Rue Saint Honoré in Paris—partly new leather, partly jasmine from Grasse. The print on her dress shimmered with rich color.

Nigel gestured to the computer. "We were just trying to get your notes ready, Miss Woo—do I call you Muffy?"

"Please do, everyone else does." Muffy bobbed her head, and her hair slipped forward like a quicksilver curtain.

"Though, we don't allow students to first-name here." Nigel's eyes dilated. "We think it breeds an unwholesome familiarity."

"Oh, yes. I agree."

Nigel sighed happily and gestured again at the Dedmarsh computer. "I'm afraid you'll find us a bit compromised at the moment. There's been a computer failure, and Dr. Dedmarsh's teaching files are unobtainable. We were hoping to hand them to you when you walked in."

Gracefully Muffy clipped over to join them at the computer. "Who taught his Chinese Empire class today?" With a dancer's balance, she leaned over to view the screen.

"No one." Nigel inhaled her. "We gave them a library day."

"And his graduate seminar meets Friday?"

"That's the one that really needs his notes." Nigel rolled his eyes. "Undergraduates, you could toss anything to them, but the graduate students are going to be upset if there's not some continuity. Dedmarsh leaned heavily toward economic theory. He's a leading authority on the Emperor Wang Mang."

Muffy nodded. "I'm very familiar with Dedmarsh's work. He was commentator for my panel at the Asian Studies Conference last year in Denver." She glanced at the gray metal file cabinets. "But he must still have notes on paper."

Esther kicked the closest cabinet. "Not here. This is all Administration."

Departmental members were gathering in the hall, anxious for a peek at the glorious new addition in red shoes. Some of the men stepped forward to introduce themselves—Wallace in American South, Lainey in Japan. They were behaving like idiots.

Exasperated, Esther closed the door. "We'll find his notes. Nothing actually disappears on computer." She called the computer center and waited for them to answer. "Czerny, I told you to call Irene Dedmarsh. She knows his password."

Nigel reddened. "Irene Dedmarsh is not answering her

phone. She's just lost her husband. I don't want to bother—"

Esther silenced him with a hand. "Hello, this is Erickson in History. We had someone try to bypass an access code and now we are getting a *Files not found* message. Do you know what we should do?"

As Esther conversed with the plastic, Nigel whispered, "She said Dedmarsh put his last name into an anagram or something. I tried everything: Marshded, Shedmard, Hedsmard. Nothing worked."

Esther called over the receiver, "And you've already checked Recycling?"

Nigel bristled. "That was the first place I looked!"

Still waiting for a response from the phone receiver, Esther peered over her glasses at Muffy. "I'm sorry for this inconvenience, Woo. If these people can't help us, my next thought is to go get Dedmarsh's old lecture notes at his house. They won't be as updated as what he has on hard drive, but at least they're a start."

Teddy said, "His files are still out at Irene's?"

Esther nodded. "When Ole and I moved him into his apartment, there wasn't enough room for everything, so Irene let him leave some stuff in the garage."

"I just told you! You can't call out there. Irene Dedmarsh is not answering her phone."

Esther glanced at her watch. "That's because she does volunteer work in the morning. The best way would be to catch her at home around noon. Then she can give you the files, maybe also tell you his password—just in case Czerny hasn't totally blown it."

Muffy took a step back to distance herself from the idiots. "Where does Irene live?"

"Out in the county. Far."

"The county is . . . ?"

"That's what they call the countryside north of town." Teddy touched Muffy's arm. "I could take you. I don't teach today, and I need to see Irene Dedmarsh myself about something else."

"Teddy, I *told* you I'd take care of the statue!"

"I know you did, Nigel. But you also just told me that Irene isn't answering her phone."

Muffy glanced nervously back and forth between the two of them. "Fine, Teddy. Should I just leave my car here? I'm pulling a U-Haul."

U-Haul? Teddy blinked. "Where is it?"

"In front of the security office."

Esther still held the receiver to her ear. "Just go, Morelli. I'll call Security and tell them to hang on to the U-Haul for a few hours."

Muffy shifted her purse. "Thank you, Esther. Thank you, Dr. Czerny."

He raised his glasses from his eyes. "Nigel."

They trotted down to Teddy's little wagon in the faculty lot. Muffy's red shoes clicked agreeably on the brick concourse, and Teddy knew that if she turned around quickly, everyone they passed would be turned around too, gawking.

"What's your field, Teddy?"

"Northwest."

"Have you taught here long?"

Teddy watched the delighted stares of two undergraduates as they approached the red shoes. "I'm finishing my second year here. Before that I had a post-doc in London, and before that I was in your department at the U."

"You studied with Fred Wright?" asked Muffy.

"And Sandinall before he retired. Who are you studying with?"

"MacKay."

Teddy unlocked the station-wagon door for Muffy. "MacKay was always on leave when I was there."

Muffy climbed in. "He's still always on leave."

They headed north to rural Whatcom County, where the Dedmarshes had custom-built on five acres. Driving up into the fertile highlands north of town, they passed the Aquí Està Fruit Stand, its colored piñatas twirling in the wind. At one narrow farm lane Muffy glanced in to examine a row of boxy migrant cabins, boarded over at this time of year. Out toward the town of Lynden, the Holstein-spotted pastures gave way to loamy furrows of low, white-blooming plants.

"Those are strawberries," said Muffy.

"And the other crop you'll see, trained up on wires, is raspberries. If it weren't for flavored yogurt, this place would be an economic disaster area."

They passed a fruit stand shaped like a giant strawberry. "Do a lot of faculty live out here?" asked Muffy.

"Some. The ones who do the gentleman-farmer thing."

"Do the real farmers mind?"

"All they ask is that you not complain about the smell when they spray manure on the fields."

Muffy readjusted herself in the seat. "What is Dr. Dedmarsh's wife like?"

"Well, yesterday she was kind of snappy. That was before we knew he was dead. But basically I've always thought of her as sort of the same kind of person he was—quiet, caring."

Muffy screwed up her face. "Are we talking about the same man? Ira Dedmarsh?"

"What's the matter?"

Muffy examined Teddy closely. "Nothing."

"What is it?"

Muffy shook her head.

They passed a young blond man on a John Deere, carefully turning over gorgeous toast-colored silt between rows of strawberries. In the town of Lynden, they rolled up to the single traffic light and waited. Teddy glanced down the side street and spotted the sign for Saints Peter and Paul Catholic Church. It was a sixties A-frame with rough-hewn trim.

"Oh," Teddy said. "That's where the statue goes."

"What statue?"

Teddy rolled her eyes. "You haven't seen my office yet. For some reason, Irene Dedmarsh had a nine-foot church statue delivered to the history department rather than to—I assume—that place. I just got moved into a retired guy's office, which has lots of room because he ripped the bookshelves out, so they put the statue in with me. Now I need to get Irene to move it."

Muffy stared straight ahead. "I see."

Outside of town they drove cautiously past construction at the side of the road, topsoil laid up in sable-colored mounds. Finally they turned into a long dirt two-track, the Dedmarsh driveway. On the left were two acres of unmown front yard, on the right, vast strawberry fields dotted with the occasional blue Porta Potti.

"Do the Dedmarshes grow strawberries?" asked Muffy.

"I don't think so. I don't know where the property line is."

There were no cars at the house. They got out and knocked, then Teddy went over and peered in the garage windows. It was cleanest garage she had ever seen, the windows sparkling, the concrete floor either waxed or varnished. No file cabinets were inside, only a tool bench, garden equipment, and a riding mower.

Down by the road, a car pulled into the drive. Muffy and Teddy turned and waited. A woman got out; not Irene Dedmarsh. The woman was wearing a powder blue sweatshirt appliquéd with blue garlands which were highlighted with glitter and textile paint. Her stretch pants and running shoes were matching blue. She had a sunny smile. "Hi, I'm from next door." She pointed to a tiny house a quarter-mile away. "Can I help you?" She had driven over expressly to check them out.

Teddy gestured to the Dedmarsh's house. "We were hoping to find Irene. No one's been able to get her by phone this morning."

"That's because Irene helps with the lunch shift at Mountainview Extended Care Center." The woman looked away from Muffy's red shoes. "Irene's trying to keep her regular schedule. You do know about her . . ."

"Yes, we do. He was in my department." Teddy checked her watch. "Do you think it's okay if we go see her at her job? We really need to talk to her."

"I'm sure it's just fine." The neighbor gestured north, where the spectacular Canadian front range loomed like a set of misplaced alps. "Just take The Hannegan Road up about a third of a mile, turn left on Osnaburg, it's the last road before the border. You'll see Mountainview on the right."

"Thank you." They walked to the car.

Teddy turned to Muffy. "I'm sorry this isn't working out."

"No, fine." Muffy smiled bravely. "This is very interesting."

They followed directions and found themselves turning into the lavish grounds of a modern low-roofed complex with hidden parking lots and lawns like putting greens. Farther up the asphalt, there actually were putting greens. They gawked at the exercise building and tennis courts, and Teddy finally said, "I didn't know you could volunteer in a place like this."

"Me neither."

They parked at the main building and went inside. Nat King Cole was Muzak. Beyond the broad reception area, a delicious-smelling dining room bustled with pink-smocked aides hovering over ancient diners. Off to their left, a pink-smocked receptionist waited for them to see her. They walked over, and she lit up with professional regard.

"We're looking for Irene Dedmarsh," said Teddy.

The receptionist's lipstick matched her smock. Silk flowers in a pink vase were close by. On the wall a framed garden scene was washed in pink Victorian twilight. She pointed to broad windows overlooking a patio at the other end of the dining room. "Irene is helping take Mrs. Wilder back to her room. You can probably catch them on the terrace."

"Thank you."

They walked through the dining room and saw that most diners had left their meals intact—chicken in sauce, ground-up indeterminate greens, bread pudding in a bowl. Outside on the terrace an overweight Irene Dedmarsh wore a pink smock, as did the sweet-faced, equally overweight Hispanic boy she was talking to. Beside them in a wheelchair a tiny silver-haired woman listed to the right. She was no bigger than a third-grader.

Irene Dedmarsh glanced at Teddy and Muffy. Her quizzing look said she couldn't quite remember who Teddy was.

"Mrs. Dedmarsh, I'm Teddy Morelli, from the history department."

"Of course, Teddy. How are you?" Irene turned sideways, as if to hide her size.

"And this is Muffy Woo," said Teddy. "She'll be teaching Dr. Dedmarsh's classes for the rest of the term."

"He probably left a mess, didn't he?" She was instantly sorry she said it. Graciously she extended a hand. "Dear, what a dear you are. Muffy. I'm so glad to meet you."

Teddy turned back to the widow. "Mrs. Dedmarsh, I'm sorry to bother you like this, but we have some problems, and Esther thought you might be able to help."

"Of course, dear, what is it?" Under her smock, Irene's fifty-year-old belly bulged alarmingly, as if she were pregnant. Turning to the young aide, she said, "*Necesito hablar con ellas.*" To Teddy and Muffy, she said, "Let's take Mrs. Wilder for a walk."

Without a word the young man aimed the wheelchair toward a broad, pebble-paved sidewalk leading to a shady glen. But Irene Dedmarsh wouldn't let him off that easily. She grabbed his arm and said, "Carlos, I'd like to introduce Teddy Morelli and Muffy Woo. Teddy and Muffy, this is Carlos Castillo. He's just moved up from Yakima and is going to make a wonderful health care professional. Carlos, *estas mujeres son profesoras de historia en la universidad."*

"H-h-h-how do you do." Carlos shook hands and quickly grabbed the wheelchair again, pushing ahead so that the three women could walk together behind.

"This is a beautiful place," said Teddy. The pebbled walkway beckoned to a wooden bridge over a dry streambed. Last summer's ferns were still proud and green, protected from the nor'easter by a thickly planted copse.

Irene looked around. "They do a good job here. The problem comes when we place aides trained at Mountainview in facilities where they're not given the time or resources to provide the same level of care. It can be immensely frustrating for everyone."

"Is that your job, training aides?"

"No, not at all. I'm the English language liaison for the Opportunity Council. At present we're trying to place Hispanic pre-assimilants into entry-level employment, not just in health care, anywhere we can find it. Our five-year goal is to have at least one English-proficient family member in each Hispanic household in the county."

"That's very impressive."

"Day by day," sighed Irene.

Muffy's heel caught on a wooden strip between the sidewalk sections, and she stumbled forward but caught herself. Teddy grabbed her arm. "Okay?"

"Serves me right for not changing shoes."

Irene glanced at Muffy's pert red shoes, then at Teddy's sturdy wing-tip oxfords. "You girls have such tiny feet."

Which made Teddy look at Irene's. Irene's feet were as broad and upright as the woman herself. She had thick ankles and archless soles that hugged the ground in a no-nonsense way. She wore navy leather walking shoes and white socks.

"Irene," said Teddy, "we've had a computer error trying to download Dr. Dedmarsh's files for Muffy. Esther said you know the password."

"Aigues-Mortes," she said curtly. "With a hyphen."

"Egg?"

Irene shook her head. "A-I-G-U-E-S, it's a place in southern France: Dead Marsh. Ira thought his wordplay was *so* clever." Her anger was involuntary—bilious poison green.

Teddy stared. "Oh, yes. I see. We'll try that. But if you don't mind, we'd also like to take his old file folders, just in case. Esther said they were in your garage."

"No." Irene frowned sourly. "I made him haul all that stuff out. He said he was going to bring it to the cabin on Gilbert Island because he didn't have room at the apartment."

"You have a cabin on an island? I didn't know that."

"Not me! Ira just bought it a few weeks ago. He'd been hiding money from me all along. Doesn't that sound just like him?"

"I . . . uum." Teddy stepped back out of range of Irene's venom. "Gee," she said brightly. "Gilbert Island, I don't even know where that is."

Irene glanced again at Muffy's prancing walk, trying to distract herself. "Ira said Gilbert is just off Lummi Island, but I couldn't find it on the road map. It must be one of the small ones."

"So you don't have a key?"

"Hardly. I make a practice of never going near anything of Ira's. I've never even seen his apartment, much less his cabin."

They crossed the footbridge, where the wheelchair made an agreeable rumbling sound, like a car boarding the ferry. Tiny Mrs. Wilder looked up and said something to Carlos, who turned the wheelchair around and went back and forth over the bridge several times. The three women stood off to the side and waited.

"Oh, Irene," said Teddy. "I know what I meant to ask

you. Our Lady of Guadalupe is still in my office. What shall I do with her?"

"Teddy, I completely forgot! I'm so sorry. The man who said he would take it for me called back and said he didn't want to get involved."

"Involved?"

"I'm afraid there's a problem at my church. I haven't been attending Mass there lately. We ordered Guadalupe in the middle of our house-building two years ago, and Ira assured me there'd be no problem with delivering her to the department." She muttered, "I should have had it rerouted to that horrible yellow apartment of his—wouldn't that have shown him?" Irene lifted her chin pluckily. "But we have to get it out of your office. I can hire movers, but I don't think the box will fit in my garage. The garage door covers the whole ceiling when it's up."

"Actually, Irene, I don't think we're allowed to hire off-campus movers. Something about liability. But if you could just rent a locker and tell me where, I'm sure I can schedule Maintenance to come move it."

"Perfect. I'll rent one as soon as I get off work."

"Thank you."

They walked back up the short rise to the terrace, and Carlos stopped the wheelchair in front of a sidewalk leading off to the cottages.

"Well, goodbye, Mrs. Dedmarsh. Thank you very much. I'm very sorry about what happened to Dr. Dedmarsh."

Muffy, too, stepped forward, extending her hand. "Thank you for your time, Mrs. Dedmarsh. I'm sorry about Dr. Dedmarsh."

The sentiment ricochetted off her. "Don't worry. I'm afraid this isn't the time to be sorry for Ira Dedmarsh. His problems started far too long ago."

"Yes . . . well. Goodbye." They watched her walk off with Carlos, conversing in Spanish. Her graceless shuffle was on the verge of a waddle because of her added weight.

"Muffy, we should call Nigel from here and tell him 'Aigues-Mortes.' "

"Oh, I'm glad you got that. I wouldn't have known how to spell it if it bit me on the nose." She looked around. "Do you think there's a bathroom somewhere?"

"Probably in the main building."

They walked inside, and Muffy disappeared down the hall. Teddy went back to the receptionist, who was missing: *Back momentarily.* Teddy picked up the receiver but couldn't get a dial tone on the complicated phone. She punched 9 without success. Then 1 then 7. Still no dial tone. Wandering down the hall, she came to a glass-windowed office with a white-smocked aide inside. Teddy stepped through the doorway.

"No!"

Teddy leaped back. The aide was actually a nurse: "Taggert, R.N."

"I'm sorry," said Taggert. "I can't let you into this room."

Teddy gestured to the desk, "If I gave you the number, could you make a call for me? No one's out at the front desk."

Taggert frowned. "Is it long distance?"

"Just Bellingham."

Taggert rolled her chair forward. "What's the number?"

Teddy gave her Nigel's department number. As Taggert dialed, she said, "I'm sorry to be such a bear, but we're having problems with shrinkage." She gestured to the medication cabinet behind her. "You're responsible for everything that disappears on your shift now."

Nigel wasn't in, so onto his voice mail Teddy pronounced and spelled the word "Aigues-Mortes" several times. Muffy came back and stood by, waiting.

They climbed into the car and drove to the university. Teddy pulled up in front of Campus Security and let

Muffy out in front of a metallic bronze sports van coupled to a U-Haul. Then, with Muffy in her rearview mirror, she drove slowly out to the north shore of the lake and into her own cul-de-sac.

Muffy's rig was too long to fit in Teddy's short drive, and after a few attempts at angling, Muffy finally abandoned her rolling stock on the street, breaking at least three neighborhood covenants.

"We need to unload the U-Haul quickly and get it out of here," said Teddy.

"Teodora!" Out the front door came Uncle Aldo wearing a kitchen apron and rubber gloves.

Muffy stepped back. "I didn't know you lived with your dad."

Teddy stiffened. "My uncle. He's just visiting." She turned for introductions. "Uncle Aldo, this is Muffy Woo. She'll be teaching with me until mid-June. And staying in my front bedroom."

"Wonderful, wonderful. I sleep on the patio. I'm making us nettle soup tonight. Electricity makes m—"

"Uncle Aldo, isn't Marjorie worried about you?"

"No problem, I called her. She's going down to visit her sister in Seattle. They're twins. Teodora, I used your old Polaroid today, I hope you don't mind. The Arawaks are all over Stewart Mountain."

Noisily Teddy banged back the U-Haul door. "Aldo, we could use your help in unloading."

"Of course!" He peeled off his rubber gloves and tucked them in his apron. "Have you ever had nettle soup, Muffles?"

"N-no."

"Tastes like asparagus. Don't touch the nettles on the counter until I get them boiled. They sting like the dickens. That's why I use gloves."

Inside the U-Haul were three rolling wardrobe racks, their rich, colorful contents half concealed under cleaning bags. On the floor were tiered cedar shoe racks, fragrant with the smell of Ozark hillsides. Teddy tried not to stare at the glorious array.

"I hope I haven't brought too much . . ."

"No, Muffy, no. There's plenty of space in my front bedroom."

Aldo pulled down the door ramp and scrambled up into the truck. "You girls go inside and make yourselves comfortable. I'll take care of this. And look at your phone message, Teodora. A man named Nigel said the password doesn't work."

The phone was ringing as she walked inside. She dashed over to pick it up. "Teddy Morelli speaking."

"Teddy?" It was Nigel. "Your blasted password did exactly nothing."

The same message was on her blue pad. "I know, my uncle told me."

"The computer center thinks Dedmarsh downloaded a Vigilance file to foil hackers. Muffy will have to make do with his old manilas. Does she think they're still current?"

"Nigel, his files aren't in the county. Irene says they're out at a cabin he bought on Gilbert Island."

"Gilbert Island? Why, the old devil! I'm chairman now. Does this mean I'll be able to afford a cabin?"

"Nigel, what do you think we should do? Just tell Muffy to wing it?"

"Where is Gilbert? Is it far?"

"I don't know. Someplace off Lummi."

He was silent, and she knew what he was thinking: he needed to ask Esther what to do next.

"Teddy, let me think this through and I'll call you back."

"I know you will, Nigel." She hung up to find Uncle Aldo spreading a series of Polaroids out on the kitchen counter for Muffy. He looked up, eyes glowing. "Teodora, her name is *not* Muffles. Come here, I can show you, too."

"Show me what?"

Aldo pointed to the first one, a shady forest scene. "Okay, this one shows the secret Arawak sign they leave for each other so they never get lost." Teddy and Muffy scrutinized the ferny path. "Where?"

"There." Annoyed, he pointed to three fallen sticks askew in the trail. "See how they're arranged in an A? And the top of the A shows the direction to follow. Here's the next A, it's a half-mile further on." He showed the next picture with its homey, funky A.

"Oh, Aldo."

"Amazing, isn't it? But this is the one I'm most proud of." He positioned the third picture. "I took it to document where I found the hair sample. Which, if you know where to look, is right *there*, in the huckleberry bush."

Nothing of interest was in the blurry photo. "What hair sample, Aldo?"

Aldo took a sandwich bag out of his shirt pocket. Inside was a coarse, foot-long black hair. "Feel it, Teodora. It's very different."

Teddy pulled out the hair. "Aldo, how do you know this isn't from a horse? See? Look at the picture. This trail is awfully chewed up."

"It's not from a horse because it's from an Arawak."

"And Arawaks actually have hair this thick?"

Aldo frowned. "Not them. Their bearskins."

"The Arawaks wear bearskins?" she clarified.

"Yes, that's the reason you people think Sasquatches are big hairy men. The Arawaks have been wearing bearskins ever since their Spanish clothing wore out."

Teddy looked him straight in the eye. "And that would have been around 1639? 1640?"

"Yes," he agreed. "The Arawak Indians of Whatcom County have been wearing bearskins since 1639."

She didn't know what to say.

Muffy smiled sweetly. "But no sightings yet, Mr. Morelli?"

Sheepishly, he grinned, knowing when he was being kidded. "Of course not. They won't even reveal themselves to me. That's the only reason the Arawaks have survived all these years in the first place, by being totally reclusive."

The phone rang, and Teddy picked up the receiver.

"Teddy?" It was Nigel. "I've been advised that the graduate seminar needs to continue its current syllabus. The students have too many projects out. Also—listen to this—Esther says that it's not a cabin on Gilbert Island, it's a big new house at the south end, and that Dedmarsh kept a boat at the marina to get there."

"Wow. Did he come into an inheritance or something?"

"I have no idea. But Esther says if we like, she can get Ole to take you over in his fishing boat this weekend and pick up the files, but we have to pay for gas because his boat is a big hog and Ole is very stingy."

"Nigel, the weekend is too late. And I can't go anyway, I'm busy."

They breathed together into the receiver. "I wonder if we could rent a boat," said Teddy. "Or maybe get Dedmarsh's boat keys."

"Oh, Teddy, would you? I can't think how to get out there otherwise. Also, Esther says if you're agile enough to climb around his dock gate, you can probably let yourself in with a house key he kept under the last flagstone in the path."

Teddy sighed. "People are so astonishing about security."

"It's to prevent your getting out there then realizing you've forgotten the key."

"I know."

Uncle Aldo was squaring up his photos into a tidy pile. He called over, "Teodora, if you need to go somewhere in a boat, Marjorie will lend us hers."

"Just a minute, Nigel." She put a hand over the receiver. "What did you say, Aldo?"

"I said we can use Marjorie's boat. She hates the water. The boat was her husband's."

Into the receiver Teddy said, "Nigel, we have a boat." She looked at her watch: two-thirty. "And I think Muffy and I could actually make it out this afternoon, if we try. Are you sure the key is under the last flagstone?"

"I only know what I've been told: a large shingled house at the south end of Gilbert Island, key under the last stone."

"Okay, let me see what we can do. If this doesn't work, I'll call you back."

"Oh, bless you, Teddy. Bless you."

"Thank you, Nigel, we're going to need it."

6

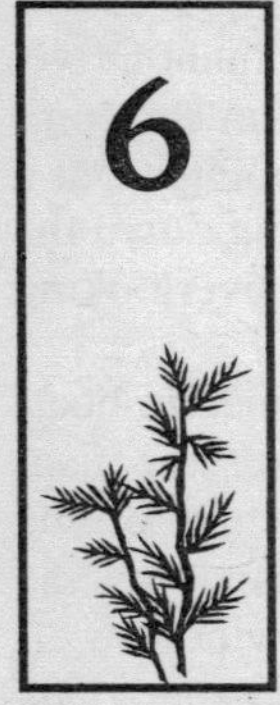

"Aldo, how are you going to ask Marjorie about her boat? You said she's in Seattle."

"No, no. She wants me to use it. It's just been sitting there since her husband died and it's getting in terrible condition. But Teodora"—he gestured toward the front of the house—"I only put Woofy's clothes in the garage. I'll need help carrying them upstairs."

Without missing a beat, Muffy clipped smartly out to the garage. "Don't bother, Aldo, we'll do it when we get back." She turned on the light, calling back over her shoulder, "What should I wear on the boat?"

"Something warm, Woofy. Something dry."

Teddy followed her out to make sure the garage door was locked and watched Muffy rifle through the scented racks, selecting khaki pants, a navy-and-white-striped French sailor's tee, and a red designer parka. At the shoe racks, Muffy had trouble deciding between the khaki-colored Keds and the red ones.

When Muffy came downstairs, changed, it was an amazing transformation. Under five feet tall, asexual, childlike, she had lost any authority she had had in a dress and high heels. From her spot in the passenger's seat Teddy glanced sideways, admiring the Muffy Woo Show more and more. Tiny Muffy sat on a cushion so she could see over the dashboard; in the luggage hold was a short utility ladder. No wonder she wore high heels.

Aldo directed the trip down woodsy Chuckanut Drive, a seaside road so beautiful it was used to film car commercials. Five miles down the coast Aldo pointed out a hidden driveway, and Teddy turned in, rolling down the broad concrete drive to a twenties colonial overlooking Wildcat Cove.

Down in the water was a home-made concrete boathouse as thick as a gun turret. Inside, over the fish-gutting counter, hung a tattered nautical chart of the surrounding sea. Teddy matched up the islands on the chart with the verdant lumps outside the window: directly beyond Wildcat Cove was triangular Vendovi Island, and out beyond Vendovi was Gilbert, a curving green zucchini floating in the middle of the Anacortes Channel.

Aldo clambered happily over Marjorie's spiffy upmarket cruiser. Having laid fiberglass in the Seattle boatyards for thirty years, Aldo was acutely aware of the difference between the floating mediocrities he had built at Kozy-Kraft and Marjorie's Alaska-duty C-Sport.

"Look at those corners, Teodora! Look at that cleat! And underneath the fiberglass is knitted like a *tee-shirt*. You can see in the lockers inside!"

The sturdy twenty-two-foot cruiser had heavy-duty chrome and a triple-layer canvas dodger over the outside seats. Down three steps, below the forward deck, was a tiny cuddy cabin with sleeping room on a V-shaped berth.

They cast off with Aldo at the helm, heading out toward the north tip of Vendovi. Muffy and Teddy stayed under the dodger with Aldo, sitting back to back in the two passengers' seats. After a few minutes in the wind, they had both zipped and cinched every part of their jackets, and Muffy shivered against her will. Aldo leaned over, calling. "You girls go inside. You need to get out of the wind."

With no protest they went down to the cuddy, throwing themselves on the cushions and listening to the delicious quiet. Aldo's half-used tin of carnauba wax was open on the shelf with a rag; the whole cabin smelled like expensive, well-kept furniture. Teddy capped the wax tin and tucked it away. "I'm hoping we get back by dinnertime. The guy I date usually calls on Tuesday night."

"Does he live out of town?"

"Seattle. He's the orthopedic surgeon for the Seahawks, and I don't think he remembers that I can't come down this weekend."

"Cool. What's his name?"

"Aurie Scholl. And actually, it's not cool. He broke up with me six years ago to marry somebody else. They're divorced now . . ." Teddy spotted a Kleenex box, plucked out a tissue, and blew. "Shows you what a loser I am that I'm even dating him again."

"Teddy, don't say that! Is he, like, one of those guys who's sort of socially out of it because they go to school too long?"

"A little bit, I guess. But actually, he reminds me a lot of Dr. Dedmarsh—totally professional about his work, absolutely clueless about everything else in the world—can't understand why everybody doesn't think exactly like him."

"This kills me." Muffy pulled off her red satiny hood, shaking out her curtain of hair. "Every time we talk about Dr. Dedmarsh, it's like you and I are talking about two different people."

"But you didn't really know him, did you?"

Muffy looked away, sighing. "I wasn't going to say anything, because you seemed to like him so much, but what I didn't tell you about Dr. Dedmarsh is that after my session at the Asian Studies Conference in Denver, he said he had some bibliographies for me, he wanted to bring them up to my hotel room. I said, 'Okay, fine,' but I didn't like the way that felt, so I asked a girlfriend to be there with me. Dr. Dedmarsh came and stayed and stayed, and then it got where he just wouldn't leave. So finally we asked him to go away, but then he said he had to use the bathroom. And when he came out, he turned on the water at the sink—it was like, outside by the closet, and instead of washing his hands, he just stood there with the water running, pawing through my clothes. We could *see* him in the mirror! So finally my friend went around the corner and asked him what he wanted. He got really embarrassed and left. But the whole thing was very creepy."

Teddy stared at middle space, at the pathetic image of Ira Dedmarsh pawing through Muffy's beautiful, scented clothes. "I guess . . ." She didn't know what she guessed. "I guess he really needed a divorce, didn't he?"

Muffy's delicate eyebrows rose in surprise.

The engine sputtered and was silent a full half-second. Then it went to humming again. Teddy looked at her watch. Three-fifteen. "If we can get in and out of there in thirty minutes, we ought to be able to get home before dark."

"That'd be nice. I have so much work to do."

The engine sputtered again and went dead. Teddy and Muffy climbed out into the cold air and found Aldo on his knees in the cockpit, unbuckling the engine housing. The boat rocked back and forth at the mercy of the waves.

"What's the matter, Aldo?"

"Something. I told her to get a tune-up," said Aldo. "We're too far from land for this to be any fun." He lifted the housing to reveal a brutish but beautiful Volvo-8. Reaching down into the engine well, he worked off a metal cap the size of a small beret. Underneath were eight round black nubs in a circle, the distributer cap. "Ugh!" He looked around for a tool to work with, then took out his penknife and began scratching the nubs.

Bright metal showed under the black. When he was satisfied, Aldo put the cap back on, rebuckled the housing, and turned the key. The engine sang happily, as if never sick a day in its life.

They rounded the north tip of Vendovi, where a lone cabin flew the Stars and Stripes on a homemade white wooden flagpole. Aiming for a navigation triangle on the south tip of Gilbert Island, Aldo piloted easily down the passage until midway, where the engine sputtered and caught again. Then, stiffly, he began listening with his whole body.

Rounding the south point of Gilbert Island, they came to a row of boxy, flat-roofed summer cabins on a low-bank shore. The cabins were empty and winter-worn, with gull-splatted picture windows and bough-strewn decks as big as the cabins themselves. All down the deck rails were festoons of white buoy line. Perched on corner posts were inquisitive wooden seagulls, their feet nailed in place. Past the cabins—on a rocky precipice deemed unbuildable by the last generation, was perched a brand-new cedar-shingled cottage—as in the Newport sense of the word.

Wrapped in broad porches, with a turret at the end, the gabled two-story house was varnished to keep the shingles a fresh-wood color and trimmed in pristine white enamel. Above all the windows were handsome fanlights with beveled panes, and up on the second floor were twin sets of white French doors opening onto shoe-box balconies. Altogether, the house hung dreamlike in the trees—a cold-coast fantasy, an invitation to hearth-fires and ease. It was if someone had started out building for the Hamptons but ended up remembering Frank Lloyd Wright.

The dock below the house was a complicated affair, a floating raft connected to the base of a massive boulder, a small island itself, really. A heavy aluminum ramp led up to the crown of the boulder and at the top of the ramp was a fearsome metal gate. On both sides of the gate were imposing wings of heavy galvanized mesh, and behind the gate itself a steel bridge gave entrance to the land.

"Teodora! Is that the cabin?"

Teddy scanned the shoreline. "Got to be. There isn't anything else like it on this end of Gilbert."

"I don't know, Teodora."

They tied up at the dock, and the two women padded up the ramp: *No Trespassing.* Washington State legal codes were mentioned in fine print. The gate had vicious steel combing welded to the top and was protected by a keypad lock.

"How're we going to get in?" asked Muffy. Teddy punched random numbers on the keypad. "Didn't the secretary say we should climb over?" They craned their necks to look at the spiked metal combing.

"Not over, around."

The heavy wings on either side of the gate were triangular, widest at the bottom and tapering diagonally to the top.

"We can't climb around," said Muffy. "My fingers couldn't hold that mesh, and anyway, there's no place to put your toes."

The only other way to get to the little island required leaping eight feet of open air.

"Let's make our own bridge. Maybe there's something in the boat." Teddy tramped back down to the boat, where Aldo was kneeling once again in front of the open engine box. "Aldo, we need something long and thin to make a bridge out of. No, we need two things long and thin, one to walk on, and one to use as a handrail."

Stiffly Aldo rose and looked around. "How about the boat hook?" He handed her the telescoping metal pole. "And I don't know what else. A fishing pole?"

"Only if it's cheap and we can trash it."

"Nothing on this boat is cheap." Aldo disappeared

down below and came back with a black graphite salmon rod. It wasn't long enough.

"That won't work," said Teddy. "How about plain nylon rope?"

"Rope we have." Aldo knelt down and banged open a lazaret, displaying a tidy locker of neatly wrapped boat lines. "What size?"

"Half-inch?"

He tossed her the hank. "Be careful. I'll be there in a minute."

"We're fine, Aldo, don't worry." Tucking the nylon rope in the back of her pants, Teddy carried the boat hook up the ramp and began pulling out its telescoping lengths. Then she climbed over the ramp railing and hung on with her knees, reaching the boat hook to the far bottom end of the gate wing.

"Teddy!"

"Teodora, be careful."

"Don't spook me, now." She latched the brass claw of the boat hook into mesh fence of the gate wing. The claw caught. "Okay. I think that'll work. Now all we need is a handrail." She scooted higher up the aluminum ramp and held on again with her knees, taking the rope from the back of her waistband. Reaching out as far as she could, she poked the end of the rope through the steel mesh and worked it out again, tying it off in a knot. Aldo and Muffy hovered anxiously.

Teddy climbed back inside the railing, much to Aldo's relief, and tied the other end of the rope onto the ramp railing. They now had a two-part bridge across to the boulder, a stiff boat hook to walk on, and a rope handrail higher up. "I hope this works."

"Let me try." Muffy was already over the railing. Testing her weight on the boat hook, she found the rope handrail too wobbly to use. "It's too loose."

"Come back a minute, Woofy." Muffy stood outside the railing, hanging on, as Aldo plucked out Teddy's knot and tied one back so tautly it twanged. "Now try."

Muffy stepped onto the pole and clutched the taut rope in her hand. It held. Angling her footsteps, she slid her hand down the line, walking step by step until she hopped onto the boulder. She turned, elated. "Come on, it's easy."

Teddy climbed over the rail and clutched the nylon rope in her left hand. Creeping out onto the boat hook, she took two more steps, slid her hand forward, took two steps, slid her hand, then was across. Muffy pulled her onto the rock, and they turned to Aldo. "Come on, Aldo. It's not hard."

Aldo shook his head. "I can't."

"It's easy. All you have to do is hold onto the rope."

"It's not like that, Teodora. I'm a man, I can't go breaking into houses like you girls." He waved them on. "Go ahead, you'll be fine. I'll wait here."

"Are you sure?"

"No! I'll tell you. I'm going down to Anacortes and pick up some new points for the engine. I'll meet you back here in two hours."

"Aldo, we don't need two hours." Teddy was already on the bridge to the house.

"Maybe not, but I do."

"Okay, Aldo. *Two hours*."

"Fine, girls. Be safe." Aldo turned the key in the ignition, grinning goodbye as the engine turned over happily. Casting off his lines, he gunned the engine and plowed down the center of the Anacortes Channel.

Teddy and Muffy scrambled up a flight of sandstone stairs dug into the cliff, then hurried down the flagstone path in a newly laid formal little garden. The garden was entirely deer-proof—tiny boxwood hedges surrounding beds of sage, lavender, and Saint-John's-wort. At the last flagstone they stopped.

"Here," said Teddy. She lifted the stone and found nothing but black landscaping soil. "Maybe they meant the flagstone at the other end."

They trotted back to the beginning of the path, already

knowing the huge rock was not what was meant. "Teddy, we're not going to be able to lift this."

"I know."

They looked around for help. Aldo's wake was a white V far down the channel. The shingle cottage was boxed up, tight and new. Two hours. "Maybe one of the windows is unlocked."

"Or something upstairs."

They scampered onto the porch and began trying the window sashes and looking for ways to climb to the second floor.

"May I *help* you?"

Stunned, they looked down to see an astonishing red-haired woman standing in the yard at the corner of the house. She was wearing bedroom slippers and a home-made necklace crocheted from metallic yarn. The hair itself was a rich burgundy color, but her scalp and ear-lobes were tinted bright orange from the hair dye. She wore a dark green sweatshirt and black jersey pants, the whole effect being that of a rare hothouse vegetable. She stood with her arms crossed, waiting.

"Hi," said Teddy. "We couldn't find the key."

"I know. I've been watching you since you rounded the point."

Sweetly Muffy smiled. "Do you live here? We thought the cabins were empty."

"I know. That's why you thought you could break in. Everybody and his mother seems to think they have a God-given right to come up here and start poking around."

There was an awkward silence. Finally Muffy asked, "Where do you live?"

The redhead turned and pointed. "Third house down the row. Took the shore path around."

Muffy gestured to the shingled wall. "It's such a beau-tiful house. Did Dr. Dedmarsh build it himself?"

"Hardly, he just gave the money for it two months ago. People from California built it, wanted to get in

Architectural Design. Brought out an architect, contractor, two queers to decorate. They all came over and took photographs, then just packed up and left, never came back. Dead flowers still in the vase."

"Amazing." Teddy shook her head sympathetically.

The redhead shifted her weight. "You're not with that Californian, are you?"

"They're trying to buy it *back*?"

"No!" The redhead was exasperated. "Not that Californian! This is somebody different. They're all Californians, though."

"We're not Californians at all. We're just friends of Dr. Dedmarsh from the history department at Rainwater." Teddy rapped her knuckles on the doorjamb. "We had hoped to get in so Muffy could find his files. She needs them to teach tomorrow."

The redhead considered Muffy a moment, then opened her hand to show a brass key.

"Oh!"

She snapped her hand shut immediately. "When I heard he died, I came over here and got this. You have no idea all the people show up thinking they need to get in." Magisterially she placed the key on the porch boards and walked toward the woods. "Lock it up when you leave. Put the key under the rock."

"Thank you!" they called.

"Key's to the *front* door, girls."

"Thank you!" Teddy snatched the key and ran down the long porch. She turned the bolt and swung open the front door to a bright entry hall with a broad hardwood staircase, a fireplace, and blond oak floors edged in a dark Greek key pattern. The stairs soared to the landing, where a stained-glass goddess presided in the window. The goddess wore a milk-glass gown and held an apple: Pomona, goddess of fruit and harvest. On the stair wall leading up to the goddess were abstract prints echoing her colors—golden spirals, green ovoids, blue swirlies, each print more outrageous than the last.

They stood in the entry and gawked. "We should take off our shoes."

"Right."

Kicking off their Keds, they padded around the main floor. In the ivory-carpeted living room were plump, creamy sofas and English antiques. Cascading down one wall were Kwakwala Indian masks. Down another was a set of bright Imari plates. The oak-paneled dining room was custom-made for the fruitwood table and matching breakfront. Beyond the dining room was the empty butler's pantry and a spacious kitchen with counters of dark green stone. Teddy wandered out to read the geology of the kitchen counters and found a pair of refurbished antique binoculars on the window sill above the sink. She picked them up and focused: the binoculars were for spying on an eagle aerie not twenty yards away.

Muffy came in. "I don't see his stuff."

"Let's go upstairs."

They bounded up the stairs, stopping halfway to admire the glass goddess. At the top they were bowled over by the view. A window seat overlooked the entire San Juan archipelago, and the islands melted away, wave after wave, starting with deep forest green and ending in smoky blues. On the window seat lay chintz pillows of all sizes in shades of forest green and dove blue: someone had decorated the window seat to match the outside view perfectly.

"Muffy, how could he afford this?"

"I don't know."

To the left was the opulent master bedroom. They went in to explore. On the far wall were the French doors they had seen from the boat. The doors opened out to a vestigial balcony with sweeping views down the channel. The floorboards were littered with faded tribal rugs, and against the blue-ticking wallpaper were English highboys. In an alcove to the right, a four-poster bed belied its Chippendale pretensions by being queen-sized.

Through the bedroom was a dressing room with built-in oak armoires, and beyond that an old-timey white-tiled bathroom looking like the Claridge Hotel.

"Cool bathroom," said Teddy.

"Yeah."

They padded through the dressing room to a door at the far end. It opened to a room identical to the master bedroom, except that this one was set up as an office. The same twin French doors offered an unobstructed view down the channel, but lining the walls were built-in oak bookcases. In the center of the room a mahogany companion desk was covered with files and books.

"Hurray!" Muffy rushed over to rummage the desk.

Useless for the task, Teddy explored the room. Only a few feet of books had been shelved; the rest were still in boxes on the floor. Thumbtacked to bookshelves behind the desk was a brittle, yellowing X ray with Chinese characters at the bottom. Teddy examined it carefully: the paw of some strange animal.

Muffy held up a pair of tiny silk Chinese booties embroidered all over with bright, swirling flowers. "Aren't these cute?"

Teddy smiled blandly and scanned titles on the shelf: *Salvatore Ferragamo: Shoemaker of Dreams*; *Chinese Footbinding* by Howard S. Levy; *The Commemorative Catalog* from the Bally Shoe Museum in Geneva, Switzerland. "Oh, Muffy, Dr. Dedmarsh liked shoes!"

"Yeah."

Muffy went back to the desk, and Teddy traversed the room. *The Sex Life of the Foot and Shoe* by William A. Rossi; *House of Pain* by Baroness de la Bretonne; a handsome red leather German edition of Goethe. The Goethe was so beautiful she pulled it off the shelf. It seemed to be a compilation of his letters to a Marianne von Willemer, mostly describing his own collection of women's shoes. In each letter, though, he made mention of the pair of red and gold slippers Marianne had given him, thanking her profusely. Something prickly was happening to Teddy. She reshelved the book. "Did you know that Johann Goethe collected women's shoes?"

"No, I didn't know that."

"Muffy, these books are all sort of, um . . ."

"Yeah, I know," said Muffy.

On the shelf was a neatly squared pile of magazines: *Puss n' Boots, Stiletto, Leg Show, Bitch in Charge.* Teddy pulled out the top one and gawked at the cover. The bitch in charge wore thigh-high black leather boots and carried a bullwhip. Teddy put it back on the shelf.

Muffy said brightly, "He's got all the academic literature on foot-binding. Here's Dorothy Ko."

"Who's Dorothy Ko?"

Muffy ignored her, reading: " 'Feng Jicai, *The Three-Inch Golden Lotus*.' Oh, no, Teddy! Yuck!"

"What's the matter?"

Muffy walked over to the pinned-up X ray. "This is a lotus foot."

"A what?" Teddy padded over to join her.

"It's an antique X ray of a bound woman's foot from Imperial China."

They gawked. It was a bizarrely formed appendage. The long white footbone was arched like a croquet wicket, the heelbone bent so vertically it looked like the spike of a white high heel. Into the black void under the arch the tiny toe bones curled back like burrowing grubs.

"I wonder who she was?"

Muffy read the Chinese: " 'Third Prefecture Hospital, Woman's Lotus Foot.' That's all it says."

"Poor lady."

"Actually, she was probably treated pretty well because of this."

Teddy looked around the room. "I'll be right back. I've got to go to the bathroom."

She went out to the hallway bathroom. There were no fixtures in it, only plumbing holes. She wandered back to the master bath. The toilet flushed with a sulfur smell. And when she washed her hands, the water from the faucet smelled the same. She dried her hands on a plump white towel, reflecting on the strangeness of the house. The contrast between rooms photographed for *Architectural Design* and rooms not used was comical: no plumbing in the main bathroom, but the master bath had a five-gallon apothecary jar filled with different-shaped white soaps; no dishes in the butler's pantry, but the sunroom had a dusty mah-jong game arranged to look half-played.

Back in the office Muffy rifled through boxes on her knees.

"Find anything?"

Muffy frowned. "These are his notes from *graduate* school!"

"I still have mine," Teddy sang. She plucked a half-used legal pad off the desk, Ira Dedmarsh's double-spaced first draft of something he was writing:

> Denny Ireland was a shoe salesman—and a good one. At his posh Madison Avenue shoe store, he had put more women into good shoes than anybody else in the business. Ireland knew all there was to know about the language of high heels—how the thin straps of bondage around the ankle could drive a man wild, how the open-toe shoe coupled with red toe polish flirted like a cheap tart, how the backless high-heel mules screamed "fuck me" without saying a word.
>
> Yes, indeed, Denny Ireland was so good he was responsible for at least a dozen marriages—grateful women told him every day. But his biggest challenge came the day he got a call from Mrs. Clarissa DeVere, Park Avenue socialite, size five AA, who never left her apartment.

Teddy put the pad down, unable to read any more. She looked at Muffy, then at file folders on the top shelf of the in-basket. She picked one up. It was labeled with Chinese characters, and inside was an aging, brown Chinese newspaper article. The only line in English was *The Taipei Daily Journal*, April 14, 1972. She closed the file and opened a second one. Inside was a copy of Canada Customs Form #14-46, a receipt indicating that Peter Maxwell of Victoria, British Columbia, had surrendered "2 kil. of panda gland, ½ kil. of dried tiger penis, 4.6 kil. of long civet musk," and several other items named only in Chinese. A second paper, a xerox from the *Canadian Biographical Directory*, indicated that Peter Maxwell—"b. 1954, m. 1982 (Felicity Brommine), B.S. (Leth.), M.A., Ph.D. (U. of Tor.)"—taught in the University of Victoria anthropology department and had authored several books on Northwest Indian herbal medicine, including *Healers and Shamans* and *The Quaking Root*. In the margin was Dedmarsh's familiar writing: "Potential client, acquire pertinent customs documents A.S.A.P."

Client? Dedmarsh wasn't a lawyer. And anthropologist Peter Maxwell wasn't even American.

She picked up another file: *Irene*. Inside was a month-at-a-glance calendar from last year. Slashed across some weeks and weekends was Dedmarsh's notation in red: "Irene in Akron," "Irene in San Francisco." Overlapping in blue ballpoint were long arrows labeled "Lainey in Chicago," "Handy in L.A."—travel schedules for most members of the department and administration. In the margins were notations: "Layover in Denver?" "Possible two days Minneapolis??" "Nota: both clients fly Northwest." Teddy flipped through the months with growing alarm—as far as she could tell, Ira Dedmarsh had been trying to correlate his wife's out-of-town trips with those of almost every man on campus.

She closed the file and glanced at another: *Czerny*. Stiff with curiosity, Teddy opened it and found a perplexing letter from the Winneshiek County District Court in Decorah, Iowa. The letter was three years old. Teddy scanned: Nigel Anton Czerny was to show cause why he should not raise his child support payments to Tawny M. Bullock from $417 a month to $738. Mind-numbing. But why did Dedmarsh have a copy? The letter was addressed to Nigel, care of the department. Dr. Dedmarsh must have—what? Steamed it open?

Cheeks burning, Teddy put down the three folders and trotted over to the file cabinets. The top drawer bore a neat label, *Clients.*

"Teddy, I've already checked those. It's not his class notes."

Teddy pulled open the oak drawer. Inside were fresh new manila files: *Handy, Lainey, Wallace, Erickson.* Erickson? The secretary? Files for members of the department and almost everyone over at Old Main. *Morelli.* She took it out.

In her file were two white letters and a murky xerox copy of the six-page article Aurie Scholl had published while still in medical school in *Annals of Athletic Medicine.* She had helped Aurie with the writing of it, giving him her research notes from a History of Science Seminar and her translations from turn-of-the-century German medical journals. But what in the world was Aurie's article doing in Dedmarsh's file on her?

In the margin Dedmarsh had scribbled: "Client collaborated in this elaborate plagiarism scheme." Teddy was too stunned for words. She checked the two letters. *"In her teaching Professor Morelli continually promotes left-wing causes, espousing both the gay and lesbian agenda and arguing against the Second Amendment Constitutional Right to Keep and Bear Arms."*

It was a copy of the horrid complaint filed by Brad Bertrand Walker, founder of the Campus Libertarian Committee, who had treated the history department like his own private minefield last year and had now moved on to Poli Sci. But why was this copy here? Six departmental members had been hit with BBW complaints.

The second letter was on University of Washington stationery. Unsigned, this was a formal complaint to Professor Gottschalk, history chair when Teddy was in graduate school. *". . . find it unwholesome and ill-advised for Professor Daniel Platte"*—Teddy stiffened. She had dated Dan Platte after Aurie had dumped her—*"to have relations with the aforesaid female graduate student."* She scanned quickly. Her name was not there—thankfully. The "aforesaid graduate student" was not named at all. It had been a miserable incident; Dan Platte had very quickly gone back to live with his wife. *". . . invites favoritism and provides scurrilous fodder for taxpayers and legislators ill-disposed toward the university."* But why was this complaint against Dan Platte here? She had never seen it before. And how had Dr. Dedmarsh learned about it? At the bottom in Dedmarsh's hand was scribbled: "Client seduces married professor."

Calmly she glanced down at Muffy busy with the boxes. Ever so casually she tucked the file into the back of her pants and pulled her sweater down over it. "Anything I can do, Muffy?"

Muffy patted a pile. "They're all here. I think *Economics* is his graduate seminar, but it looks like upper-level *Empire* used to be three separate classes."

"Not at Rainwater, it didn't. That must have been when he taught at Cal-Davis."

Muffy scooped up a handful of files. "I'll just take them all." She glanced outside, down the channel. "What time is it?"

"Five-fifteen."

"Hope your uncle doesn't take the whole two hours."

They checked the rooms to make sure everything was in order, and while Muffy was closing doors in the master suite, Teddy folded the stiff *Morelli* file and zipped it into the rain pocket of her jacket. They locked the front door of the house and deposited the key, sitting on the steps to wait for Aldo.

But Aldo didn't come. Another hour went by, and the sky turned from pink to rose to dusky gray. Lights went on in the third house down the row. Finally Muffy said, "We better eat something." They unlocked the door again.

Evidently being photographed for *Architectural Design* did not require owning kitchen utensils or food. They banged open cabinets one after another and finally found the few things Dr. Dedmarsh had brought over—salt, pasta, instant coffee, a cheap aluminum pot. Teddy filled the pot at the sink and sulfur again rolled up, reminding her that the chief limiting growth factor on islands was access to good water.

The canned pasta sauce was so awful Teddy dumped sugar on hers. After dinner they cleaned up, and Muffy went upstairs to do lesson plans. Teddy was restless in the house, so went outside to wait for Aldo in the dark. She shuffled down the white gravel paths between the boxwood parterres, fingering the file in her coat pocket. Should she dispose of it here or bring it back to town? Bringing it back was better. She could peruse the file in her locked office, then take it home and burn it in the fireplace, utterly assured that no one else would ever find a cinder. A scent caught her nose in the night breeze—lavender. She leaned over and plucked a pungent stalk, sniffing. Gorgeous night, despite her turbulence.

The white gravel garden path led luminously off into the woods, and she followed it to see where it went. Gravel quickly gave way to soft dirt. She stumbled forward in the dark, finding her way with the soles of her feet rather than by sight. After twenty yards the path ended at a bluff overlooking the salt water. Down below, a small crescent beach of fine sand glowed in the moonlight. It was impossible to get down to the sand. A ladder or steep staircase was needed. Perhaps the next owner would make it accessible. She inhaled the cold, wet air a minute, then turned and walked back to the house.

Upstairs the lights were on, and she found Muffy in the office still working, her feet up on the desk. "Muffy, I don't think he's coming tonight."

Muffy closed her files. "Where do you want to sleep?"

Teddy gestured toward the master bedroom. "Not in *his* bed."

They wandered around upstairs. The two remaining bedrooms had no furniture or paint or ceiling fixtures. The walk-in linen closet had no shelves. They pulled the quilted silk duvet and pillows off the Chippendale bed, finding only a mattress pad underneath. If Dr. Dedmarsh had actually slept here, he hadn't even put on sheets. Dragging the bedding down to the living room, each woman claimed a sofa, Teddy volunteering to wrap up in the mattress pad. She was instantly asleep.

Next morning they awoke to knocking. "Teodora? Teodora? Are you there? Teodora, let me in."

Teddy leaped up and unlocked the door for Aldo. He looked more urban than yesterday, with sharper edges—less a creature of the woods.

"Teodora, I'm so sorry, the boat broke down. Teodora, they've heard of me in Anacortes, the Chamber of Commerce, they want me to walk their beaches." Muffy came in, stretching and smiling. "Woofy, are you girls all right?"

"We're fine, Aldo. How'd you get over the gate?"

"Oh, no. I already took down your little bridge, then I tied up down the row. There's a nice lady there, she showed me the shore path."

"Does she have red hair?"

"Ooh boy," Aldo helped them pull off the bedding. "That's really something, isn't it? She's nice, though, Roxie."

They cleaned like Scouts and locked the house, leaving the key under the last flagstone. They took the shore path back to Roxie's where, gracious and smiling, she fed them coffee and cinnamon crumb cake, all the while trying to interview for a job as Aldo's Norwegian cook. When it was time to leave, she walked down to the dock with them, refusing to let go of the bow line until Aldo promised to come back and play pinochle.

"I will, I will," called Aldo. "I have to get the girls home now."

They waved goodbye, watching the burgundy hairdo pick up highlights in the morning sun. "Are you really going to come back and play pinochle, Aldo?"

Aldo cautiously reversed the cruiser. "Teodora, I'm a man of my word."

"In Marjorie's boat, huh?"

"Hush, Teodora."

They motored back to Wildcat Cove in less than an hour. Aldo shooed them up to the car while he stayed down in the boathouse, putting things away.

At home they showered and changed, Muffy emerging from the front bedroom in an elegant taupe pantsuit over a white silk shirt. Around her neck was a taupe and black scarf, on her feet were high-heeled black granny shoes—real ones—that she must have filched from her grandmother or bought at Magnin's before it went out of business.

Proud of her stylish new associate, Teddy led Muffy down the hall to Esther for her office assignment, hoping nobody but her students would notice she had just missed morning classes. Leaving Esther to explain to Muffy the thermostat in the office of a woman on sabbatical in India, Teddy slipped away and let herself into her own office, slithering past the Virgin. Her phone light was on. She punched it.

"*Liebchen*! Where are you?" It was Aurie. "Just in case you don't get the same message at home, I've just been handed some wonderful tickets for *Die Fledermaus* Saturday night, and there's a new Cajun-Fusion sort of thing on First Avenue we're supposed to try. Howard McCollum is positively swooning over a Blackened Marinated Ahi-ahi. Doesn't that sound positively post-modern? Call me."

"Aurie, for Pete's sake, please look at your calendar." She had told him weeks ago she was busy this weekend. The machine chirped and started again.

"Dr. Morelli? This is Conrad Voltz, in Resheveling at the Archives. You and your assistant were the last users of a volume that has come back with two of the pages stripped. The book I am referring to is"—*thump* went the heavy volume—"Whatcom County Deed Book of 1888. If these pages have ended up in your possession by mistake, we would certainly appreciate your returning them. As you know, we're required to suspend your research privileges when something like this happens. We will also notify the library that your circulation privileges should be suspended. If you could call me back at extension 3125 as soon as possible, perhaps we can work something out about the return of the manuscript pages."

"Shoot!" Poised over the phone, she heard voices in the hallway—the police detectives who had interviewed her the other day. One was asking where Room 247 was—her office! Dedmarsh's *Morelli* folder was right there on her desk! In one motion she picked it up and stuffed it between the slats of the Virgin's crate. She looked up to see the great bulk of the detectives, same sports coats as the other day. Teddy smiled and struggled to remember their names. The Asian was Bao, the other one . . .

"Hi," she said, craning around the Virgin. At the same time she poked a fingernail between the slats and slid the folder farther down the crate.

Detective Bao was stone-faced. The Caucasian scowled. "You're hard to catch up with."

"We just got back. We had to make a quick trip to the islands."

"We know. You want to tell us what you were doing out there?"

Teddy scootched around the Virgin to join them in the hall. "We have a new person filling in for Dr. Dedmarsh. She needed his files so she could teach his classes."

"Which made you break into his house."

"We . . . I just . . ."

Esther and Muffy had just come around the corner, ready to enter the copy room.

"Tennant, Bao!" called Esther. "They haven't sent you guys home yet? I thought you'd be the first people to hear about Dedmarsh's cardiologist."

"Farnum?" Tennant's eyes widened. "What about him?"

Coming close, Esther lowered her voice. "My cousin's a dietitian at the hospital, and she says the only reason Dr. Farnum's making such a stink right now is that he's been in trouble before—with the Tissue Committee over bypasses. My cousin says the reason Dr. Farnum is asking for blood tests is to make sure it doesn't look like it was his fault that Dedmarsh died, that he gave Dedmarsh the wrong medication."

Tennant squinted unhappily. "We don't know anything about that, ma'am. What we're working with is information from the prosecutor's office supplied by the path lab. Pathology seems to think that large amounts of a heart drug called Lanoxin had been mixed with the sugar, yogurt, and instant coffee samples from the victim's apartment."

Teddy turned. "Yuck, Muffy! We ate his food."

"Out on the island?" Detective Tennant eyed Teddy carefully. "I wouldn't worry about it if nothing's happened yet. It's doubtful anyone had access to both food supplies."

"Access?" Teddy had to look up over Tennant's chest he was so tall. "Dr. Dedmarsh was supposed to take Lanoxin. You told me that."

"No, ma'am. We didn't tell you that. His prescription was for something called Rythmol."

"But you said—I don't get it. Why was there Lanoxin in his food?"

The detectives grunted, their eyebrows rising. "Ms. Morelli," said Tennant, "the scenario we're working with is that someone introduced high doses of powdered Lanoxin into Dr. Dedmarsh's food over an extended period of time. Our problem right now is that you and Ms. Woo have just engaged in suspect activity by gaining illegal access to the property of an assumed murder victim."

"Murder? You mean they put Lanoxin in his food to poison him?"

"Yes, ma'am, that'd be right." Tennant folded his arms. "To poison him."

7

Detective Tennant turned to Muffy. "Are you the one who took files from the Dedmarsh property?"

She drew her shoulders back to stand up to his withering gaze. "Yes."

"Can we see them?"

Muffy pivoted neatly, leading the men down the hall. Esther followed. Left alone, Teddy padded the few steps back to her office, staring unseeing at the vinyl tiles. Poisoned him? One of his "clients?" That would make her file important now, the *Morelli* file. The police needed it. They would need everything.

"Professor Morelli?"

She froze.

"Would you mind joining us?" Detective Tennant called back down the hall.

Turning stiffly, Teddy tucked her hands in her pockets and shuffled toward Muffy's office. Tennant casually fell in beside her. "Oh, by the way, I wanted to ask you about the black cabinet you took from Dedmarsh's apartment for safekeeping after he died. That was something you gave him and wanted back?"

"The what?"

"The medics said there was a black Chinese cabinet on the table in his living room, little drawers in it."

Teddy nodded the whole time as he spoke. "I saw that. Some sort of elaborate tea caddy. Are you saying it's missing?"

On his open palm Tennant wrote the words "tea caddy," then drew a question mark. "Yes, that's what I'm saying. There wasn't anything like that by the time we got there."

"Then I don't know what happened to it." She stopped at Muffy's doorway, watching the little historian hand over four fat manila files to Detective Bao. Bao, in turn, gave two of the files to Tennant, and they both leafed through the yellowing thirty-year-old pages.

Muffy hovered anxiously. "It would be better if nothing gets out of order."

"That's true." Bao looked her squarely in the eye. "They've been taken from the house of a murder victim."

Muffy winced.

"And the rest of the things you took . . . ?"

"But this . . . this is it! The economics folder and three on Imperial China." Muffy looked back and forth between the officers.

"We were just out at the island. It looked like Dedmarsh was keeping other kinds of files, too—files on people."

Color rose in Muffy cheeks, plummy veins engorging under the skin. Coolly she met his gaze. "Yes, Officer. I saw those, too. I didn't touch them, because they were none of my business."

"So you didn't take *any*?"

"No, Officer, we didn't."

We? Teddy jerked in surprise.

Tennant closed his two China files and tried to straighten the edges against the desktop. "We're going to have to take these."

Muffy flittered anxiously. "But . . . I have to teach from them."

"No problem, Woo." Esther surged instantly into the

hall, sweeping Teddy before her. "We'll copy them. Let me get the Xerox key from my drawer."

Detective Tennant and Muffy went to wait for Esther in the copy room while Detective Bao strolled the hall, peering through open doorways. No one was interested in Teddy anymore. She slipped back to her office and closed the door. She stood behind it and leaned her cheek against the dense oak slab, face buried in the academic regalia neatly hung on a coat hanger from the hook on the door. Her nose was in the blue velvet on her hood. How on earth had she done something so stupid? She had to tell the police she took her file. They'd find out anyway. It was their job. And the information in hers wasn't all that bad, actually, except the part about Dan Platte. And maybe Aurie, too, come to think of it. The word "plagiarism" killed careers. Oh, God, her tenure . . .

She knelt down in front of the crate and peered into the thin line of darkness between the slats. She needed something to pry open the slats—a crowbar—so she could just hand them her file—slap it on the desk and say, "Sorry, I took it. Didn't know it would turn out to be evidence in a murder case."

On her desk the phone rang. She looked up, watching it make noise, refusing to give herself any more trouble today.

It chirped and voice mail began: "Dr. Morelli, this is Conrad Voltz in Archives. I'm sorry we haven't been able to reach you by phone, but I'm going ahead and having your library research privileges suspended—temporarily, of course—until we find out how you want to resolve this problem with the Deed Book. I'm sorry I have to do it, but I've been told that lendables are considered to be in jeopardy in your possession until it's proven otherwise. Thank you very much."

Stupefied and defeated, Teddy plopped down on her bottom on the floor. Under her desk the space looked dark and inviting, a nice place to disappear. She realized she was in trouble. Somebody had killed Dr. Dedmarsh. Who was it? And his tea caddy was gone, too. But she couldn't think about that now, she had her own problems—like getting this file out to give to the police.

Through the crack between the crate slats she could see the name tab on the file, *Morelli*. She could probably grab hold of it if she could tease it out. She got up on her knees and opened the desk drawer, deciding on a letter opener. She slipped it into the crack and pried out the name tab on the edge of the folder. She got hold of the tab, but if she pulled, all she would get was an empty file, the contents would crumple up inside the crate. She pulled the tab a millimeter and surveyed the situation. Then she reached up into the desk drawer and grabbed a ruler, using it to pin the folder to the crate slats, but the ruler was too fat and stiff to work with. Switching the ruler to her left hand, she slipped it under the name tab, then stabbed the letter opener into the front of the file.

The file was now squeezed thin enough to slide out of the crack, but she needed a third hand to lever out the bottom corner so it wouldn't get jammed inside when she tried to pull. She put down her tools and rummaged again through the desk drawer. Okay, how about a paper clip? A paper clip and . . . Scotch tape. She unbent the paper clip and used it to lift the bottom file corner out into daylight. Then she taped the bottom corner against the outside slats. Picking up her tools again, she slid the ruler under the name tab and used the letter opener to stab the front of the file. Pinching viselike, she pulled the file out of the crate.

Quickly she ripped off the tape and ran into the hall, just in time to hear Tennant and Bao moving toward the stairwell, making the small talk of goodbyes.

"Stop!" She dashed down the hall.

They stared.

"Sorry." She slapped the file into Bao's hand. "I took this from Dr. Dedmarsh's house on the island. I didn't know it would be evidence in a murder case." Bao opened it, leafing through documents. "This is yours," he said.

"Sorry. I took it from Dr. Dedmarsh's house on the island, I didn't know it would be evidence in a murder case."

He eyed her curiously. "And why didn't you tell us earlier?"

"Yes, that's right." She was trembling all over. "Earlier you were talking to Muffy, that's when I came down here and got it for you. I didn't know it would be evidence in a murder case."

He close the file. "Thank you, Ms. Morelli. We'll be in touch."

Esther was standing there watching, as were Nigel, Beauclerke Wallace, Tim Lainey, and three more of her colleagues. Teddy went back to the office and closed the door.

Her phone light was blinking: Conrad at Archives. Good, it was time to get the Pickett-Patchetts off her back. There was too much going on here, with a murder investigation in the works. She punched in Conrad's four-digit campus number—but his phone was busy. So she punched in President Rhodes's number. He would be forced to kick the P-Ps off campus when he heard about the Archives caper.

"Office of the President."

"Hello, Penny? This is Teddy Morelli over in History."

The wonderfully efficient secretary breathed quietly, waiting to dispatch Teddy to almost anywhere else. Teddy sat up straight—she had less than six seconds to get through to the Great Man. "Penny, some *close personal friends* of President Rhodes's, who I think will be *big donors,* have gotten themselves in trouble at the Archives. It would be much better if Rhodes talks to them himself, rather than their being confronted by the Archives staff."

"Is there a message I can give him?" Too bad, honey, you lose.

"Umm . . ." Teddy closed her eyes, concentrating on the delicacy of the task. "Could you please tell Dr. Rhodes that Sally Pickett-Patchett was researching yester—"

"Just a minute. He'll want to talk to you."

Teddy listened to Muzak for a full two minutes, then Rhodes came on. "Dr. Morelli, thank you for following through. I'm sorry for the delay. I've been on the horn with the *Tribune*, sorting out what should go in tomorrow's paper about Ira Dedmarsh. Some days I feel like one of those carnival clowns they throw the balls at to dunk in the water."

"We just heard over here he was poisoned."

"Us too, and I'm hoping that's not really the case. But I'm glad your department found itself a real, practicing Chinese historian."

"You're a real Chinese historian."

"Five years behind on my journals. I wasn't looking forward to coming over there and reading my out-of-date material to your graduate students. That's a pretty savvy bunch."

"They're scary, aren't they? Most of them are in Chinese history because they've already traveled in Asia."

"And I hear you and the new replacement stumbled onto some fairly hair-raising file cabinets out at Dedmarsh's cabin this morning."

She nodded. "Hair-raising is exactly the word."

"The police told me what was involved, and I sat here wondering whether to call in the legals and tell them to get ready for lawsuits from the whole history department or call the board of trustees and resign before it happens."

Teddy laughed. "Actually, I don't think it's all that bad."

"How do *I* look as a criminal? Pretty sinister, I guess."

"As a matter of fact, I don't think Dedmarsh had a file on you, at least I didn't see one."

"You don't say? Glad to hear it. Be damned if I could figure out how I was going to sue myself."

Teddy smiled; if he could laugh about it, so could she. "At least Dr. Dedmarsh wasn't running an Internet term-paper business out of his apartment."

"Apartment? Oh, yes. I keep forgetting he lived in an apartment. I only visited the Dedmarshes together out there in the county. So, Professor, what can I do for you?"

"Dr. Rhodes, I met with Mrs. Patchett yesterday in the archives and showed her a document relating to her great-great-grandmother." Teddy sucked in air. "And now this morning I get a call from the archives and they said the pages we were looking at are missing."

"No, no, there must be some misunderstanding. I'll talk to Sally immediately. There shouldn't be any awkwardness between you on your trip out to San Juan this afternoon."

"This afternoon?"

"That's what you called about, isn't it? Sally and Herb changed their plans to work the trip in today because you couldn't get away this weekend. Herb has reservations for tonight."

"Dr. Rhodes, I can't! I just got *back* from the islands. I need to stay and work."

Pained annoyance charged the phone line. "Professor Morelli, I know you've got a lot on your mind—we all have at this point—but this morning we started negotiations with Herb about something called the Pickett Scholars Endowment, and he left feeling pretty good. We're at a very touch-and-go stage now, and we simply cannot implement a program like this without the support of everybody involved—especially our faculty, tenured and non-tenured alike." He let that sink in. "I—I don't know what else to say, Professor. We need you on board. Today."

Teddy sighed, and said nothing.

"I hear you, Professor, but we just can't do this without you."

A dull throbbing started halfway back in her skull. "Well, could you please at least ask Mrs. Patchett to bring back the deed pages to the archives? They've already taken away my library privileges. Without a library card, I'm dead in the water."

Humor and good feeling oozed through the phone lines. "Ha-ha! And that really is unacceptable, isn't it? I'll see what I can do. Meanwhile, we've given the Patchetts a city map and shown them where you live; they said they'll pick you up at three to make the four-fifteen ferry out of Anacortes."

"Fine." No, it wasn't. "Thank you, Dr. Rhodes." It was 2:02.

"Thank *you*, Dr. Morelli."

She hung up the phone and poked her head out into the hall. She had to get rid of the Pickett-Patchetts now—that's all there was to it. She scurried out to Nigel's office and found his door open, the office empty. Around the corner in the lounge Nigel was reading the ingredients on a tin of Amaretto coffee. Teddy went in and stood across from him, waiting.

"Dear girl! What *is* the matter?" He propped his glasses on his forehead. "I told you Maintenance is coming for the statue. You're not still upset about Ira Dedmarsh, are you? If it turns out that Irene was just trying to move him along with extra heart medication, I'm sure she thought it was a mercy killing."

"Nigel, stop it. Irene did not give him extra heart medication. And it's very scary to me if somebody did kill him on purpose. But right now I'm having a meltdown situation with Old Main."

He put down the coffee tin. "Old Main is my bailiwick. What's your problem?"

"I'm hoping you can talk to President Rhodes for me. I am being pushed into an untenable situation with the Pickett-Patchetts."

"Now, remind me who the Pickett-Patchetts are again."

"The Pickett-Patchetts are the people who want me to write about General George Pickett. I'm going out to San Juan Island with them this afternoon and I'm going to tell this woman some brutal truths about her ancestor, which upon hearing, she and her husband will end up *not* donating 3.4 million dollars to the university. Rhodes has already indicated the whole episode will go in my tenure file."

Nigel rasped, "He has not! That's not permitted."

"I know it's not permitted. And the last thing in the world I want is to be threatening lawsuits when I'm up for tenure."

At the word "lawsuits" Nigel jerked straight, mortified. "So, I see. It's come to that, has it?" He crossed his arms over his chest. "Well, then. We'll have to be very, very careful from here on out, won't we?" He looked at the clock, surveyed the room. He was already documenting this meeting for her personnel file.

"Nigel, I didn't mean that. I'm sorry. What I mean is, I'd love to help the institution any way I can, but this is simply not a good project to undertake."

"Dear girl, then just keep saying, 'This is not a good project to undertake, this is not a good project to undertake.' They're like students, Teddy. When the fog finally lifts, yours are the words they'll come away parroting: 'This is not a good project to undertake.' "

"Nigel, you're not helping me at all."

"Yes, I am! Trust me! I care terribly about your welfare. I care terribly about all my personnel."

Without a word, she turned and paced back down the hall. She had forty-five minutes to get home, pack, and become agreeable for her trip to the islands with the Pickett-Patchetts.

At afternoon tide change, the rain started, a fine mizzle from clouds like used Kleenex. Out in Teddy's cul-de-sac the rhododendrons held up their leathery leaves in thanksgiving while yellow banana slugs slithered about in anticipation of a wet and gluttonous evening. At 3:07 Herb and Sally pulled into the driveway in a rented red sports van, as tousled and dismayed as rained-out campers.

"When will this quit?" asked Sally. She wore a pleated rain bonnet over her brunette coiffure, not yet having realized that she would wear it fulltime for the rest of her visit if she actually cared about her "do."

"Let's see," said Teddy. "August?"

All the way down Chuckanut Drive Herb stopped at scenic overlooks to peer down at beaches. Sally took in everything—blue islands, leaden sea, gulls sleek as modern sculpture, quoins of Chuckanut bedrock exposed like ruins of ancient cities. Teddy and Sally watched Herb out in the weather, his thick blond mat darkened brown by the rain.

Sally smiled cheerfully. "You have to humor Herb. He's got this thing about reverse osmosis from salt water, and he's trying to buy up beaches."

"He won't have much luck here, then. The ones on this road are more like mud flats."

"That's what Walter Rhodes said, too. But Herb likes to even just look at real estate. I think it lowers his blood pressure."

Brightly Teddy tried, "Speaking of President Rhodes, did he tell you about the manuscript pages that were missing from the archives?"

Sally made a face. "That's already taken care of. They've been checked back in. I only checked them out in the first place to make color copies. But listen"—she put on a pair of gold-rimmed reading glasses and pulled an antique buckram book out of her bag—"I've been so excited to show you. I had so many good ideas, thumbing through Grandma Sally's book last night."

"I didn't know she wrote a book, too."

"Oh, yes. Grandma Sally was a prolific writer. That's how she supported herself after Grandpa George died."

Herb came back to the car, dripping wet, happy as a dog.

"Find anything, Snickerdoo?"

"Gray mud. Kind of beach you let the tree-huggers have."

"Don't catch cold, baby." Sally patted him on the arm absentmindedly, then showed her book to Teddy. "When I started reading, I realized we could base three whole chapters of our biography on Grandma's Sally's book alone." She pulled a pencil from her bag.

"Really?"

"Oh, yes. See if you agree. We've got George Pickett: Scholar, George Pickett: Pig War Negotiator, George Pickett: Indian Fighter. It falls right into place." Sally marked a book passage with her pencil. "And I know this is a sensitive subject, but I thought we should talk about it now so there won't be any misunderstanding later," she turned, "Don't you think the cover of our book should have my name first? I don't mean to sound selfish, but I think it'll sell more copies that way: LaSalle Corbell Pickett—that would pique people's interest, wouldn't it?" She scrutinized Teddy's face. "Unless, of course, you think Theodore Morelli, Ph.D would be better."

Teddy's mouth had fallen open. She closed it.

"Here." Sally held the book out to Teddy. "This is the material on Grandpa's linguistic work. Evidently he was well loved by the Indians, and he even translated the Lord's Prayer into Nootka—and some other language, too."

"He what?" Teddy snatched the book: *Pickett and his Men* by LaSalle Corbell Pickett (Mrs. G. E. Pickett), published by Lippincott, Philadelphia, in 1913. It was a sturdy, handsome volume, with a cameo frontispiece of the middle-aged George Pickett in his Confederate general's uniform.

"Read the part about the Pig War I marked."

Teddy read:

> Captain Pickett was greatly distinguished in this war, not only as a soldier, but as a promoter of the arts of peace. He made friend even of his enemies, learning the dialects of the different tribes, that he might be able to teach them better principles of life than any they had ever known.
>
> Over them he exerted an almost mesmeric influence. The red men were all his friends, but the most devoted among them were the Nootkams and Chinooks, who greeted and spoke of him always as Hyas Tyee, and Nesika Tyee—'Great Chief' and 'Our Chief.' He translated into their own jargon, and taught them to say, and to sing, some of our most beautiful hymns and national airs, and the Lord's Prayer:
>
> *Nesika Papa klaksta mitlite kopa saghalie, tik-egh pee kloshe kopa nesika tum-tum Mika nem: Kloshe pee Kloshe Mika hyas Saghalie Tyee kopa konaway tillicum: Kloshe kwah-ne-sum Mika tum-tum kopa illahie, kakwa kopa Mika saghalie. Potlatch konaway sun nesika muck-amuck.*

"Actually," said Teddy, "this isn't an Indian language, and he probably didn't do the translation."

"No?" Sally bridled.

"This is something called Chinook jargon, which was a pidgin language everyone out here spoke in the 1800s—Indians and whites alike. It was a conglomerate of lots of different languages, and I've seen at least eleven different versions of the Lord's Prayer. I imagine if we check old missionary sources, we'd be able to see if this version is the Oregon Catholic, the Walla Walla Methodist, the Portland Congregational . . ."

"But what if this is his translation for the Chinook tribe?"

"No, no." She still didn't get it. "The Chinook *tribe* of Indians is something completely different. They had their own language. The way you can tell this is a composite jargon is to look at the words. *Nesika Papa*—'Papa' is English, isn't it? And look, further down, *Potlatch konaway sun,* which means 'Give each day.' You've heard the word *potlatch,* haven't you? It's Nootka for 'give.' And 'sun' is the English word, used for 'day.' See? Some English words, some Nootka words, some Chinook tribal words, all mixed up in the jargon." Teddy handed back the book. "My thought about this passage is that your great-great-grandmother found this Lord's Prayer in her husband's papers and spun some fine prose around it to make your grandfather look more accomplished than he was." Teddy made sincere eye contact.

"Well," Sally sniffed. "That's interesting. Maybe you should read Grandma's book and find out what we can use."

"Good idea." Teddy tucked it in her bag.

At Anacortes they loaded the van onto the ferry and made their way to the upper lounge. Herb pulled out a topo map of the islands, heavily annotated in ballpoint pen, and they helped him match up the snatches of sandy beach outside the picture window with locations on his map. They off-loaded at dusk in the island town of Friday Harbor and drove immediately down to the barren south end, where Captain George Pickett of the Union army was posted before he resigned to join the Confederacy. The park gate was already locked for the night, and they left the red van in front of the chain and crunched down the gravel road. Silver breath rose in the evening air. Teddy found walking-tour brochures in a covered box, and she took out three, handing one each to Herb and Sally.

They hiked down the bleak road in the mizzle, and as they came out from a windbreak of gnarly trees, the westerly smacked them from the side. They trudged out along the stark peninsula to the lone remaining building of Camp Pickett, a white clapboard house used as officers' quarters. They clomped up onto the porch. The house was locked and needed repair.

Teddy turned up her jacket collar. "This wasn't built until after George Pickett left. I think I remember its being very shabby inside."

"That's too bad." Sally stood on the porch, surveying the barren, windswept site. She seemed deeply moved.

They tramped across the sour soil out to the gun redoubt; wind whistled from unknown hollows. At the highest viewpoint of the redoubt they stood and surveyed the leaden sea to the south. Gray clouds hung like hospital curtains, blocking all views of anything glorious or majestic.

Teddy unfolded the brochure. "This earthwork (or redoubt) was built by Henry Martyn Robert, who later wrote a little book on parliamentary procedure called *Robert's Rules of Order*. Robert was two years out of West Point when he came here on August 22, 1859, as a young engineering officer, designing and supervising construction of the redoubt. After leaving two months later, he enjoyed a long career in the Corps of Engineers, retiring as its commanding general."

"Now, that's interesting. Can we put that in our book?"

Teddy shrugged. "It'll amount to about two sentences."

They stood silently and surveyed the cold, gray water in the cold, gray rain. Camp Pickett was as dreary a spot as there was on earth. Dry grass, glacial boulders, prevailing westerlies, stunted trees, overcast as far as they could see.

"Now, what were they fighting the British about?" asked Sally.

"Well, as I said Sunday, the precipitating incident was that a Hudson Bay Company pig from a farm down in"—Teddy turned and pointed—"*that* hollow was shot by an American farmer who lived pretty close to the place where we parked the car. But the reason both were living on the island in the first place was that when the Canadian-American border got drawn in 1849, the boundary commissioners said the line should cut south through the main channel between Vancouver Island and Washington Territory. Well, it turns out there are two main channels, with this group of islands between."

"So when did they fight?"

"That's the good part. They didn't. The Brits set up their camp at the north end of the island and the Americans here at the south. Both sides just sat in the rain, drinking, playing cards, trying to find something to do. There were an awful lot of desertions to the gold fields up north." There was a popping sound in the wind. Beside her foot the dirt mysteriously erupted in a tiny explosion—rabbits, she thought. Warren holes were everywhere.

"And Grandpa George was here for . . . ?"

"Four months in 1859 and a few more in 1860."

"So basically, he just sat in that farmhouse in the rain?"

Again Teddy made sincere eye contact. "That's about the size of it."

The air popped a second time, and the wind whistled next to her face. Were they being shot at? She looked around and saw nothing. The spring-bare trees hid no one. The hollows in the cliffs looked too shallow to hide a man. But something made her walk very quickly down from the exposed ramparts. Sally was out of the wind already, scraping her muddy shoe against a rock.

"Herb, honey, let's go. I'm cold."

Car heater noisily going full blast, they drove back to town and checked into the posh San Juan Inn, with hot tubs and balconies overlooking the harbor. Thirty minutes later in the dining room, they wolfed down a Copper River salmon and sweet potato ravioli. Afterward Herb ordered a single piece of chocolate hazelnut cheesecake that he cut into thirds and put on everyone's coffee saucers.

Delicately Sally put a fork through the rich chocolate chunk. "You haven't mentioned anything about the you-know-what, Theodore."

"The book?" asked Teddy.

Sally frowned. "Never mind, we can talk about it when you're ready. You do know we're willing to pay?"

"That's good. Because sometimes research costs money. Travel, buying books . . ."

"You don't want to talk about it yet, do you? I can understand that." Thoughtfully Sally broke off another forkful of cake and began again. "Tell me, Theodore, why do you think there's such a mystery about Grandpa? Grandma Sally had to work so hard to promote him. He was such a peaceful man for a general, almost like he didn't like to fight."

"Sal, you're not saying he was a coward, are you?"

"No, but . . ."

Teddy nodded. "There is something very odd about George Pickett. About his not wanting trouble or perturbation of any kind. He's just so . . . passive for somebody in that position. I've never understood what made him tick."

"Maybe we could call him the thinking man's general. I mean, all his strategy during the Indian Wars . . ."

Indian Wars? Teddy put down her fork and calmly sipped coffee. "Well, it's too late to call Etta Egeland tonight, because she's one hundred and two years old, but tomorrow before breakfast I'll try to get ahold of her and see if she's up for a visit. She can tell you anything you want to know about George Pickett and the Indian Wars."

"A hundred and two!"

Teddy smiled. "She was born in 1896. She has been the town historian for most of the twentieth century."

"A hundred and two," repeated Herb.

Sally grew misty-eyed. "There's always somebody like that, isn't there?"

Teddy nodded, swallowing coffee. "People with memory. It's easy for them, because they just seem to understand that things will always flow."

"That's so amazing." Sally turned to Herb and squeezed his hand. "Well, Snickerdoo, it's been a long day. A hundred and two!"

Herb delicately put down his coffee cup. "I'm ready to turn in, too. Though I don't think I'll join you tomorrow for the old lady. We drove by a real estate office on Main Street, and the boys inside look like they might know what they're doing."

Sally wrinkled her nose. "Herb says a good real estate agent can read your net worth off your shoes."

Champagne-haired Herb covered the rim of his cup, stealing its warmth. "These boys didn't even see my shoes. I just looked in and could see they'd both been selling property for a long time. Figured if I asked about any beachfront on the island, they'd probably've played on every single one of 'em when they were boys."

Teddy shook her head. "I can't imagine there are any nice, big beaches that don't already have developments on them."

"Doesn't have to be big. All I need is a couple of yards of five-micron diatomaceous silicate. Need it to run a reverse osmosis system."

"And reverse osmosis is . . . ?"

"Reverse osmosis is the hottest thing going for making a halfway decent fresh water from salt. You pressure-run it through porcelain filters. Trick is, you've got to find your five-micron particulate for first-stage filtration. Cuts down the cost. Let Mother Nature do all the work for you."

"Reverse osmosis."

Herb nodded. "Gonna be all over the place this century, you watch."

"Herb's a visionary," said Sally.

Teddy imagined strangling him with her napkin. "Well, this is really going to change things on the islands, isn't it? You're saying it's now actually cost effective to make fresh water from the sea?"

"Oh, absolutely."

"And no one's tried it up here yet?"

Herb raised his hand modestly for the check. "I like to think of us as pioneers."

They said good night and went to their rooms. Teddy tried to stumble through a few pages of *Pickett and his Men* but found it to be the most unmitigated cant she had ever seen. The only interesting part was trying to figure out why old Sally Pickett had written it in the first place. Was there a pension involved? Or was she trying to cover up something else about Pickett? The last thing Teddy remembered was the popping sounds on the gun redoubt. They couldn't possibly have been gunfire.

First thing in the morning, Teddy called Etta Egeland, explaining that she was from the history department at Rainwater and that she and a visitor from California were hoping to visit Etta, if she was up to it. Graciously, Etta invited them over for ten o'clock.

Over a breakfast of coddled oysters and milk toast, Teddy outlined the morning agenda to Sally and Herb. Herb, too, had had good luck. His realtors had called him back within moments of his leaving a message at eight. As the waitress cleared their plates and poured fresh coffee, Teddy looked at her watch. "When's your appointment, Herb?"

"Oh, anytime. I need to take the van, though. I'll drop you two off. Realtor says his Caddie won't like some of the places we have to go."

It was nine o'clock—still an hour before Etta would be ready for them. "Speaking of places to go, I just thought of something you might like to see while we're waiting. It involves the Pickett family and it's right up the street."

"Let's go."

They checked out of the inn and drove up the hill to San Juan County Courthouse, which was just opening for the day. A turn-of-the-century redbrick, the courthouse had high, echoing hallways and frosted-glass transoms above the doors. The hallways were entirely empty, like a school with class in session, and halfway down the main hall Teddy stopped and pointed to a huge, life-sized oil painting in a black enameled frame.

"Here he is," she said.

Not George Pickett. The man in the picture was a nineteenth-century European gent with muttonchop whiskers and a blustery face. Under his short suit jacket he wore a red diplomatic sash. Someone had worked very hard to make this common little man look distinguished and clever.

"Who's that?" asked Sally.

"Kaiser Wilhelm of Germany. Remember I said he was the one who arbitrated the Pig War and assigned the islands to the U.S.? Well, your"—Teddy thought for a moment—"great-grandfather, George E. Pickett, *Junior*, donated this painting to the courthouse in 1938."

Sally touched the frame. "It's a nice painting."

"It's a nice painting," said Herb.

At 9:55 Herb drove them three blocks over to Etta's on the hill back of town. "Bye, Sal. If you gals finish before I do, just walk down to the ferry and wait for me in those shops. I'll pull into the ferry line as soon as I get back."

"Bye, Snickerdoo. Have a good time."

They knocked on Etta Egeland's door, and she welcomed them into the eighty-five-degree heat of her living room. Tiny Etta wore a heavy sweater and a pair of glasses so thick they glinted blue around the edges.

"You'll have to speak up," she said, "I'm a bit hard of hearing."

Teddy shook her bony little hand. "I hope that's my only problem when I'm one hundred and two." She presented Sally. "Mrs. Egeland, this is Sally Pickett-Patchett, the great-great-granddaughter of General George Pickett. Sally, this is Etta Egeland."

"How do you do?" The women shook hands.

Etta seated them in the living room and served tea and homemade banana bread. This was a familiar assignment for Etta, and Teddy watched her listen to the small talk, waiting to hear what they wanted from her. After listening to Herb's beach adventures, she turned impatiently, focusing on Sally through the thick lenses. "So you're a descendant of George Pickett?"

"Yes, ma'am." Sally broke off a small piece of banana bread. "And Professor Morelli and I are collaborating on a book about him. As you probably know, most of the books out are very biased. Of course it was a terrible thing he took the blame for at Gettysburg, but he was really at his best during the Mexican War, also out here during the Pig War." She turned to Teddy. "Though I don't think we'll be able to make a whole chapter out of the Pig War, will we?"

"It'd be a stretch."

"But I was reading the book you recommended about Pickett and the territorial governor . . ."

"Isaac Stevens."

"Yes, him. And it sounds like the Indian Wars were terribly exciting." Sally rolled her eyes. "I can just see it like a movie. Those great big war canoes coming out of the coves, and Grandpa shouting out, 'Fire the cannons.' I mean, forty thousand angry warriors, that's a monumental battle."

"When was that?" asked Etta.

Teddy pressed her teacup firmly on the plate. "Sally, I believe forty thousand was the entire estimated population of Indians on Puget Sound in the 1850s. And George Pickett was never involved in a battle."

"No wonder I couldn't find it."

"And as far as I know, the only Indian troubles this far north were with Alaskan Indians coming down in raiding parties."

"Yes. That's what I found. And Grandpa George helped guard against them, didn't he?" Sally turned to

Etta, who had been silent. "You people must have really been thankful for the military during that time."

Etta didn't bat an eye. "Hard to say." She raised herself from the chair and went out to the bookshelf in the dining room, returning with a manila envelope. "My people didn't come here until the 1870s. And the Indian raids were long, long before." She stretched her arms out to read and flip pages. "And too, you have to remember George Pickett was on the mainland in Bellingham during the Indian raids. And if I remember, it seems like the locals were none too confident about his ability." She passed a thick xeroxed article to Teddy. "Could you find what I'm looking for? It's something about letters to Governor Stevens from a Bellingham man named Mason Fitzhugh."

"Sure." Teddy quickly skimmed the article, *Raiders from the North,* by a park ranger named Mike Vouri. She found "George Pickett" and the Fitzhugh letters indented and offset. "Do you want me to read them?"

"Please do," said Sally.

" 'We might all be killed as we expect no assistance from George Pickett's Military Post, they having as much as they can do to protect their own perimeter, their pickets not being finished, and many of the soldiers being in irons in the guardhouse.' "

Teddy looked up. "Do you want the other one?"

Sally said nothing.

" 'Bellingham miners and others on the Sehome side of the bay have formed a Volunteer Company, and intend to build their own blockhouse. . . . All we need now to feel cozier is our own cannon, which would inspire confidence in our forces. Otherwise we might just beat a path south and leave Bellingham Bay to the Lummis, the harbor seals and Henry Roeder.' "

Teddy said kindly. "Henry Roeder ran a sawmill in Bellingham. The Lummis are the local tribe." She folded the article smoothly and set it on the coffee table.

Everyone was silent, and finally Sally said, "Well, I

don't know. This whole thing must have been so hard on Grandpa. Building forts with incompetent men, not getting all the supplies you need. It would have driven me to drink."

Etta said, "Yes, exactly, I think you've put your finger on it. It may be that I'm just sensitive to this because of my age, but I've noticed whenever I'm reading about George Pickett, there's always a mention of rum, spirits, whiskey of some kind. And I believe he died of a ruptured liver. So my thought has always been, when trying to understand George Pickett, that he was an alcoholic—he needed to get quietly soused every evening after work. But of course, I may be wrong." This time Etta made sincere eye contact.

"An alcoholic?" A light went on in Sally's eyes, but she lowered her lids to hide her thoughts.

Quickly Etta said, "Of course, I'm much too old, but if I were writing a book on George Pickett in the Northwest, I would write about little Jimmie Pickett." She rose again and went out to her cache of manila envelopes. "That's the interesting story. And there's so much material."

Opening the envelope, Etta let the brittle brown newspaper clippings flutter onto the coffee table. "For instance, when George Pickett's widow, Sally, was out here visiting after the Civil War—1888 I believe it was—she gave Jimmie Pickett the general's cavalry sword. And when Jimmie died the next year of tuberculosis in a Portland boarding house, the sword was stolen from his room during the funeral. Isn't that heart-rending?"

"She *gave* that boy Grandpa's sword?"

Etta pushed over the heap of newspaper clippings. "That's what my friend Dolly Connelly said. She wrote an article in 1977 for the *Tacoma News*, researched for months."

Sally touched the fragile newsprint. "I think people who say George Pickett had a half-breed son want to drag him down."

Behind her thick glasses Etta considered. "I believe the Bible George Pickett gave his son Jimmie is in the State Historical Society in Tacoma."

Sally's pretty face twisted ugly with fury. "That doesn't mean the boy was his son. Anybody could give anybody a Bible!"

Teddy picked up Dolly Connelly's article. "Oh, Sally, look, here's the Bible inscription: *'May the memory of your mother always remain dear. Your father, George E. Pickett.' "*

"Well." Sally's eyes bulged. "Well. That proves it, doesn't it?" She sipped her tea.

There was no conversation after that. They made a few more pleasantries, said goodbye, and walked down the hill to town. At a café near the ferry terminal, they ate lunch silently, keeping an eye out for Herb's red van. When he finally showed up at one-thirty the roof rack of the van was loaded with twelve-foot lengths of fine hardwood wrapped in green canvas.

The sight of her husband put Sally back in good humor. "Herbert Patchett, what on earth have you bought this time?"

Herb tucked the boards lovingly under the tarp. "Teak. They took me to a boatyard where they make the most gorgeous little wooden boats. I ordered us a little dinghy, Sal. It's a honey of a boat."

"What are we going to do with a dinghy, Herb?"

"Put it in the backyard. You can grow flowers in it."

Sally danced with vexation. "Did you buy any property?"

"Nope. Seen better."

The ferry chugged neatly into its slip, and they drove on. Upstairs in the overheated lounge, Sally turned to Teddy. "She was wrong about the Indian boy. If you go get Grandma's book from your things, I can show you the part about the great chief giving Grandpa his son."

Teddy considered: they had winged Sally, but she wasn't dead yet. Now might be a good time to give her the lecture on reliability of sources. "Sure." Teddy stood, waiting.

"Herbert, give her the car keys."

Dutifully, Herb reached in his pocket and handed Teddy the keys. She went down to the car deck and pulled *Pickett and his Men* from the side pocket of her duffel. She relocked the van, noticing that underneath the lengths of teak was something large and flat, probably sheets of marine plywood. But no, whatever it was was painted, not raw wood.

Curious, she unhooked a bungee cord and pulled back the canvas to peek. It was the back of a painting—the black enameled frame of Kaiser Wilhelm from the courthouse.

8

At five o'clock they dropped her off to find a thirty-foot Land Yacht motor home in her driveway. *Sassy Lady* was scripted across the back, a pair of dice dangling from the last *y*. The vehicle's utility panel was open, but no one was in attendance. Teddy made her goodbyes and dumped her bag inside by the door.

"Aldo?"

He came out from the kitchen, carrying a fragrant latte. "Teodora, how was your trip? I hope you don't mind the Land Yacht. It's Marjorie's sister's, the inside lights don't work. And don't worry, I've already moved my things out there for tonight and as soon as I get the lights fixed, I'll go."

"You don't have to go." She glanced around the kitchen. He had been sitting at the table with the Yellow Pages open. Her espresso machine was back together. And she needed to call President Rhodes immediately.

"Of course I have to go," said Aldo. "Woofy can't stay here any longer with a man on her patio. It's not good for her reputation."

"Her name is Muffy, Aldo."

"I know, Woofy is somebody else. She just called to say the computer is running and she has all the students' names, she's going to stay late and work. Last night we moved her clothes upstairs, but there wasn't enough room. We left a rack in the hall."

"I'm sure it'll be fine." Teddy pulled out the campus directory. It was 5:07. If she was lucky, Rhodes was still at the office.

"Excuse me again." Aldo held up a short silver cylinder in his gnarly fingers. "I need to buy a bunch of fuses at the Land Yacht dealer in a town called Lynden. Is that close?"

"About thirty minutes away. Can it wait until tomorrow?"

"Don't worry. I can hitchhike."

"No, you can't." She thumbed the campus directory.

Aldo pulled over an open copy of the Bellingham *Tribune*. "And one last thing: guess what? I was sitting here reading the article about your dead professor, and they said *she* did it. Next thing you know the phone rings, and it's her! She wants to talk to you, she has something for you. Now isn't that something?"

"Muffy?"

"No, no. The dead man's wife."

"What?" Teddy rushed to the table and scanned the *Tribune*.

DEATH OF RAINWATER STATE UNIVERSITY PROFESSOR

Ira Dedmarsh was upgraded to a homicide, said Bellingham Police spokesperson Sergeant Richard Davies, in a press release Wednesday. Davies said that new evidence indicates that the death was not from natural causes, but could give no further details, as the case is still under investigation. Dedmarsh, 58, was found at 11:37 Monday morning by emergency crews in his apartment at 808 High Street and pronounced dead at the scene. Spokesperson Davies said that Dedmarsh's estranged wife, Irene Dedmarsh, 56, of 4708 Lynden Road, is considered a "person of interest" in the case.

"She's only a person of interest, Aldo. And if you'll excuse me, I have to go upstairs and make a phone call."

Aldo was gone, out in the driveway.

She punched in Rhodes's campus number and waited. On her blue telephone pad was Aldo's perverse notation: "Irene *Dead*march (Is it something she can give to you???) Call her. 671-2626."

"Office of the President."

"Hello, Penny? This is Teddy Morelli. I need to talk to Dr. Rhodes about the Pickett-Patchetts. Is he still there?"

Instantly came a voice: "This is Walter Rhodes."

Easy-peasy, once you knew the magic words. "Dr. Rhodes, this is Teddy Morelli. I think we have a big problem."

He chuckled. "Bigger than trying to explain to the legislature why the chairman of my history department was keeping personnel files in his private residence? That's what we're calling them now—personnel files. Think the legislators'll buy that?"

"I don't know. I think if I had to go see the legislature right now, I'd just try to distract them with pie charts about our terrible budget."

"Not pie charts, can't give away my pie charts anymore. As the kids say, pie charts are so five-years-ago." He cleared his throat. "So, Professor, what can I do for you?"

"Dr. Rhodes, I'm afraid I showed the Patchetts an oil painting today in the San Juan County courthouse, and later Mr. Patchett had it concealed under a tarp on the roof of his car."

"So what are you saying? Herb Patchett bought a painting from the San Juan County Courthouse?"

"Well, I can't imagine he bought it."

"I see. And what was it a picture of?"

"Kaiser Wilhelm. The painting was given to the

county by Mrs. Patchett's ancestors in 1938."

"I see. And Herb had old Kaiser Bill on the roof of his car, eh?"

"Well, I didn't actually see the kaiser, I only saw the frame."

"So you're saying, maybe Herb bought a picture someplace else, or maybe he stole a picture of Kaiser Wilhelm from the San Juan County Courthouse—is that what you're saying?"

"Yes," she said meekly.

"Well." His mind was already on the next agenda item. "If you find out if the painting is actually missing, will you please get back to me?"

"Thank you, Dr. Rhodes, I will."

She stared at the phone, then she called Irene. The phone rang for a long time, and Aldo came in cradling a whole handful of silver cylinders in his leathery hand. He leaned against the counter, waiting.

"Hello. This is Irene Dedmarsh."

"Irene? This is Teddy Morelli, from the history department. My uncle said you called."

"Yes, dear, thank you for calling back. I was afraid no one would want to talk to me after the *Tribune* article. I'm so angry, I just . . ." She exhaled and started again. "Teddy, I have something of yours, and I was hoping you could come get them tonight. I wanted to bring them in myself today, but the car broke down and it's in the shop. The police won't let me have Ira's truck."

"Can't you just send it?"

"Actually, it's 'them,' and it's better if you just come quickly, so I can explain. There'll be a lot of people here tomorrow, and I'd like to get these back to you before they come."

Teddy glanced around the room. "As a matter of fact, Irene, I have to bring my uncle out to the Land Yacht dealer anyway." She smiled at Aldo and said to the plastic, "Is that okay?"

"Any time tonight is fine, dear."

"Then I'll see you at your house in about thirty minutes?"

"It's more like forty." Irene hung up.

Thoughtfully Teddy cradled the receiver. "Aldo, how late is the Land Yacht dealer open?"

He poked a bony finger into the Yellow Pages: " 'Open nightly till nine. Closed Sunday—see you in church.' It's a religious town, Lynden?"

"Four flavors of Dutch Reform, each more fundamentalist than the last."

"Oh, dear. Do they like Catholics?"

"I'm sure they pray for your soul."

"Good." He slapped closed the phone book.

In Teddy's little beige Subaru wagon, they drove the farm roads to Lynden. Evening had tinted the eastern pyramid of Mount Baker in pink alpenglow, the same shade as the sunset in the west. It was a holy time of day, especially among growing things. They drove into town. Aldo read a bumper sticker out loud: "*If you ain't Dutch, you ain't much.* Teodora, these people are worse than Italians."

"Every culture is like that, if it has any self-worth at all. It's very important to think your group is the best."

"But Italians *are* the best."

"Good, Aldo."

At the main intersection of Lynden, Teddy stopped for the light. "Where's the Land Yacht dealer, Aldo?"

"10700 Guide Meridian."

She swatted her blinker. "This is Guide Meridian." They turned left, driving past Saints Peter and Paul Church, its parking lot filling for an evening meeting. Teddy said, "This is the church where Our Lady of Guadalupe is supposed to go."

"She's still in your office? Look! There's the patch of Land Yachts."

Teddy turned into Vanderpool R.V. and Travel, with its fresh black asphalt spread like frosting into the potato fields. Blue plastic flags whapped loudly in the wind, and gargantuan motor homes beckoned to buyers with open doors and tiny Rubbermaid stairs. Aldo clutched his handful of funny fuses and shouted over the flag noise, "I'll just wait here until you pick me up."

"Fine," she shouted back. She drove past the church again, its lot almost full, heavyset women entering the basement for an evening meeting. Out past the strawberry fields, she had to drive cautiously around the construction work—a great ditch was being dug alongside the road. She found Irene out in the yard, deadheading azaleas. The bushes must have been spectacular two weeks ago, because each now wore a blanket of burned-over brown. Irene held a cupped handful of dead blossoms, waiting for Teddy.

"Hi." Teddy got out of the car.

"Thank you for coming, dear. I'm hope you don't mind being in the presence of a suspected criminal."

"You're the wife. They're always going to say you're a person of interest."

Irene paced, barely able to control her rage. "Of course, the distressing part is I can't even feign surprise for them that Ira was murdered. He was spying, I always knew he was spying, but they showed me this calendar he was keeping on me—I had no idea it had gotten that bad, the man was *so* sick. They also seem to know all the terms of the divorce settlement and that I was at the lawyer's last week trying to get it stalled."

"You were?"

"Ira knew about the city annexation, did you know that? He knew, and he deliberately stuck me with the assessment for the sewer."

Teddy stared quizzically.

Irene seethed. "I'm not making much sense, am I? On paper it looks like we made an equal split: he gets the retirement pension, I get five acres and the house. But the retirement has doubled in the past two years, and I get stuck with balloon payments on the house—he didn't even tell me we had a floating rate. And to top it off, the city of Lynden has just annexed the whole east side and wants fifty thousand dollars to put me on the sewer. Ira knew it was going to happen. The only reason I found out is that his lawyer spilled the beans. Maybe if I hadn't spent my whole life dutifully following him from job to job, I wouldn't be so bitter. The deceit is just . . . killing." She tossed a handful of dried blossoms into the flower bed and started toward the open garage door. "I'm sorry I'm out of control. I'm just having a really hard time with this."

Silently Teddy followed her into the open garage. They climbed two steps and went into the mudroom. On the dryer sat a clutch of plastic Rainwater State University ballpoints, five or six copies of a postcard, and, astoundingly, Teddy's black-and-white pool scuffs, the ones she'd lost at the departmental picnic last summer. Irene pushed the pool shoes toward her.

"I—I don't understand."

"Ira stole things, dear." Irene grimaced. "He'd take little things from people that they wouldn't miss—cheap pens, papers he could xerox and put back, boxes of Kleenex." Irene shook her head furiously. "Stupid, stupid things." Her eyes burned with fury. "Burrowing into other peoples lives was Ira's way of having power over them, he had so little self-esteem himself. In some ways I'm glad I fina—, I'm glad *it's* finally over." She smiled awkwardly.

Teddy stared at the replicated scene on the postcards, a brilliant orange sunset behind a London bridge. "Well." She picked up the stripy shoes, hugging them to her chest. "Well, thank you very much. I guess I should just take these and go."

Irene continued, "When the police come tomorrow, I'd like things to be as straightforward as possible, so they don't go off in all directions. And these aren't particularly important to the case, are they?"

"No. I guess not." The prickliness started on the back of Teddy's neck. She tested: "And I guess also the police will have to conclude that neither one of us poisoned Ira because we didn't have a way to get into his apartment."

Irene's contorted face was a gargoyle. "Sorry, dear. I told them that, too, but then they started quizzing me about what I do Mondays at noon. It seems the apartment manager goes to the Bellingham Landlords Association at that time, and police are wondering whether someone slipped in and out on a regular basis. Evidently the manager's safe is broken. The keys are readily accessible."

"Yes, that's true, the safe is broken. But Monday noon I'm always around the department. And you're at Mountainview during the day."

Irene's eyebrows arched in self-deprecation. "Actually, dear, I take days off whenever I like; Mondays aren't always my best day."

"Oh . . . well." Teddy backed toward the door. "Well, thank you for the shoes. And hang in there."

"Thank you, dear. Be safe."

Outside on the drive Teddy tossed her scuffs on the backseat and swerved erratically down the dirt two-track, almost afraid Irene would follow. Something was the matter, something about what Irene had said. Taking Mondays off—no, that was too obvious, she'd said that on purpose, just to make sure everybody knew. There was something else. Ah, yes, there it was: Irene had said the shoes "weren't particularly important to the case." But how would Irene know that—unless she herself knew what *was* important? Was this logical thinking? Teddy glanced at her reflection in the rearview. Or did fancy French analytical methods even apply to real life? "Too clever by half, Morelli." The mirror did not answer.

She drove through Lynden, noticing for the first time the serious sewer work going on. Two miles down the highway she remembered Aldo. She made a U-turn and went back. Aldo sat in the waiting room of Vanderpool

R.V. and Travel drinking stinky, all-day coffee and reading magazines.

"Teodora, you're back." He jiggled a small paper bag. "Strange little fuses. We get it all nice and fixed up, Marjorie and her sister can take it wherever they want. Did I tell you they're twins?"

"You did." Should she tell her theory to Aldo?

"Their names are Marjorie and Mae. Marjorie is six minutes older."

"That's great, Aldo." No, Aldo would be baffled at her logic.

They drove down the Guide, again approaching Saints Peter and Paul. The parking lot was entirely full now, but quiet, the parishioners all inside. "Teodora, what did the Mrs. Deadmarch say about Our Lady of Guadalupe?"

"I forgot to ask."

"Turn here!"

Teddy jerked the wheel to turn into the parking lot. "Why?"

"You can't work with a statue in your office. We'll find somebody to take care of it."

"Aldo, I've got a lot—"

"Come on, let's get this done with."

They parked on the grass at the edge of the lot and went in at the basement door where they had seen the women go earlier. In the dark hallway the only light was from the little square windows in the swinging doors; everyone was inside the big multipurpose room. Teddy and Aldo tiptoed over to peek through the glass.

The room was packed with heavyset women. Out in the hall was an unattended card table with a signup sheet and religious books for sale: *God's Answer to Fat, More of Jesus, Less of Me.* There were foods, too—diet crackers shaped like eucharistic hosts, olive oil decked in raffia and red sealing wax. Free bookmarks listed wholesome Mediterranean foods that were part of a biblical diet. Aldo popped a sample cracker into his mouth.

They peeked inside the meeting room again.

The women wore pastel sweats and were very chunky. One stood among the seated crowd, deep into her testimony. Some looked away, embarrassed. Others were weeping into handkerchiefs. ". . . knew it wasn't a food that Jesus approved of, but I put it in my mouth anyway—my need was *that* strong. What do you think? Can you imagine Jesus coming out of the supermarket with twelve bags of potato chips, one for each disciple?"

The room broke into titters.

"Jesus knew I had a spiritual hunger, even if . . ."

"No," said Aldo. "Not here." He padded farther down the hall where the janitor's utility closet was open and the light on. He pointed to the open door. "Let's find this one."

They trotted the rest of the way down the hall and took the stairs up to the sanctuary. The last tier of ceiling lights lit the back of the church, and the red sanctuary lamp glowed on the altar. Down the side aisle a middle-aged man was mopping the vinyl tile. He wore a plaid outdoor shirt and jeans buttoned to logging suspenders: much, much more than a janitor.

"Hello, sir." Aldo approached confidently. "I'm looking for somebody who knows what's going on in this place."

The man grinned, enjoying the possibilities of his answer. "Well," he said, "In this place, the only people who know what's going on are God and the women downstairs. Downstairs, they change their minds about three times a week, and God, he ain't talking."

Aldo pointed through the colored glass panes in the window to the sleek modern rectory next door. "Your priest is home?"

"Oh, no. We ain't had a priest in that house for year and a half. Share him with Blaine and La Conner now."

Aldo pointed to Teddy. "My niece is a college professor. In her office she has a statue of Our Lady of Guadalupe that's supposed to go where your . . ." He squinted at the statue of the Virgin on the side altar, not recognizing her totemic signals. "Who is that?"

"That's Perpetual Help."

"Perpetual Help, yes. I always thought Our Lady of Perpetual Help was flat." He drew a rectangle in space. "She's a what-cha-ma-call-it."

"An icon," said Teddy. "Usually she is. She's Byzantine."

"She's Byzantine," added Aldo. "So"—he turned back to the janitor—"why is she being replaced?"

"Nope." The janitor shook his head. "That ain't happening. The Martha's Guild squelched that one."

"Who is Martha's Guild?"

He gestured to the floor with his mop. "The women in the basement. Like I said, when we lost the priest, they sort of took over as pooh-bahs in the parish. Anything they want, they get, there're so damned many of them."

Teddy said, "But they're a weight-loss group."

"Yep, that too. But they do anything they want now, no priest around."

"Then why did they order Guadalupe in the first place?"

"No, that would be your Saturday evening crowd, your Mexicans. They finally got their own Mass Saturday night in Spanish. Next thing, they wanted a Guadalupe on the lady altar. The old priest, he says 'Fine,' so they raise the money, then the priest gets canned and Martha's Guild reneges on the deal—they never wanted her in the first place. It's like: why can't the Mexes learn to pray to Perpetual Help like everybody else, you know what I mean?"

Aldo nodded sympathetically.

"One group, the daytime Marthas, they signed a petition. Said they weren't coming anymore if they got to pray to the wetbacks' Madonna. Personally, I think that's going too far."

"Oh, yes, me, too."

Teddy asked, "And Irene Dedmarsh was working with the Mexicans?"

The janitor brightened. "Oh, yeah. Mrs. Dedmarsh was doing a lot for those people. She's the one set up the *Clase de Inglés* program. She quit coming to church, though, about a month ago. I heard she goes up to Blaine for Mass."

Aldo sighed. "And that's why my niece has a very big statue in her office."

Thoughtfully the janitor spun his mop onto the floor. "Sorry, can't help. If I tried, I'd be making more trouble for myself than it's worth."

Aldo nodded. "We understand completely. Thank you for your time."

"My pleasure."

They went back downstairs and peeked in again at the Marthas Guild. A salon-dyed blonde in a well-cut business suit now held the floor. She couldn't have been more than fifteen pounds overweight—a role model. ". . . prayed for weeks when we heard the university had to close the women's restroom in the dining hall because they were tired of cleaning up puke from bulimics. So our Sunday night group is sponsoring International No-Diet Day as a way to involve college girls in our ministry. It's designed to be a celebration of God's love for each person's unique body size and dietary needs. It will be a picnic potluck at Boulevard Park, which is walking distance from the college. . . ."

"Let's go," whispered Aldo.

"Yes."

They drove home in silence, Aldo clutching his little bag of fuses. Muffy's sports van was in the driveway, and she herself was reading in the living room, tiny and barefoot. "Hi." She came out to the hall. She wore a skinny designer tee-shirt over her flat, little girl's chest; her blue jeans must have been size two.

"Hi, Woofy." Aldo went to the kitchen and filled a

glass with water. "Don't worry about me tonight, I'm sleeping in the Land Yacht."

Teddy said, "You can't do that, Aldo. It's not allowed in our condominium covenant. As a matter of fact, I don't think you can even have an RV here for more than forty-eight hours."

Aldo gulped his water and set down the glass. "I'll be out by morning. No one will even know I was here. Good night, girls."

Teddy went back to the living room with Muffy, and they both settled into the upholstery. Teddy gestured to Muffy's stack of papers on the couch. "Are you getting caught up?"

"I'm okay for tomorrow. And I found the topic notes for seminar, and a kid was going to deliver a critique anyway, so we'll get through just fine. The graduate students want to take me out for beer afterwards. Should I go?"

"Absolutely. But only have one, and only stay an hour. They drink like fish."

"Oh." Muffy nodded to the phone pad, "A man named Aurie called. We had a nice talk, and he wanted to know if you're coming down this weekend."

Teddy closed her eyes. "I wish he'd look at his calendar."

"So Aurie really is your boyfriend?"

"Something like that."

"And you really weren't having an affair with Ira Dedmarsh?"

Teddy jumped out of the chair, shouting. "Where did you hear that?"

"Campus." Muffy examined Teddy's face. "I glad you're not."

"Me, too. Jiminy, how does this stuff get around?" Teddy sank back in her chair, and Muffy turned to the papers beside her. "Oh, Teddy, I wanted to show you something." She held up a paper. "See if you think this is important. Everywhere I looked in the computer files, I kept finding this Chinese newspaper article. Dr. Dedmarsh scanned it in under, like, six different document names."

"I saw that!" Teddy darted over. "The original of that was out on Gilbert Island. It *is* important, if he's got it scanned into his computer. What does it say?"

"Well, it's pretty yucky . . ." Muffy cleared her throat. "It says, *'Visiting scholar Wah T'e Lu was cleared of all charges involving the death of housemaid Miss Hsue on July 14 of this year.*

" *'Miss Hsue Mei Ying, from the village of Shanglou, near Kuohsiong, committed suicide and, from autopsy reports, showed evidence of . . . torture and was revealed to be three months pregnant at the time of her death.'* "

"Oh, my god."

"I know. *'Professor Lu and his lawyer, Hu La-hsia, met with Miss Hsue's family yesterday at the justice palace in Taipei and arranged a burial and compensation fee of a hundred and twenty thousand New Taiwanese dollars to be paid immediately to the family. In return, Professor Lu was absolved of all legal responsibility for the death.'* "

"Wow! Who's Professor Lu?"

"And more importantly, why does Dr. Dedmarsh keep an article about him from *The Taipei Daily Journal* from 1972?"

Teddy plopped down next to Muffy on the couch. The printed Chinese page was simply undecipherable. "How much is a hundred and twenty thousand New Taiwanese?"

"About five thousand dollars back then."

"So Professor Lu tortured his housemaid, got her pregnant, and she committed suicide."

"Actually, that's not even the strangest part. Listen to the last paragraph.

" *'Dr. Lu has been an active intellectual and strategist in the Nationalist cause, having been a recent recipient of the Chang Shang Kuo Foundation grant for service involving journalistic and scholarly endeavors. Total grant monies recently received by Mr. Lu were a hundred and twenty thousand dollars N.T.' "*

"The same amount of money. So what are they saying? A foundation paid his bill? What's the foundation?"

"I'm not really sure. I think it's Nationalist—Chiang Kai-shek, you know. So there might be government money involved."

"I don't know what this means." Teddy sat on the arm of a chair. "Okay. This means that Professor Lu was important enough that someone in the government paid his bills to hush up a really big scandal. But who's Professor Lu? You said he's a *visiting* scholar."

Muffy frowned at the page. "There're tons of Lus in academia, both here and abroad, but I can't think of any Lu with this given name. But my question is, should we tell the police? Didn't you say Dr. Dedmarsh bought the house with a lot of money nobody knew about? What if Professor Lu is now some powerful Chinese politician and Dr. Dedmarsh was blackmailing him?"

Teddy shook her head. "I thought about blackmail, too, but it can't be. Because besides my file out at the cottage, I also found one on . . . somebody we both know, somebody in the department. Okay, I have to tell you: Nigel—"

"I saw that." Muffy nodded.

"Then you saw what it says, about the—"

"Child support."

"Yes. Anyway, I was talking to Nigel and told him about Dedmarsh's cottage, and he said something like, 'Why, that old devil! I'm chairman now. Does this mean I'll be able to buy an island place?' See? It was like Dedmarsh's money was a brand new thing to him."

"Umm." Muffy made a face, thinking. "Who do you think killed Dr. Dedmarsh?"

"I don't know. Irene just told me the police think it was somebody who slipped into his apartment when the landlord was away at noon on Mondays. The safe is broken, and whoever did it could have possibly had a duplicate key made."

"Oh, a key, that's right. How do they know it wasn't the landlord himself?" Then Muffy groaned. "Oh, no, this is terrible."

"What?"

"Dedmarsh was into wordplay. This one is foul." She held up the file. "The guy in the article is Wah T'e Lu, and he's called the document *Waterloo.* Wah T'e Lu: Waterloo."

"That is awful."

Muffy looked at the scanned article and pressed her lips together. "I need to ask you something, Teddy. I didn't see one out on the island or on the computer today, but Dr. Dedmarsh didn't have a file on me, did he?"

"Muffy! Why would he? You two just met in passing. Didn't you?"

Muffy exhaled, letting go of gray air. "No reason. Just wondering." She held up the Chinese printout. "If you want, I can ask my grandfather what he thinks about this. I'll see him this weekend."

"Is he coming up?"

"No, I'm going down. My cousin is getting married Saturday, and she's asked nine of us to be bridesmaids."

"Nine! You must have a huge family."

Muffy rolled her eyes. "You better believe. There's a hundred and eighty of us now, fourth-generation Seattle. You've probably seen the pharmacy on Jackson Street."

"That's *your* family?"

Muffy nodded. "We all put ourselves through school working there—I close my eyes at night and I'm still counting pills. As a matter of fact, my great-aunt, the grandmother of the cousin who's getting married, was the first woman pharmacy graduate at University of Washington."

"When was that?"

"1934."

"I love your pharmacy. Every time I drive past I wonder why it isn't on the national register."

"Because three years ago, when we tried marketing the old-timey Chinese pharmacy thing, someone stole an antique apothecary chest that Grandpa said was about two hundred years old. It just about broke his heart. He's not into tourism anymore."

"Oh, I'm so sorry." Teddy stretched and looked at her watch. Too late to call Aurie. E-mail in the morning. "Well, I hate to leave Aldo alone this weekend, but I won't be here, either. I'm going out on a research boat to date Indian burial caves on the wild and woolly west coast of Vancouver Island."

"I thought Northwest Indians used trees for their dead."

"That, too, but out on the coast in the nineteenth century so many people died from smallpox and scarlet fever they started stuffing them in sea caves. Also, it was around the time missionaries were trying to get everybody to start using Christian cemeteries, but people hated the missionaries so much they hid the bodies in the sea caves just to keep their relatives to themselves."

"You get such interesting gigs."

Teddy yawned, standing up to go to bed. "Actually, it'll be cold, wet, and dirty, and when I get back, I'll still be in terrible trouble, and my work will still be piled up."

"But maybe they'll have figured out what happened to Dr. Dedmarsh."

At 8:54 Friday morning Teddy unlocked her office, said hello to the boxed Virgin, and dashed downstairs to chalk an outline on the board, beginning with Bernard DeVoto's famous quote: "The history of the West is the history of water."

On the map, she showed them the renowned Nebraskan 100th meridian of longitude, west of which falls less than twenty inches of rain a year. She ran through the material on John Wesley Powell, mentioned Reisner's *Cadillac Desert* and Worster's term, "hydraulic West." And when she could see the glazed eyes in front of her begin to think that none of this desiccated topic applied to the wet, green place they called home, she held a mock vote on who should have priority at the free-for-all that would be the Nooksack River water conference next fall—Dutch berry farmers, Indian clam growers, corporate pulp mills, spawning salmon, or yuppie river rafters like themselves.

Trotting across the hall at 9:55 for her Intellectual History class, she chalked up the outline for the Romantic Movement, and before they could become lost in the dreamy vagueness of the term, she asked what they thought the New England Calvinist ministers they studied last month would have done to Walt Whitman, who declared, "I worship . . . the spread of my own body" and "I am not the poet of goodness only, and I do not decline to be the poet of wickedness."

She gulped down her bagel and cheese at lunch, then at one o'clock was utterly unnerved in seminar when the graduate students began taking notes on the Santa Fe New Western History Conference, a symposium she'd taken part in, but they considered a mythic event of the past. She came out of seminar and sensed a disturbance in the hallway air. There were visitors in the department. She unlocked her office, and ten seconds later the hallway darkened; there was a knock on her doorframe.

"Professor Morelli?" It was Tennant and Bao. "May we see you a minute?"

Teddy stood, gesturing to the Virgin. "We'd better go to the lounge."

They walked to the faculty lounge, and she spotted the negotiated pot of departmental caffeine—half French roast, half decaf espresso. "Would you like some coffee?"

"No, thank you." Tennant watched to see what she would do next. She sat on the sofa. He quickly followed.

Detective Bao surveyed the whole room, including the ceiling, then walked over to a defendable nook by the door and stood with his arms crossed.

Teddy looked back and forth between them. "I hope this won't take too long. I need to catch a seaplane in downtown Vancouver in two hours."

Tennant lowered his eyelids, utterly passive. "We won't keep you. We just need to clear up a few things here."

"Certainly."

"For instance, you only showed us three items in the file Dr. Dedmarsh was keeping on you."

She nodded. "That's all there was."

He waited, wanting her to talk more. She smiled.

"So I imagine you've destroyed all your other correspondence with Dedmarsh, deleted all your E-mail?"

"I don't think I have any correspondence with him, except my hiring letters. And we never used E-mail. We talked in the hall."

"But the two of you had been seen a lot in the coffee shop recently."

"Well, yes, the coffee shop, too."

"And the Faculty Club."

Teddy reddened. "Yes, that, too. We had a lot to talk about. I just took over Intellectual History this year, when Dr. Patterson retired. Dedmarsh and I had a lot of fine-tuning to do, because it's not something I was originally hired for."

Tennant grunted sympathetically. "Had Dedmarsh said anything recently that made you upset or angry?"

There it was again, the boyfriend stuff. Where was this coming from? "No," she said. "I'm telling you, it wasn't like that. Dr. Dedmarsh was just a very nice—" No, he wasn't, he was appalling. She couldn't finish the sentence.

"Is there something you want to tell us, Ms. Morelli?"

"Only that I haven't done anything. And that I have to go to Vancouver right now."

Tennant stood. "You'll be in Bamfield at the research station all weekend?"

She looked up, stunned. "Yes."

"And back Sunday night?"

"Yes."

Tennant exchanged glances with Bao. "Professor Morelli, please feel free to get in touch with us if you can think of anything else we should know about your relationship with Dr. Dedmarsh. Sometimes people remember things later on. Phone calls, arguments . . ."

"No. Nothing like that." Teddy stood and walked resolutely into the hall.

"We understand. Thank you for your time."

Teddy nodded curtly and watched them disappear down the stairs. Mortified, she shuffled back to her office, packed her book satchel, and went down the hall to tell Muffy she was leaving. Muffy was sitting at the desk with her feet up. When she saw Teddy, she swung her feet down, standing to say goodbye. She wore her black granny shoes and a stylishly severe black pant suit with stovepipe trousers. Artfully framed in window light, she looked like a miniature professional model.

Teddy stepped into the room. "The police came to see me. They think I killed Dr. Dedmarsh."

"No, they don't. They were here, too."

"Oh, Muffy, this is so awful." Teddy glanced at the work on Muffy's desk. "What did you tell them about the Chinese newspaper article?"

"Detective Tennant recognized it right away. They saw the original out on the island. He asked if I could write out a translation and fax it downtown."

"I guess Detective Bao doesn't read Chinese."

Muffy raised her elegant little eyebrows. "Hardly."

"Then they must have all of Dedmarsh's files."

"I think so. I've got an appointment with Nigel in a while and I got the impression they asked him about his, too."

"Don't tell him I know he pays child support."

Muffy nodded. "I'm going to pretend I don't know, either."

"Oh," Teddy groaned, "I just want to die." She sighed. "But I didn't do anything. And nobody else did either. All these files. It's just people being people."

Muffy soberly tapped the Taiwanese newspaper article. "Some of them."

Teddy shook her head. "Dedmarsh's files aren't important, don't you see? They're just something he did for a fantasy life, like playing James Bond. I mean, look at it. He hadn't tried to blackmail anybody—not me, at least, and not Nigel—and I bet this article is just something he cut out of the newspaper years ago when he was on research in Taiwan."

"But what about his big house?"

"I haven't figured that out yet. When I get back from Vancouver Island, I'm going to start making inquiries. And the place to begin is with the fact that somebody was breaking into his apartment—no, *entering* his apartment—and peppering his food with heart drugs. That's where we start: who could've gotten into and out of his apartment? Also, who had access to heart drugs? When we figure out those two things, we'll know who killed Dr. Dedmarsh."

"No, Teddy, you shouldn't be doing this. What if you get in the murderer's way?"

Teddy set her book satchel on the desk. "I won't. All I'm going to do is think about it, hang out in my own head. That's where I spend all my free time anyway."

"Teddy, be careful."

"I always am." She put out her arms for a hug. "Well, I need to get going. I hope you have a lovely time at your wedding, and I'll see you Sunday night."

With mock irony, Muffy mugged, "It's not *my* wedding."

They both giggled at their pathetic mutual predicament, and Muffy went back to her desk. "Have fun on the island. And don't do anything rash about Dr. Dedmarsh, okay?"

"Thinking—that's all I'm going to do."

But as Teddy drove home to change into khakis and long underwear, she was vaguely aware that something was missing from the equation—somebody who knew about Dedmarsh's apartment and was being overlooked. Irene, Esther, Nigel, surely, but who else? That awful Scotto actually had a key, but maybe that wasn't important, since his safe was broken. Or maybe he broke his own safe—that would throw the police off the scent.

Up in the magnificent city of Vancouver her mind kept churning as she parked the station wagon in the downtown Harbour Airlines seaplane lot. They called her flight to Bamfield, and she was surprised to see that she was the only person who followed the pilot down the floating ramp to the six-passenger Beaver. He helped her onto the pontoon steps and invited her to take the seat next to him, after which he filled out his clipboard. But who was missing in the Dedmarsh fiasco? Who else could have gotten in? She glanced up at the new skyscrapers going up dockside. The pilot fired the twin propellers and taxied out onto Burrard Inlet, then called over the earsplitting noise, "You're the one looking for the university research boat, right?"

Jerked back into the present, Teddy explained the obvious. "The research boat is at Bamfield."

"Not right now, it isn't." The pilot buckled in. "You and I are going to have to go find it."

9

To the ear-drilling noise of the seaplane's takeoff, Teddy watched the shrinking city gather in all the things that made it wonderful—the downtown beaches, the cliffside front yards, the winding inlets, craggy coves, and beloved Stanley Park, a forest next to downtown. To the north the whole empty province of British Columbia fell away in a tumble of snow-covered mountains and blue diamond lakes. To the west the vast furry greenness of Vancouver Island spread like badly laid carpet. They crossed the Straits of Georgia in five minutes, as Teddy peered down at the comets left by boat wakes. Finally she leaned over and called in the pilot's ear, "Will it be hard to find the research boat?"

"Not really. Your friend said to look for her in the Alberni Ditch."

Teddy shook her head. "I don't know what that is."

"Alberni Inlet. Channel between Port Alberni and Bamfield.Traffic's all up and down there."

"How will you find one boat?"

He pointed to the complicated instrument panel. "Channel sixteen."

"Oh."

Forty-five minutes later they flew over Port Alberni, a gritty lumber town on a finger of Pacific salt water, yet still in the heartland of Vancouver Island. The waterfront was astonishing for a town so small—vast log booms, loading cranes, Japanese freighters, pleasure boats, waste ponds for the pulp mill, lumber mills, sort yards, fishing boats, warehouses. Something bigger than the little town was serviced here, perhaps even the whole inside of Vancouver Island itself.

The pilot switched on channel sixteen and listened to static and the boat traffic below. Mostly it was fishermen hailing one another, asking about hot spots, and talking trash. The pilot picked up the radio receiver. "This is Harbour Air Delta-12, Harbour Air Delta-12. Looking for the research vessel *Pickford.* Go to channel 6, *Pickford.*" He waited and repeated the message.

After a short silence there was a burst of static, and Teddy heard the cheery voice of her friend Willo Thompson, of the University of Victoria anthropology department. "Harbour Air Delta-12, this is *Pickford.* Meet you at channel 6."

The pilot reset the dial and asked, "*Pickford*, do you copy?"

"Roger, Twelve. Is Teddy there?"

Teddy smiled broadly.

"Roger, *Pickford*, she's right beside me. Where do you want me to set down?"

Willo paused. "I am in the center of the channel off Ten Mile Point, heading south-southwest. I am a white, thirty-three-foot troller with a dark green cabin. I'm pulling a blue-pontooned Zodiac."

"Roger, *Pickford.* Will find."

He flew over the busy shipping channel, Teddy peering down at all the white fishing boats. He didn't bother to stop her, but after a few minutes he pointed to a looming hillside projecting into the channel. "There's Ten Mile Point." He dipped low, and they started examining boats. Down on the water, on the deck of a funky, old-fashioned fishing boat with a green cabin, a woman with straw-colored hair started waving. The pilot dipped his wing in reply, then banked sharply in a circle and set the plane down a hundred yards from the *Pickford*. They ferried over to *Pickford*'s stern, and Teddy hopped out onto the plane's pontoon. The pilot handed her her duffel. "Have a good trip, now."

"Thank you. Goodbye."

She threw her duffel on board and climbed into the open arms of Willo Thompson.

"Teddy!" she squealed. "Did you have a good flight? Sorry I couldn't meet you in Bamfield. I had to run to Alberni to change a gasket on the head." Willo was a tomboy blonde with impossible corkscrew curls and skin ruddy from the outdoors. Anytime of year Willo Thompson looked like she had just come down from the ski slopes—which, considering where she lived, was entirely possible. Today she wore baggy khaki pants and navy polar fleece. Clamped around her tan pouf of hair was another band of fleece, an earwarmer, that made her head look like a well-formed peanut. Her whole outfit was functional and outdoorsy: don't mess with Willo Thompson, it said, unless you can roll a kayak and rock-climb twelves.

"The flight was beautiful," said Teddy. She held up her canvas duffel. "Where do I stow this?"

"Bunkroom. In the fore."

Teddy padded through the extended cabin, with its unwashed galley pots and crumbs on the table. She dumped her gear onto the single remaining bunk—of four—that was not littered with Willo's junk. Willo was not into housekeeping. On the way back through the galley Teddy tossed knives and a plate into the sink so they wouldn't knock around when under way.

Willo was rolling up the ladder, and Teddy went back to help. "Where're we off to? I wanted to tell a friend where I was going, but I realized I didn't actually know."

"On purpose, if you don't mind."

"So I'll be off the coast of an island, on an island that I don't actually know the name of?"

Willo looked up cheerily. The squint lines next to her tawny eyes were cut deep from use and wind. "On purpose, if you don't mind."

"Guess I can live with that. We've had such a horrible week at school, it'll be good to be someplace where nobody can find me."

"What happened?"

"The chairman of my department died Monday, and the police think somebody poisoned him."

"Teddy! His wife?"

"Not unless you know something about church ladies that I don't."

"Church ladies! The worst kind."

"Actually, for a while a friend and I thought he might be blackmailing people—he kept these awful files on everybody—but as it turns out, I don't think he actually did anything with them."

"Why not?"

Teddy shrugged. "He kept one on me and he never tried to do anything with it."

Willo sniggered. "What did *you* do?"

"Nothing worth blackmailing about. That was his problem."

"Rats. I thought you were going to tell me some unsavory secret about your past." Willo stowed the ladder in a stern locker and led Teddy inside. The yellow and blue nautical chart for Barkley Sound was perched above the helm, and Teddy studied it. "Are we going wherever-it-is right now?"

"Not tonight. Tonight I'd like to make it most of the way down the channel, though, so we can putter on out to the island for low tide tomorrow."

"Sounds good." Teddy stood next to the helm as Willo piloted them down the spectacular flooded valley. On their flanks, walls of evergreen plunged straight into the sea. Out in front, the misty blue unknown beckoned from around the next craggy cliff. Willo turned on the VHF, and they listened to breaker static and good-humored ship-hailing over channel 16.

Teddy said, "Do I really not get to know where the cave is?"

Willo considered, her taffy-colored eyes scanning the horizon. "Caves—plural. If you're the logging company, they're on Princess Maude Island, but if you're in the Ohiaht Indian Band, they're on Tapaltos Island. Open the chart out, I'll show you."

"What does the chart call it?"

"Princess Maude in big type, Tapaltos in parentheses."

"Well, that's a start." Teddy spread out the dog-eared chart of Barkley Sound. Centered in a white-colored bay off the west side of Vancouver Island was the Broken group of islands, tinted softly yellow. Undulating around the Broken group were swirling blue fathom lines marking the deadly reefs, bars, and high-tide rocks that helped give this coast its other name: Graveyard of the Pacific. Princess Maude (Tapaltos) Island was just south of the Broken group in a cluster of ragged seaward isles named after Queen Victoria's more obscure cousins.

"How far do you want to get tonight?"

Willo drew a wide circle on the chart with her finger. "One of these log dumps at the end of the inlet."

"How long's that?"

"Two hours."

They motored down the inlet, letting the engine noise and the radio static lull them into travelers' silence. At the occasional oncoming barge or sport fishing boat Willo raised a hand in greeting and veered off-course to charge the wake head-on rather than be slapped from the side. At dinnertime they tied up next to a gargantuan log boom in a silent cove. The boom itself was the size of a football field, each log worth several thousand dollars. It seemed as if half the wealth of Vancouver Island was floating there beside them—straight, knotless, with diameters the size of king-size beds.

Huddled in the galley, they ate thick home-canned soup from Mason jars sent along by Willo's mum. With pilot crackers and Braeburn apples, they made a simple meal, their overboard fishing lines not picking up a bite.

Teddy spooned up the delicious soup. "So get me up to speed on the caves."

"Okay." Willo broke off a piece of flat, round pilot cracker. "Stafford-Bleusen contracted to clear-cut the west side of Tapaltos last September. It hasn't been logged since 1912, so the timber is really ready to go. The Ohiaht Indians objected this time around, said there were burial caves all over the place. Staff-Bleu sent in a private firm to do an impact study, and they came back saying that the burial caves were a hoax, the whole place had been salted."

"Salted?"

"You know, like new objects brought in to make it look like an old site."

"Nobody does that."

"Well," Willo munched cracker and swallowed. "Except in one cave they found a bunch of bones in what looked like one of Effie Wate's shopping baskets."

"So *that's* why you wanted me." American Makah basket weaver Effie Wate had been a big part of Teddy's dissertation. She had died in 1994.

"Their noses were fairly out of joint that I asked for a Yank. I hope you're as good at basket I.D. as I told them you were."

"I can probably do Effie, but she's not even Ohiaht. Does the tribe—I mean, the band—have an explanation for why it's there?"

"The Ohiahts' best thought is that somebody—maybe a relative—came in not too long ago and tried to clean things up a bit. But the Department of the Environment is pretty keyed up over the whole thing and has the cave sealed off with a steel net." Willo touched a lump of hidden keys in her pants. "We're supposed to verify that we found the cave locked, that we examined it, then locked it back."

"Poor Ohiaht."

Willo blew on her soup. "Teddy, I hate to break this to you. But the Ohiaht can play hardball as well as anybody else—better, because they live out here. But the second cave is the one I'm more concerned about. It's pretty exposed to boaters, and the Ohiaht say that artifacts are disappearing at a fast clip. We're to do a bone count and take pictures—hasn't been one for the last ten years."

"People don't still steal stuff, do they? That's so nineteenth century."

"Oh, I love the naïveté. Teddy, everybody steals. Boaters, loggers, Indian teenagers. The whole island is still talking about the loggers on Hesquiat who pulled skulls out of a shore cave, lined them up, and used them for target practice." She read Teddy's face. "Documented—1972."

They finished dinner listening to tomorrow's weather and then turned in for the night. Nestled in the narrow bunks, they let the lulling waters of the inlet rock them silently. Teddy was just about to nod off when Willo murmured, "Say, your department chair who died?"

"Umm?"

"He isn't the chappie who tried to bilk Peter Maxwell last year, is he?"

Teddy was instantly alert. "He had a file on a Peter Maxwell, he's in your department."

"Oh, this is utterly amazing. Peter's going to wet his pants when I tell him."

"What was Peter doing? It was something about Customs."

"High farce, high farce. Peter was in a bit of hot water over some imported tiger penis or some such—we were giving him a terrible time. Customs had just tightened the ban on endangered animal parts. The whole thing eventually worked out, but then this American chap calls up trying to do this cloak and dagger stuff: 'I'll ruin your career.' Peter thought the whole thing was hysterical."

"Then it was Dedmarsh. He was a blackmailer. Or at least, he tried."

"Sounds like he was too stupid to pull it off." Willo reached up to screw down the porthole. "I bet his wife killed him."

Teddy lay in the bunk, staring at the ceiling. But it was too hard to think about Irene sprinkling heart medication in her husband's food. It was too hard to think about anything. Her body fell in with the delicious lulling of the troller, then her eyes fluttered and closed of their own accord. In the middle of the night one wild boat skimmed by, knocking her awake, but Teddy turned over and fell back to sleep. In the morning, she got up to a blustery gray wind, her stomach heavy and knotted. The corners of her mouth turned up sourly and she turned to Willo. "I don't think I want breakfast."

Willo's brow furrowed in discomfort. "Me, either." They put on rain jackets just in case, and Willo fumbled in the larder, pulling out a box of gingersnaps. "Here. Mum always makes me take a box; they quiet your stomach."

They nibbled gingersnaps all the way down the inlet, bucking into whitecaps. Willo slowed to chart her way cautiously through Robber's Passage on the way out to Imperial Eagle Channel, where they found the ride even rougher. Thirty minutes out, they rounded a somber, forested island, coming out on its blustery ocean side. The sea instantly lifted the boat and Teddy's stomach. She darted to the rail and upchucked the toasty gingersnaps. Willo leaned out the pilothouse window and hurled hers onto the deck. Waves slapped *Pickford* around like a toy.

Teddy heaved and heaved again. Gingersnaps came up a thick brown sauce. After a half-dozen spasms there were no more gingersnaps, but her stomach kept heaving, trying to clear itself. She spit and spit again, glancing over to see Willo off the other side, her face powder green, the whites of her eyes a ghastly yellow. Teddy realized she must look just as bad. "I think I'm going to die."

Willo wiped her mouth with her sleeve. "I know; that's what they say. There's two kinds of seasickness: the kind where you think you're going to die, and the kind where you wish you would."

"That's not even funny."

"I know."

Resolute, Willo motored through the swells, her face puckered as a peach pit. Teddy hung on to the stanchions and stared at the dark shore, forcibly demanding that her stomach achieve the same horizontality. To the right was the rolling gray Pacific. To the left were the steep cliffs of Tapaltos Island. Random black shadows painted the cliffs in places where shadows shouldn't have been. Teddy perked up, growing curious. The boat moved in closer, and she saw that the shadows were actually sea-level caves, triangular openings where fissures in the gray sandstone had been flushed of loose rock. Each cave had a tiny sand beach, size of a doormat, slapped incessantly by waves. Landing craft would be instantly pulverized.

Teddy watched to see what they would do. Willo steered south past the caves and around a point at the far end. Behind the point, out of the wind, the water hardly riffled. Willo motored in as close as possible, cut the engine, and dropped anchor. They lowered the rubber Zodiac raft and climbed in, carrying their life jackets, day packs, and Willo's camera bag. Willo zipped across the cove, running the raft full speed onto the rocky beach. At the last second, she expertly cut and tipped the nine-horse engine.

"Willo!"

"What's the matter?"

Teddy climbed white-knuckled from the boat. "Aren't you afraid of rocks when you do that?"

Willo looked baffled. "Don't you see the landing site?"

"What landing site?"

"Look."

The beach was littered with skull-sized rocks except for a cleared driveway stretching deep into the water and far up on the shore. "The Indians cleared the rocks away for their canoes hundreds of years ago. Every rocky beach has a place like this."

"Cool." Now that Willo had pointed it out, the cleared section of beach was as obvious as the yellow brick road. They dragged the Zodiac up the cleared strip and lashed it to heavy driftwood. Teddy's stomach unknotted incrementally. She took a deep breath and felt her face relax.

At the back of the beach, exactly where you'd expect it, was the shore path. Long-legged Willo tromped uphill in laced boots, her camera bag bungeed to her daypack. Teddy in cross-trainers scampered to keep up. "Can we get down to the caves this way?"

"Not the tidal cave," Willo called back over her shoulder. "For that one we have to land the Zodiac at low tide, about three this afternoon, if the weather breaks. Right now what we're doing is checking out the cave in the woods that Staff-Bleu said was salted."

They tramped through the wet woods, dead calm behind their thick mat of wind-locked spruce. Occasionally the dense undergrowth parted, flashing views of the ominous gray Pacific. In about thirty minutes, they came to a thin creek dripping down a rock face. Mosses and tiny ferns fuzzed the sandstone.

"Up," said Willo.

They climbed the damp earth, passing the camera bag back and forth. Tall firs and hemlocks held the slope intact, their roots woven like gnarly fingers. Teddy glanced up to see a schist overhang, below which were tumbled rocks. Underneath the schist was a black hole covered by cabled screen the size of a cargo net.

"I see it."

They climbed the rest of the way, using tumbled rocks for footing, following a faint path.

The mouth of the cave smelled dank and cold. They nestled their gear in the uphill nook of a Douglas fir, and Willo unlocked the padlock that secured the wire net. Peeling back a section of net, Willo took out two heavy-duty flashlights and handed one to Teddy.

"Here."

They crouched over, walking in, yellow flashlight beams swirling across the web-hung ceiling. *This* was what cold smelled like.

The floor was littered with ashen bat guano. Everywhere hung fat black spiderweb streamers, plump as hand-spun wool. The walls were mottled with beautiful iridescent algae—reds, emerald green, dapple gray. On a back ledge was an old-timey wooden beer crate, collapsed, showing complicated brown contents. Baskets lined the wall. In the corner was a caved-in steamer trunk, its wood slats shredded like broom straw. The whole atmosphere was a swirling mixture of moist, dry, cold, must.

"Ah-choo! Ah-choo!"

"Bless you," said Willo.

"Thank you." Teddy trained her flashlight on the baskets. The finest one was definitely Effie Wate—tightly woven, with a traditional Makah whale-killer design, but in Effie's modern beach-bag style with convenient shoulder handles. Teddy pulled back a collapsed side, expecting the worst. Inside were china mugs, plastic plates, a rusty tin of chewing tobacco. Underneath were undetermined fabrics. Toweling. A bit of pink jacquard polyester. The plates were funky, square-sided Melmac from the eighties.

"Willo, I don't think we need to remove this to date it. The plates are from K-Mart. If we take pictures *in situ,* I think we can nail down the exact time frame when we get back."

"Excellent."

Willo darted outside for photo gear and came back, handing Teddy a small spotlight to hold in an awkward position. Willo took pictures of the basket from all angles, then cleaned the spider streamers from her hair. "What's in the other ones?"

Teddy pulled back another basket side. "Pork and beans, a can opener, some round leather thing. I don't know, I can't tell. These are definitely Effie Wate. The ones with wave designs are her early things."

"Environment isn't going to like this. I don't think 1980 is old enough."

"That's too bad." Teddy trudged over to the steamer trunk and shone her light. The black lid was sunken, the sides were bowed out. The shredded wooden slats of the lid were held together by what was left of the thick yellow varnish. "Willo, this is much older than the baskets."

Willo came over and washed it in light. "Should we open it?"

"What if it falls apart?"

They examined it carefully. The lock plate and hinges had been reduced to furry rectangles of rust. Willo trained her flashlight on the hinges. "Look, someone has already ripped the lid off at least once." The hinges were broken at the knuckles, no longer attached to the trunk.

"But they've also put it back. Which is good, because"—Teddy scanned the floor with her light—"maybe we can figure out how they did it."

On a ledge were two whippet-straight alder shoots. She duck-walked over to get them. "Here, this is what they used. Slide them under the lid."

There were already indentations in the lid edge where the saplings had been used before. Teddy tried to line them up exactly.

"Remember to say in your report the grooves were already here." Willo adjusted her poles.

"I was thinking the same thing." Teddy grabbed her end of the makeshift stretcher. "Ready?"

Carrying the trunk lid on two poles, they set it on the floor. They beamed their flashlights into the trunk and gawked in amazement. Inside was a green, hollow-cheeked man, mummified, luminous as a June bug. His torso ended at the groin.

"Wow!" breathed Teddy. "Why's he green? Where're his legs?"

His hands were crossed over his chest, fingernails the color of good jade.

Willo swallowed loudly. "He's green because that's the kind of mold that got him. It feeds on moisture from the cave mouth. And his legs were probably cut off so he'd fit in the box. Usually they're underneath."

Teddy ran her flashlight down the half-body. The man wore a homemade dark suit and an elaborate bead and shell necklace almost the size of a breastplate. His closed eyes were wrinkled bronze pods. He was missing most of his teeth, but the three bottom ones that showed were as long and thin as snake fangs.

"What color are you going to call this?' asked Teddy.

The man shimmered iridescent under the flashlight, rich emerald with highlights of turquoise and purple. His swollen knuckles were like dried greengage plums.

"Wet moss green," pronounced Willo.

"Shimmering green velvet," tried Teddy.

"Good enough for government work. But how're we going to date this?"

"I don't know. These clothes are really old." Teddy's eyes followed the shoulder seam with its irregular hand-stitching. "The jacket's pre-machine." The lapels were weirdly shaped, odd triangles of fabric stitched on like afterthoughts. The pants were button-fly, pre-zipper, but that could have been anytime before 1931. Wool, twilled, English, probably black. Impossible to date.

The lowest coat button showed underneath his crossed arms. It was military brass, utterly black, maybe with a spread eagle. "Could we lift his arms?" asked Teddy.

Willo propped her flashlight on the corner of the trunk and gamely wedged her fingers under the corpse's forearms. She lifted slowly. The arms came up together. The coat button underneath was dull camel-colored brass, protected from oxidation by the man's arms. Centered on the button was a spread bird, crowned; underneath was written "No. 27" and a halo of unreadable Latin. Teddy scrutinized the writing in the terrible light. *Renais.* Not Latin—French. "Willo, it's a phoenix button! They're all phoenix buttons! We've got to take some pictures."

Willo quickly set down the arms and moved to set up the shot. "What's a phoenix button?" She propped her light on the trunk corner and squinted into the viewfinder. "Teddy, get above his head and hold up his arms."

Standing at the man's head, Teddy straddled the trunk. Leaning over his face, she held up his arms, her back muscles straining. "Phoenix buttons are probably the most identifiable trade goods on the whole West Coast, next to Hudson's Bay blankets." Her lower back was not going to hold out very long. "They're all from the same cache brought out to Oregon in the 1830s by a Yankee trader named Nathaniel Wyeth. He came to Astoria to start a salmon salting business, but one of his earlier ventures was shipping New England ice to the West Indies, where everyone is pretty sure he bought all the surplus military buttons made for King Christophe of Haiti."

"Haiti didn't have a king."

"Haiti had a king from 1811 to 1820, Henri Christophe. He was the black military leader who helped kick out the French. Committed suicide in 1820, I can't remember the details. But what happened after that is that the military uniforms he ordered from Massachusetts never got made and the buttons ended up in Astoria, Oregon. It's really rare to find them this far north. Hurry, I can't stand like this much longer."

Willo fidgeted with her floodlight. "I can't get proper light on the writing."

"We've got to be able to see at least one word."

"What does it say?" Willo clicked pictures.

A shiver rippled down Teddy's spine. *"Je renais de mes cendres."*

"That's Frog language."

" 'I am reborn from my ashes.' "

"Got it—phoenix. But this doesn't necessarily mean this tomb dates from the 1830s."

"I'm thinking the suit would date him from the 1870s or 1880s. A local seamstress using buttons bought much earlier. Willo, I have to let go. I can't hold him anymore."

"Fine. I got him." Willo took more pictures, and Teddy went over to explore the beer box. Inside was a tobacco-brown skull, adult male, with high native cheekbones; femurs and arm bones visible underneath. The bones were clean and tidy, clearly brought from someplace else. The only words left on the box were "Molson's Dark A" in sleek thirties Art Deco letters.

They moved the trunk lid back into place, and Willo took a few more photos to document how they were leaving it. They stepped outside into the sparkling air and sat down with their notebooks, each describing the baskets, trunk, and beer box. They clipped the padlock back on, Willo took a final picture, and they slogged down the slope, which spilled loose soil into Teddy's running shoes.

Down on the path Teddy shook her foot. "Wait a minute, I have clean out my shoes." She took them off and emptied out the dirt.

"What are we going to recommend?" Willo gestured up at the cave.

"I don't know. But I think Mr. Green Jeans is authentic."

"Righto. He's not really something you can fake. So

maybe the beer box bones and basket stuff were brought in later?"

Teddy tied her shoe. "Yes, but the one thing that doesn't figure is why would anyone waste Effie Wate baskets on a burial cave. Those hummers sell for thousands, tens of thousands in the States. They're all in museums now."

Willo grimaced. "These are all going to get stolen sooner or later."

They walked solemnly down the path.

"Okay," said Teddy. "Assume the cave is legit. How would we explain everything there?"

"How 'bout this? We would say that Mr. Green Jeans was laid out in the steamer trunk in the late 1870s in his best suit. Then, about 1930, somebody brought in an adult male in a beer box, maybe a family member of Mr. Green Jeans, because . . . because the place where he was previously laid was getting overrun with people."

Teddy prodded, "And the Effie Wate baskets?"

"Right. Okay, sometime in the 1980s somebody else came along and left gifts in some valuable Effie Wate baskets because—I know! They used Effie Wate baskets because by that time the culture had become so self-referential that they put offerings in expensive Effie Wate baskets rather than old beer boxes and steamer trunks."

They paused. Everything rang true except the last part, where Willo had used the woolly academic word "self-referential" to pad her thoughts. They walked on in silence, Teddy trying to piece together what she knew about family, memory, and mourning.

"You know, Willo"—Teddy watched the trail move under her—"Effie Wate lived down with the Makahs all her life, but she would never talk about her father, I always got the impression it was, like, a sensitive subject. I just stayed away from it."

"And?"

Teddy glanced ahead at the waffle soles of Willo's

sturdy shoes. "What if the bones in the beer box are Effie Wate's father. And Mr. Green Jeans is one of her early ancestors."

Willo turned brightly. "So you're saying Effie herself cleaned up the tomb and brought the baskets?"

"Who else would use Effie Wate baskets that way?"

"Teddy, excellent! Let me run some genealogy, see what the Ohiahts think about that. Teddy, that's a good idea."

"Thank you. Thank you."

In a while they came out on the shore. The wind had died down, and the rocky beach was twice the size it had been when they left. The Zodiac was gone. They were stuck on the beach.

"Oh, shit!"

But there it was, far away, two fat blue sausages nestled in the rocks a hundred yards down shore.

"Damn. I'm sure I tied it up." Willo dropped her pack and tromped down the shingle beach, hopping from rock to rock, making her way around tide pools. Superfluous for the task, Teddy plopped down on a boulder to wait, wondering how the Zodiac could have teased itself loose and blown away in this sheltered cove. What if somebody had come and set it free, a malicious trick? She looked at the Indian driveway. There were no tracks other than their own. Oh, well, it must have just worked itself loose.

She watched Willo hop in the boat and use an oar to push the Zodiac away from the rocks. Then Willo started up the little nine-horse and zipped back over to pick up Teddy. When they were safely back on board *Pickford,* they ate lunch, listening to weather reports on VHF. Soup again. Teddy carved apples with her Swiss Army knife.

"We're not going to bring the *Pickford* around the outside of the island, are we?"

"No way. There's no place to anchor out on the weather side."

"I hope the sea's died down out there."

"We shall see."

At three o'clock they hopped into the Zodiac and rounded the point. Happily, on the ocean side of the island the sea was celebrating low tide quietly, with sedate westerlies and a glassy demeanor. They motored down past the sea caves, now all footed by much bigger beaches and lapped by calmer water. In some places the gravel extended far enough out to allow walking from walled beach to walled beach, from cave to cave. It was actually a pleasure to be here.

Willo took out a set of color photos from a ziplock bag and handed them to Teddy. "Find the one with the post-it flag. It's supposed to be the sixth cave up."

Teddy held up the picture of the craggy black fissure cave and started comparing it to fissures in the cliff. At the sixth fissure cave, the photo did indeed match up with the cave on shore. "This is it."

Willo veered the boat to shore, gunning the engine and again running the boat right up onto the pea-sized gravel.

Teddy climbed shakily over the fat, pillowed sides of the Zodiac. "Willo! There's not even a landing area here."

"This time it's the old adage: rocky beach, rocky bottom; sandy beach, sandy bottom. But you're right, I should be more careful."

They dragged the Zodiac up the gravel and tied the painter securely around silvered driftwood. Dragging the camera bag from the boat, they trudged up the loose gravel and stopped at the mouth of the cave to take out their flashlights. Long ribbons of thick algae hung over the entrance, dripping green stalactites. They ducked their heads to enter and flashed their lights inside. This was an entirely different kind of place from the cave up on the hill.

The wet walls were coated with glistening black algae. Long ago handprints and graffiti had been inscribed onto the walls, and thick ridges of algae scar had built up around each disturbance, layer upon layer, like tire tracks on a fragile meadow. Rotten wood boxes—maybe dynamite cases—had floated into skewed positions on the receding tide. Shells, sticks, wood, bone, shreds of fabric, all littered the floor randomly. Water dripped. The floor was wet sand, brown seaweed, boards, sea litter, slime.

"Careful," said Willo. "Here's the little stuff."

Bones. Teddy hopped quickly. Willo meant little bones. They were scoured as white as laboratory specimens, litter from an extra-high tide. Ribs, vertebrae, assorted parts of the hand and foot, tiny, large, from many different skeletons. Two strides later they came to the femurs, a perfect row of them lying in soldier-straight formation, the gleaming white hip balls all facing the mouth of the cave. A yard beyond the femurs was a row of skulls. Behind that was the cave wall, shiny and gleaming like black sealskin. Teddy squatted down in front of the amazing row of femurs.

"Who put them like this?"

"Nobody." Willo squatted, too. "I take that back. Crabs and otters come in here to pick them clean. Then during storms high water comes in and floats them around. When the water recedes, all the bones settle out by weight." Willo pointed out the hierarchy. "Skulls in the back, then femurs, then arm bones and stuff." She flashed her light to the front of the cave. "I think most of the really little stuff just washes away."

Willo took pictures from all angles. They counted five skulls—three male, two female, with broad coastal cheekbones bleached as white as Halloween. There were three pulpy wooden boxes, none containing bones, thirteen femurs, twenty-seven large ribs, three pelvises—all male—and uncountable numbers of vertebrae and bones from the hand and foot. Willo compared the numbers to the earlier totals and found that in 1992 there had been twelve skulls, four remnant boxes, eighteen femurs, five pelvises, unknown numbers of ribs, vertebrae, and small bones.

"Theft?" asked Teddy.

"Hard to say. But I'd like it better if we found as many skulls as last time. Water hardly ever gets back there."

There were no basket or fabric remnants to identify here nor any means of identification. The afternoon sun suddenly made an appearance on the back wall, and Willo was so thrilled she took another roll of pictures. By the time they were ready to leave, it was well past five o'clock. They lugged the camera bag outside into the air and looked around for the Zodiac.

It wasn't anywhere on the gravel.

Willo scampered up a beach rock and scanned the tide pools, the rocks, the vast stretch of water before them. Teddy climbed up the cliff wall a bit and looked even farther. Their beach was smaller than before—about the size of an urban backyard—and it was losing the battle with the sea with every lapping wave.

"I tied it up." Tears filled Willo's eyes. "I swear I tied it up."

"You tied it up, Willo. I saw you."

They scrambled over rocks south to the next crescent beach. No caves here, only sheer cliff. But here the beach was still broad enough for them to walk around the peninsula of rocks to the next cusp. They slogged around and found another tiny beach and another rocky peninsula beyond that. They trudged down to the next beach, this time across slippery rocks full of tide pool critters—sea cucumbers, miniature crabs, starfish the size of dinner plates. It was very slow traversing. Past the tide pools the rocks dropped abruptly into the sea, and a sheer cliff rose behind. Their disappointment was as thick as undulating kelp.

"Let's go back to the cave," said Willo.

"We might be able to climb the wall there. I did a little already."

"Umm."

They slushed back up the gravel, over the rocks, and back onto the beach. Lapping tide pushed white foam higher and higher up the beach, where it dissolved and popped on the pea-sized rocks.

"Teddy, I really did tie up the boat."

"I know, I saw you."

"Do you think it was the rental skiff?"

"What rental skiff?"

"The one behind us yesterday in the channel. I saw it again this morning."

Teddy scanned the swells for one of the heavy aluminum skiffs rented by city fishermen. The only thing out there was a freighter against the far horizon and the vast, molten Pacific itself. Then she turned around to look at the indentations they were leaving in the gravel. "Willo, there'd be footprints up the beach if someone actually untied it."

Willo looked, too. "Gravel's hard to tell. You could also walk on the driftwood and the rocks."

They climbed up the last tumbled outcropping of rock before their beach, which was now the size of a goalie's turf. Fear rippled down Teddy's spine. The cliff behind the cave went straight up. All up and down the shoreline the cliff rose straight and unclimbable. And unless they could find a way off the beach in the next little while, they were going to be in serious trouble at high tide. She looked at her watch. 5:52. "How long do we have?"

Willo grimaced. "Let's not think about that."

They clambered down onto their own tiny beach, tried climbing the cliff—a silly endeavor—then trudged out to the shore rocks on its north flank. Up the next gravelly beach, driftwood piled as if for a massive bonfire. They climbed over and under the driftwood, taking much too long, watching seawater lap underneath. At the next beach a slimy creek dripped from a shaley shelf overhanging a cave. They slogged over to it, still toting the camera bag, and looked up the angled shale. Earth-air from the cave breathed over Teddy.

Dropping her bag, Willo scaled about twelve feet, holding on with fingers and toes. Teddy fidgeted, fighting the urge to tell her to come down. Three minutes later Willo dropped back down to the gravel, exhausted.

Teddy looked out at the next surging wave. It smothered the shore rocks, then receded. Passage to the next beach would soon be blocked.

"Willo! Let's go. Hurry!"

They scrambled on to the next beach. It, too, had a sheer gray cliff and a fissure cave, but the beach was even smaller and closer to the waterline than their own cave.

"Teddy, we're stuck."

"No, let's go farther."

They leaped from rock to rock, over tide pools and boulders so scabrous with white barnacles that they looked like mislaid chucks of ancient Roman concrete. Orange starfish lit the watery crevices, and tentacled anemones beckoned seductively to their prey. Past the next beach was a bony finger of rock jutting into the sea. They climbed it and peered around—the end. Deep water slapped against a sandstone cliff for at least two hundred yards before the next beach, an achingly beautiful one, sandy, long, broad, with easy access up the cliff.

"That's it, we're stuck."

"We're stuck." Teddy looked at the camera bag. "Do you have the cell phone?"

"In the Zodiac," said Willo.

Blinded by panic, Teddy looked away. Finally she said, "What do you want to do?"

"Get to high ground. What do you wat to do?"

Teddy waved to the tiny freighters on the horizon. GEARBULK, read one. "Maybe we could attract attention if we stood out on the rocks."

"There aren't going to *be* any rocks in fifteen minutes."

"Then we'll just have to get to the best place . . . in case we're stuck for a while."

"What about the beach with the creek? We could always climb up the cliff a little. That way, we'd be out of the high tide for sure."

Teddy imagined the two of them clinging to a sheer rock face for hours at a time. "What about our cave?"

"I am not going to get caught in a cave at high tide. It's a stupid way to die."

They were already walking back to the original beach. "I disagree. If we're stuck out here all night, the weather's going to get us first. And the Ohiaht probably chose that cave in the first place because it's the highest. I don't think we'd get in trouble. It's not spring tides."

Willo said nothing. They trudged methodically back to the original cave, now with only a bedroom-sized beach. Ducking to enter, they dumped the camera bag on the wet floor, then looked for a place to sit. Teddy briefly considered squatting on a skull, but went outside and dragged in two flattish rocks. But there was no dry wall to lean against. Willo unfolded her round reflection scoop—sixty-seven dollars Canadian—and wedged it behind their backs. As twilight took over, they walked in and out, checking their escape route, watching the gravel beach grow smaller with every third or fourth lapping wave. It was going to be a long night.

Finally there was no escape route at all. They had a cave and a doormat, that was it. Teddy sat on her rock thinking of all the things that must not happen that night—no earthquakes in Japan, no storms, no spring tides. But everything would be fine, just fine, the moon was half-made, so it wasn't even time for spring tides.

They watched the last secant of orange sun melt into the sea, and Willo said, "Teddy, I think he was an American."

The man in the skiff. "How could you tell?"

Willo fidgeted. "I don't . . . He was driving like a jerk, I don't mean that."

"That's okay."

The sunset clouds were achingly beautiful, and as night settled in, they walked back and forth, alternately standing on what was left of the beach to wave flashlights at faraway freighters and sitting on their rocks in the cave. Chill bore down as the cave took on the temperature of the water, which came closer and closer. They buttoned their rain jackets, they turned up collars. Finally they were so tired they fell asleep leaning against each other, but Teddy woke up once in the night and saw she was laying facedown in the muck, her cheek against the black slime.

10

Teddy woke in the dim light. She was lying on the cave floor, a white pelvis inches from her face. She was cold, wet, stiff. Willo was gone.

She dashed outside, and wind grabbed her wet legs. It was 4:38 A.M. The beach was gray, long, serene. Gulls swooped and cried, hours into their morning feeding. Willo was not there.

Teddy climbed the rocks and looked both ways. No Willo. She sat down in the chill, shivering, using the wind to dry her pants. Her hands were black with slime. The synthetic-fabric long johns under her clothes were all that protected her from the wind, and they were probably the only thing that had gotten her through the night.

She looked down at rippling red seaweed in a tide pool. No food since yesterday. Lying on her belly, she dipped in her arm and ripped off a piece of the rubbery red leaf. She took a bite and spit it out immediately. Then she began searching tide pools for sea urchins. They contained a kind of caviar, she remembered, if you could get past the spines.

Willo came around from the north beach. Her face was dirty. Teddy splashed water on her own, trying to scrub it.

"Teddy!" Willo waved her arms. "The water's not

deep up past the cliff. I think we can wade it."

Teddy waited until Willo was close. Her wheat-colored ringlets were felted against the side of her head. Her face was crusty with dried black slime. "Willo, it was very deep last night. How do you know there aren't drop-offs?"

"We don't. But we can't stay here." Willo grabbed the camera bag and tramped resolutely back over the rocks. Teddy could only follow, listening to the reflux in her stomach. The morning tide pools had an optimistic feel, like a library before opening, even on this gray and chilly day. The two women climbed the ravaged sea rocks paved with barnacles and rounded the point to the driftwood beach. There was shoreline now in front of the tumbled silvered logs, and passage across the sand took only minutes.

Round the next promontory was the black shale cliff with a dripping waterfall over a cave. Willo walked straight to the vertical stream and made a V with her hands, funneling water into her mouth. Teddy waited her turn, peeking into the crevice sending out the green earth-air. Fresh footprints led into the cave. Teddy took a few steps in, and around the corner, up on new wooden racks, found shrink-wrapped bundles in thick, cloudy plastic—amazing to see them here—Asian ideograms on the shipping labels. A row of head-sized boulders on the floor also caught her eye. "Willo, come in here!"

"Teddy, hurry. Let's go!"

Teddy picked her way over to the boulders and saw they were being used to hold down brand new wooden statues—five identical copies of a graceful Chinese lady, very familiar, a deity perhaps, smiling like Mona Lisa. High tide came across this floor. Someone was deliberately trying to age these poor gals a hundred years in a few weeks.

"Teddy, come on."

She ran out. "Willo, there's stuff in there, Chinese artifacts. The Ohiahts are smuggling."

Willo didn't even turn. "That's their business, okay? You haven't seen it. Just keep your mouth shut."

"Right." Teddy stared at the gravel, instantly remembering their terrifying situation.

They tramped down the long beach and rounded the outcropping to gaze at the next impassable cliff. But below the cliff now were sandbars—soft beige triangles and odd loaf-shapes—to use as stepping stones between wading.

Without hesitation Willo hefted the camera bag above her head and jumped in. "Jesus, that's cold!"

Teddy hopped in, too. And gasped. It burned it was so cold. Icy acid oozed into her warm foot arches, up her legs, burning hot, painfully cold. Nerve-endings screamed in protest.

Knee-deep, they slogged fifty feet through the water, climbed a sandbar, walked twenty feet dripping wet, then splashed back into the surf. Teddy was soaked from the waist down. Khaki rubbed abrasively against her legs, back and forth with every step. Then another sandbar—mercifully—then more water. Finally they had used all the sandbars and had to slog the last long stretch, which was quickly becoming chest deep. No more pretense about "the ankles." They waded, dragging eddies of weight, whole oceans, behind.

Teddy raised her hands as if held hostage. Her clothes were soaking wet. Do not fall down, do not fall down. She dragged her bit of sea as fast as possible, trying to keep up with the high-held camera bag. Willo was tall. She didn't even know Teddy was in trouble.

Breast-deep in the water, Teddy tried to catch up, desperately focusing on Willo's back. Soon Teddy would be swimming. And then the real trouble would start, with no way to get warm or dry. She surged ahead, fighting panic.

But Willo's body started to rise from the water. Waist, legs, knees. Teddy felt the sandy bottom rise beneath her, too. They were in shallows, finally. They slogged ankle deep through the surf, surveying the long, benevolent beach in front of them.

Trails honeycombed the cliff. Broad stretches of morning sand already gave off daylight smells. They scrambled up the first trail they came to and at the top looked around. The shore path was like a highway running north and south, exposed, bright, and windy.

Wet khaki made the noise of harvest scythes. Chill swirled around their legs as wind taunted the fabric. Synthetic underwear was probably saving Teddy's life. She remembered that Willo had a blue peekaboo triangle of knitted undershirt under her sweater, too. They were both probably still perky only because of long underwear. Her stomach crooned like Frank Sinatra.

"Willo!"

"What?"

"We've got to eat."

Willo answered with the silence of her back. Then, as she passed a stand of hardy salal bushes, she ripped the popcorn string of white flowers off and popped them in her mouth. "Salal," she called over her shoulder. At the next stand of salal Teddy mimicked Willo, tossing flowers into her mouth, too. They were dry and bland, the best food she had ever tasted.

They tramped into deep undergrowth, then back onto bare cliffs. From this height they could see the busy traffic in the shipping lanes—barges carrying ziggurats of yellow sulfur, freighters Alaska-bound, zippy fishing charters making their way to the Broken Islands. Back in the undergrowth they came to territory that made them slow down. It smelled like yesterday, very familiar, and they perked up, alert. A creek dripped down a sandstone slab, and Teddy looked up to see the disturbed earth of their own footprints on the slope. A happier time, unvisitable, separated by the space of one planetary rotation. The schist overhang loomed high above. Willo looked up, too, and also knew there was no reason to stop.

Thirty minutes later they broke onto the beach where the *Pickford* rocked peacefully a hundred yards out. Far across the channel a fishing charter plowed by. They ran down to the water and waved their arms. The charter did not waver. Silence took over again, and they stared at the *Pickford*.

"I'll go."

"No, Teddy, you'll die."

"It wasn't that bad, wading. And I've been training for triathlon season."

"In triathlons you use wetsuits."

"All I have to do is keep moving. It's not really that far."

Willo looked up and down the beach for alternatives. Then she turned. "What are you going to wear?"

"Long underwear." Teddy was already taking off her rain shell and canvas jacket. When Willo saw the scoop-necked polypropylene under Teddy's sopping turtleneck, she started taking her clothes off, too. "Take mine, they're English."

Willo's long johns were a fine-denier wool, powder blue, lacy at the edges. "Mum's sister in Leeds sends her a proper pair every Christmas."

"Is wool better?"

"For what you're doing." Willo took off the pants and stood on the beach in her cotton panties and undershirt. Teddy peeled off her long pants and stepped into Willo's. Too long. She folded up the cuffs. Willo was putting on Teddy's little pair against the wind. They next exchanged undershirts, and Teddy tucked the tail into the elastic waistband and folded up the cuffs. Then she put her bare foot in the water. Like being squeezed in a vise. She stepped out again.

"Right." Willo sat down on the beach and undid her boots. She peeled off a layer of ragg wool socks, then a pair of ribbed wool kneesocks. "Okay. Put the fuzzy ones on your feet and the thin ones up your arms."

Teddy sat down and put on the ragg wool socks, layering them under the pants' trim. Then she stuck her arms out, and Willo helped her tug the ribbed English kneesocks over her hands, all the way up her forearms, and over her elbows. She again stepped down to water's edge.

"Wait, Teddy, the boat's locked!" Willo grabbed her wet khakis from the beach and dug into the pocket, unfixing her personal keys from the two boat keys and their fat bobber. "Can you carry them?"

Teddy grabbed the foam float with her puppet-mouth hand and tried to tuck it down her shirt. No opposable thumb. Awkwardly Willo reached her own hand into Teddy's bra and tucked the float securely under the cup of her breast. Teddy looked away.

"Okay. This is it." Teddy walked to the edge, falsely brave, terror seizing her chest. This was a very stupid idea.

She dipped her foot in. Through the wool the water was achingly cold, electric blue, hurting. She waded out chest deep and gamely put her face in. The cheek pain was like getting clubbed with a tire iron. Dizzy with blurred vision, she lifted her head, breaststroking in a white fog, waiting for her eyes to clear. Maybe she could breaststroke the whole way out there, but no, slow breaststroke would keep her in the water too long. She put her face in again and started a crawl. The face pain was not so bad this time.

Flutter-kicking, she turned her head to breathe, stroke after stroke. Salt water stung her tear ducts until they had been scoured by the sea. Barely opening her eyes—to keep her contact lenses in—she looked down into a frothy pool of her own bubbles. The sweet water trickled down her throat, she was so hungry she thought of swallowing more. Which would be asking for a bellyache.

Her pants were falling down, sagging around her groin. She stopped to tread water and pull them up, but couldn't grab them without thumbs. She used her hands like clamps and pulled awkwardly.

Willo shouted, "Are you okay?"

Not enough energy to shout. Teddy waved her arm and went back to work. Numb all over. But it wouldn't matter if soon she got to the boat. She swam, nearly exhausted, and in a few minutes poked her head up to see the elegant curve of the bow looming fifteen yards away. Not good enough. She swam again and looked up. She was there at the bow. But the ladder was in back.

She threw her head down and swam to the stern, realizing she had not budgeted her body heat wisely. She had forgotten there would still be work to do after she reached the boat. She poked her head up and grabbed a ladder rung. Her sock-clad hand instantly slipped off. She grabbed again but could not hold it. Panicky, she trod water. The ladder was her enemy, she had to get the socks off her arms.

Treading water, she ducked her head under and peeled back the kneesock. It came down an inch, then stalled in tight wrinkles on her forearm. She trod frantically.

Grabbing the ladder, she hooked her left elbow around it and forcibly willed herself calm. Then she willed herself warm, then willed herself all the time in the world. Her body refused to buy the last part. Clamping her free hand onto the sock, she coaxed it down her left arm slowly, with her puppet-mouth grip, then peeled it off and let go. Oh, dear, it was Willo's sock—too bad.

She surged to the other side of the ladder, hooked her right elbow above the rung, and with her functioning left hand, ripped the wool sock quickly down her forearm and threw it up over the boat transom. Taking a deep breath, she grabbed the ladder and—with every last bit of effort—*hauled* herself out of the water, rung after rung, then bellied over the side of the boat. She fell to the deck, stunned. Her heart was beating red alert. She'd never felt it like that before. Barely, she could hear Willo shouting far away.

Minutes later, she got up on hands and knees and

crawled toward the galley door. But her body wasn't working for her. She knelt like a penitent, forehead on the fiberglass deck, waiting for strength to return.

After a time, she finished the crawl to the door. Summoning her hands to work, she fished out the keys and put the door key into the lock. But not quite. She tried again, this time insisting that the thin, brass blade insert itself into the dark, jagged hole. It went in. It turned.

Teddy crawled inside. Off the table she swept cracker bits into her mouth. A carton of milk. Quart, quart, it dribbled down her chin. She slowed down. Ginger snaps were vomit, she ignored them. Bread, lots of bread, she chewed. Willo.

Padding to the window, she watched Willo waving on the shore. Teddy was supposed to do something now, but couldn't remember what. Dish towels were strewn about the galley. She folded one. Something for Willo, but what was it? She padded around the galley and picked up a dish towel. Folded the blue terry cloth and folded again.

Then it came to her. She was supposed to rescue Willo. She went outside and waved, then went back into the cabin and switched on the ignition. Anchor. She'd have to raise the anchor.

The anchor had a winch handle, and she went to the foredeck to crank the dripping shaft out of the water. Back in the cabin, she shifted to Forward, then gave the boat a tiny bit of gas. The boat puttered toward shore, but how deep was the water? She had no way to judge.

Twenty yards off shore she cut the engine and ran outside. "I can't come any closer. You'll have to swim!"

Willo paced back and forth. She was wearing Teddy's silly long john bottoms, her polar fleece, and hiking boots. "Teddy, I'm not keen on swimming. And what shall I do with the camera gear?"

"If you get on board, we can at least go find somebody to come help."

Willo paced the shore.

"Come on, Willo. There's nothing else to do."

Pulling off her boots, Willo set them on the camera bag, then zipped the polar fleece to her chin. Wading out waist deep, she gritted her teeth in pain. Trying a few strokes of head-up Hollywood crawl—the most exhausting exercise ever devised—she then turned on her back and finned a bit to rest. She turned over again and tried a few more strokes of crawl, then settled into a sedate, dry-haired breaststroke. Willo had ended swimming lessons at the point at which you learn to breathe. Her trip would be terribly slow. Teddy shouted encouragement from the boat, glancing often toward shore. The boat was being swept in. But she couldn't dishearten Willo by moving farther out.

"Hurry, Willo, can you?"

Sedately Willo breaststroked.

Fidgeting, Teddy tracked Willo's progress, searching for the bottom, watching Willo approach the bow, watching the shoreline. Yes, indeed, the tide was still going out. And the boat was drifting in.

Willo finally reached the bow, and Teddy patiently walked around to the ladder, watching Willo stroke below. Finally Willo was on the ladder.

Teddy hovered as Willo hauled herself out of the water, the jerk of her body sending the boat a few feet forward, grinding it onto the sand bottom with a woeful schussing sound.

"Oh, no."

Willo collapsed on the deck, her already pale skin bloodless as marble. Shivering uncontrollably, she immediately got up and padded into the cabin, seeking heat. She stopped in the galley and stuffed bread in her mouth, gagged, and spit it out. Then she went into the bunkroom to squirrel under her sleeping bag. Teddy went in and unzipped her own sleeping bag, laying it over the shuddering body.

Teddy turned the key in the ignition, shifted to reverse, and gave it gas. The engine raced, frothing impotently. The boat didn't move. She stopped and waited, then revved again. The same results.

She cut to Idle and ran outside. Maybe she could use the boat hook to push off from the sandy bottom. The boat hook was clamped to the deck, and she pulled it out to its full length. Two days ago she had used a boat hook—what different circumstances. Uncle Aldo, he would know what to do.

Up in the bow, she leaned over the rail and poked the boat hook into the water. It didn't even hit bottom. Then she lay down and thrust the upper half of her body out over the water and tried pushing the hook down to the bottom again. She hit solid sand, but the boat was so stuck, her effort produced nothing.

Suddenly the deck vibrated with the sound of a boat motor not too far away. She stood and looked around, waiting. A fishing charter came into view out in the channel. It was towing a blue pontoon boat, maybe the Zodiac.

Willo dashed out of the bunkroom, wearing a sleeping bag around her shoulders. "The radio." She switched the radio on, waiting for it to warm up, turning to the hailing channel.

Meanwhile the charter boat skimmed by. Desperate, Teddy dashed inside and grabbed the air horn. She pressed the spray tip—*Blaaat!*—owned the world. The charter boat kept going, and she pressed again. *Blaaat!* A few seconds later the boat veered toward them. She waved. A tall turbaned Sikh in fishing waders came around and stood in the bow. He was definitely subcontinent of India—dark-skinned, bearded, and for all she knew, carrying his ceremonial dagger under his waders. Twenty yards from shore, the engines cut and the Sikh called, "What's the problem?" His accent was wise-guy Canadian, hard-core Vancouver.

"We're grounded. And if you found that Zodiac, it's probably ours."

The skipper came out and regarded Teddy. He was

also a Sikh. He wore a ribbed navy surplus sweater over his rotund belly. "Who's on board?" He meant, "Where are your men?"

Willo came out in dry pants, still hugging her sleeping bag.

Teddy said, "It's just the two of us."

"The two of you, eh?"

Willo shouted, "Does the Zodiac still have our backpacks in it?"

The Sikhs waited before answering. "We don't think this is yours. It was upside down on the rocks off Cape Beale. It belongs to the Marine Research Institute."

"Bloody hell!" hissed Willo. She then called out politely, "We're from the research station. This is a research boat, too. Listen, the tide's still receding. Do you think you could tow us out of the shallows?"

The Sikhs looked at each another. "We can give it a try."

The skipper puttered in close and threw a line to Teddy while Willo took the wheel. Teddy wrapped her line around a stern cleat, and Willo gave thumbs up out the window, gunning reverse as the fishing boat revved powerfully forward. Nothing happened. Then, finally, a dreadful rasping sound shuddered through the boat—it was as if the boat were being pulled in two. *Pickford* scraped slowly across the sand. Excruciating sound. Suddenly they were free, bobbing gracefully again.

Teddy raised her hand in triumph, and Willo motored alongside the fishing charter. Then she idled. The deck mate walked their Zodiac around and handed Teddy the painter as if giving her a pet on a leash. "Thank you."

"You're entirely welcome."

Willo called out. "You haven't seen a metal skiff around, have you? One of those little rentals?"

The Sikh shook his imposing head. "We've not been looking at boats."

"Well, thank you very much for your help." Willo waved. "Hope fishing was good."

They didn't answer for a moment, then one finally called, "We don't fish. We have only rented this boat today to come down and see the ocean." They looked at her inquiringly, reluctant to leave. "Are you sure you're okay?"

"We'll be fine," called Teddy.

The Sikhs looked doubtful. They cleared their decks and checked the chart, all the while glancing over for evidence that it was okay to leave two incompetent women out on the brine. Self-consciously Teddy and Willo walked in and out, changing clothes and outfitting the Zodiac for the still-needed trip to shore, trying in every way possible to show that the crew of the *Pickford* was up to snuff. Finally, when Teddy and Willo boarded the Zodiac wearing life jackets and waving goodbye, the men cast off.

The Zodiac engine wouldn't start, so they ended up rowing to shore with the miniature safety oars lashed to the pontoons. Willo was so adept she used even these ridiculous objects to good effect. On shore they picked up Willo's boots and camera bag, stuffed in the rest of the clothes, and silently paddled back. There was no point in offering to take the oars from Willo.

Teddy asked, "You still think it was the rental skiff, don't you?"

Willo choked. "I *always* tie the boat." She pulled on the oars. "What do you think?"

"I was wondering how somebody could sneak up on the beach without our knowing. I mean, we would have heard a boat, wouldn't we? Even inside the cave."

"Unless he landed a ways down shore and walked around from one of the other beaches. There're enough beach rocks and driftwood out there. You wouldn't have to worry about footprints."

"I'm not sure I would know footprints on a gravel beach if I saw them."

Willo worked the oars. "The thing is, that wasn't a practical joke, Teddy. People drown on the beach at high tide. Everybody knows that. There are even warning signs in German for the tourists. I hate to break this to you, but I think you're in big trouble. Somebody wants you dead."

"Not me." Teddy went numb all over. "How do you know this isn't some political situation with the Ohiahts or the loggers?"

"Teddy, this is Canada! What I want to know is what you're not telling me about your department chair, the man who was poisoned."

"I told you everything. There's nothing to tell."

They stroked the rest of the way in silence and climbed back on the *Pickford*. They stowed gear, then ate everything on board, including the boiled contents of an ancient box of cereal—Wheateena. Unbelievably, it was only a little past noon, a lifetime of change since morning. They motored up Trevor Inlet watching the woolly conifers change colors as the water valley took on golden afternoon light. Absolutely silent, Teddy stayed close to the steering console. As they approached the Bamfield docks, she said, "How are you going to report this, Willo?"

Willo stared out at the water. "I'm just going to tell them what I think. The thing is, I don't think you'll be invited up anymore. It was hard enough getting you passed through this time."

Teddy looked at the glassy channel. "I understand."

It was two o'clock Sunday when they tied up at the dock. After hot showers in the institute locker room, Willo insisted that they make a quick run around the harbor to look for the rental skiffs. None were at the charter businesses, and all the businesses themselves were closed, displaying phone numbers to call for assistance.

The seaplane landed at three-thirty and picked up Teddy at the dock; it was a different pilot. Neither woman broached the horrendous situation hovering over Teddy. They just hugged and said goodbye. As Vancouver came into view below the snow-covered Lillouet Spur, her body filled with dread at the thought of touching down into real life again. What should she do about Dedmarsh? Was it true that somebody was trying to kill her? Willo thought an American male—but who could that be?

Teddy picked up her station wagon in the seaplane lot and drove the fifty miles south to home. Muffy's van was not in the driveway, nor was the Land Yacht. Teddy walked in at the front door and dumped her bags.

"Aldo?"

No one answered. And Aldo's gear wasn't on the patio. Her blue phone pad was on the kitchen table with a note. Aldo.

Dear Teodora,

The fat women meet at 7:00 tonight. (Don't call them fat women.) Marjorie is Catholic, her sister knows, we'll fix it—you bet! Muffy is fired. Don't worry, I'm taking care of it.

Zio Aldo

"Muffy!"

Teddy ran upstairs and found the clothes racks still there. It was six-thirty. She went downstairs and read Aldo's note again slowly. He was taking care of Muffy's firing? Maybe Muffy was out in Lynden with Aldo. And maybe Teddy should get back in the car and find out what the hell was going on.

11

Black and white Holsteins like a campy joke. No tennis shoes on Dutch cows, though. Plodding through muck of their own making, the cows of the farmers of Lynden were serious, healthy, blessed, productive beyond belief.

Teddy watched the Holsteins cluster at the door of the milking parlor, silver breath rising in the evening air. Inside, to the music of Mozart and Loretta Lynn, they would trot to their stalls, tease hay from the racks, and wait their turn at the suction tubes that relieved them of their heavy loads.

The sidewalks of Lynden were busy on Sunday nights. Families walked toward lighted church basements, the women toting casseroles in colorful quilted bags. In the parish play yards swings had started to chirp, and outside parish kitchens the smokers—damned to hell—shuffled guiltily and looked at their feet. The First Reform, the Second Reform, Methodists, Lutherans, Baptists—Regular and Irregular—Catholics, Nazarenes, Assemblists, Evangelicals, Pentecostals, all manner of witnesses to whatever it was that happened in Palestine all those years ago.

Teddy turned into Saints Peter and Paul parking lot and found it full, and pulled onto the grassy play field.

She went into the dark basement hallway and peered into the multipurpose room. It was crammed with Marthas. Teddy viewed them in profile, their soft, eager faces lighted by what two women in front were saying. Aldo was in the back of the room, wearing red, leaning against the steel kitchen counter. In front, the two speakers' body language said they were intimates. Twins! Marjorie and Mae.

Teddy padded down the hall and found the kitchen door. She tiptoed through the institutional steel and came out beside Aldo. He had on a new red satin baseball jacket trimmed in black and gold. She squeezed his arm. "Where's Muffy?"

Aldo seemed perplexed. "Seattle. She had to go to a wedding."

Women in the back row threw angry looks: be quiet. Aldo and Teddy raised their chins attentively.

Marjorie (or Mae) was holding a cylindrical candle with the image of Our Lady of Guadalupe on the side. The twins were fraternal, dark-haired, with Brownie smiles, as thin as dancers. Unlike the audience in cotton-candy sweats, the twins wore neat gabardine slacks, belted, and dark leather shoes.

The one with the candle was saying, "The problem is, you have to read the whole prayer in Spanish or it doesn't work. You can't just rattle off a Hail Mary or something. I was skeptical at first, but then I started to say the prayer, especially at that terrible time, three in the afternoon: 'Dear Lord, please send your mother to help me,' then say the prayer. And by the time you're finished *"la gracia de Dios y tus maternales bendiciónes"* you can live with the hunger. If you can't, you just say to yourself, 'Hunger, you're my Jesus, I want to live with you,' and you repeat the prayer."

There was a hand raised in the back. "How do you use the candle?"

Majorie (or Mae) held it up. "The candle you light at mealtimes, and you say the prayer again or not, depending on how your family feels. Everybody seems to like candlelight, though. It turns mealtime into a special event."

"And I assume you're selling the candles."

A disapproving murmur rippled through the audience.

"No," calmly answered a twin. "Votive candles are available in any Mexican grocery store. And while you're there, you might take a look at the foodstuffs, too. Our friend in Mexico City bases her diet on tortillas, beans, and fruit. She hasn't been an ounce overweight since she was thirty-five."

The other twin nodded. "She has the most beautiful complexion."

There was a skeptical silence, and finally a hand flew up.

"Yes?"

"Can we go through the prayer again?" The questioner held up her printed sheet.

Marjorie and Mae picked up their own copies of the prayer and read it out loud, a line at a time.

"*Santa Maria de Gaudalupe . . .*"

"*Santa Maria de Gaudalupe . . .*" repeated the women.

"*. . . amparad a todos . . .*"

"*. . . amparad a todos . . .*"

As they recited, line after line, the smartly suited facilitator got up and joined the twins, anxious not to lose her crowd. After the prayer the two women were applauded, and they picked their way through the smiling audience, joining Aldo in the back. Rosary beads started coming out of pockets and purses, and Aldo, alarmed, squired all three women out of the room.

Out in the hallway Aldo beamed, "Teodora, look what they gave me." He held up his arms to display the red satin jacket. The color made his dark eyes vivid. The waist-high cut showed his toned outdoorsman's rump, making him seem much younger than his seventy-three years. Marjorie and Mae both seemed to notice the fact.

Aldo turned around to model, showing the yellow satin A stitched on the back.

"Arizona? Atlanta?" asked Teddy.

"Arawak, Teodora. This is my new Arawak jacket. The twins said I should wear it when I go out so the Arawaks get used to me, they know I'm their friend."

Teddy glanced at the twins in disbelief. Their eyes smiled sweetly, giving away nothing. But then one winked.

"But Teodora, I'd like to introduce my friends, the Madison sisters—they used to be the Madison sisters before they were married. This is Marjorie." He turned. "And this is Mae."

Mae had a slightly fuller face, with reading glasses on her head and a poochie tummy. She was the observant one, the winker. She put out a hand and said, "Your uncle's told us so much about you."

Possessively Marjorie clutched Aldo's arm. "You should hear this guy. Every other sentence is 'My niece the college professor.' "

Teddy smiled. "Thank you for letting us use your boat last week."

"Oh, fine, honey, no problem. Use it all you want."

"The twins are fixing it, about where the statue goes, did you hear them? Only two or three more meetings. Right, Twins?"

Teddy smiled wanly. Don't hold your breath, Aldo.

They walked quietly past the double doors as the rosary droned inside. Out in the parking lot, Aldo hung back with the twins. He wasn't going home with Teddy. "Well, Teodora . . ."

She pulled him aside. "Aldo, why did Muffy get fired?"

"She didn't tell me, such a sweet child. She came home Friday, she'd been crying. They fired her, that's all I heard. She had to go to Seattle for a wedding."

"Her clothes are still there."

"No, I can't tell you if they're there or not. I'm sleeping at Marjorie's—outside in the Land Yacht, of course."

Teddy raised an eyebrow. "Aldo, the Land Yacht's full of electrical wires."

"Yes." Aldo suddenly blushed. "But Marjorie and Mae are getting me used to things again."

After a fitful sleep, Teddy dashed up to her office, dropped her book satchel on the chair, squeezed back past the Virgin, and dashed downstairs at 8:54 to chalk a Columbia River outline on the board, following up with journalist Bill Dietrich's provocative quote: "If the Mississippi was the quintessential nineteenth-century American river, then the Columbia had been the twentieth-century one." She spun the class stories of the Plateau Indians and their yearly ceremony at the upriver arrival of the First Salmon. She told about the slave trade on the river, how it differed so dramatically from American chattel slavery, then talked about the Chinook tribe at the river's mouth, who controlled trade between the inland horse-loving tribes and the oceanic folks in their fabulous sea-going canoes. In conclusion, she gave the class her incomplete list of the twelve current competing economic uses of the river and ended by assigning reading from Richard White's *Organic Machine.*

At 9:56 she gulped water in the hall and bounded into the next classroom to watch two student commentators chalk up outlines for the papers they were presenting. As gently as possible, she corrected the boy who wrote that he was reporting on the impact of IWW on American intellectual life, explaining that although IWW and WWI appear in the textbook at almost the same time, he should never confuse International Workers of the World with his topic, World War I.

At 10:54 she stumbled, brain-dead, up the stairs and came out into the history department, remembering first the nightmare with the Zodiac, but then Muffy. Instantly, she girded for battle. She stomped down the hall right to Nigel's office. The door was open, Nigel was on the phone. With his mother.

". . . don't think there are any public courses in the area. I can take you down next weekend, Mother, and see what the country club is like." There was a pause. "Of course not, Mother, the weather's very healthful, lots of sun. Listen, someone's here, I've got to go now. Bye." He hung up and quickly picked up papers from his desk, refusing to look at Teddy.

"Teddy, good morning. What do you know about Alkali Lake, Oregon?"

She sucked in the mothball scent. "Never heard of it."

"Southeast Oregon State is advertising for a new president, and it's been suggested I apply."

Teddy's mouth dropped open.

"Well, you needn't wear your opinions so vulgarly." He tapped his papers into a neat pile. "I've been feeling a bit stagnant here lately, and people have always said I have a great gift for administration. One wag in the Lunch Bunch—how did he put it? He said that I tiptoe well through the twin minefields of Personnel and Purse Strings." Nigel just made that up. "And frankly it is something I enjoy."

"Nigel, where's Muffy?"

He looked away, perusing a new document. "I wouldn't know. That's not my business anymore."

"Why did you fire her? She was doing a great job."

"Teddy, no! You're overstepping your bounds. This is a personnel matter, and I can't even begin to discuss it with you."

Teddy hovered like a rabid bee. "Nigel, it doesn't matter that she knows about your child support in Iowa. I know too, and you're certainly not going to fire me."

Nigel bolted out of the chair. "Teddy, how could you? How many people have you told?"

"Nobody! Only Muffy and I know about it, and she's very discreet. Last week she was the answer to your prayers. And now I come home and she's fired. At least give me her Seattle address so I can find out what you've done to her."

"Absolutely not." Nigel stared at his document. "I would get in so much trouble for doing that."

"Nigel, how am I going to find her?" Teddy thought of the Woo family pharmacy on Jackson Street but was so mad she flitted angrily at Nigel's shoulder.

"Teddy, I'm sorry, I really can't talk about it. And it has absolutely nothing to do with any personal situation of mine, I can assure you. Now if you'll please excuse me . . ."

Teddy stared at him a moment, then heard Esther out in the hall supervising the removal of the old Xerox machine from the storage room. Teddy briefly considered asking Esther about Muffy, then remembered that Esther had taught Nigel everything he knew about being tight-lipped. Teddy tromped into the faculty lounge and poured herself a cup of the negotiated department brew and stood in the center of the room, her heart pounding furiously.

Beauclerke Wallace was on the couch, perusing the latest issue of *Journal of Southern History*. He was handsome man, midforties, wearing a pair of his go-to-hell pants—the departmental appellation for the multicolored plaid wool patchwork trousers Beauclerke ordered from the Brooks Brothers catalog. Everyone in the department understood that the nonconforming pants involved some obscure form of Southern rebellion, but no one had a clue how to help Beauclerke. Or even if they should.

Beauclerke moved his mail, making room for Teddy on the couch. "Nigel giving you a hard time? You just found out about Woo."

Teddy tested her coffee, then put it on the table, too upset to drink. "Nigel won't tell me anything. I don't even know where to call her."

"But isn't this a dandy situation? We all have a way

to work Czerny now—you just mention his child support."

"Beau, that's so cruel. You men are so cruel to each other."

"Teddy, I guess you weren't listening to yourself. You just did the same thing."

"Oh, I did, didn't I?"

"The corridor echoes." He smiled serenely. "But don't worry about Woo, it'll all work out. I think it's best right now that Woo not be found."

"Wrong! Somebody has to apologize to her."

"Teddy, I know you women fix onto each other because there's so few of you, but from what I hear of Jocelyn Woo, this department got out just in the nick of time."

Teddy twisted on the couch. "That's not right. She's a great person."

"That may be, but word up from Seattle is you don't want the likes of Jocelyn Woo anywhere near your history department. She's trouble from the word go."

"No, she's not! What'd she do?"

"Well, it seems like our little Chinese historian has a long history of filing harassment charges one after the other. Whips them off at the drop of a hat."

"That's impossible. How would she even have time? She's still in grad school."

Beauclerke shrugged. "Czerny picked up the news Friday morning and caucused the senior members, told them what he'd heard informally. They all decided that since her paperwork wasn't pushed through yet, best thing to do was cut her off right there, look for somebody else."

Teddy scooped up her coffee mug to leave. "I don't believe it. That doesn't even sound like Muffy." She turned at the door. "Who's going to take the China classes?"

"Guest lecturers from Poli Sci, until they find somebody else."

Without a word, Teddy shuffled back to her office. Her phone light was blinking and she punched it.

"Dr. Morelli? This is Archives. Sorry to bother you, but Mrs. Patchett is here again, this time asking for information on General Pickett's sword. I tried to explain to her that we have no documents on Confederate weaponry on our shelves, but she seems to think you have personally instructed us to withhold materials from her."

"Oh, hell."

But this was chaos, her whole life—too much was going on and she had to get a grip on things.

Teddy pushed the phone to the back of the desk and uncapped her rollerball. A list, that's what she needed. "Number one," she wrote. "Find Muffy." No, that wasn't number one. She had to figure out who untied the Zodiac, if anyone did. "Call police," she wrote. And tell them what? She stared at her fat, green-enameled rollerball, thinking of the strangeness of it all. Willo was certain an American had untied the Zodiac, an American who was after Teddy. But that couldn't be right. She had no enemies. Enemies were whoever poisoned Dr. Dedmarsh.

"Number two," she wrote. "Find poisoner." And that would get the police off her case, too. Why hadn't they picked somebody up yet? And what had happened to the tea caddy? Irene had said the poisoner slipped in Mondays at lunchtime, when Scotto was at the landlords' meeting. Irene herself was free Mondays. But, angry as she was, Irene was basically a nice person, hardly the type.

So who else had cause to hate Dr. Dedmarsh? Her mind went blank. Muffy again.

"Number three. Where's Muffy?" Yes, that was number three. And what Teddy needed was the name of the Woo pharmacy in Chinatown. Who could tell her that? The Asian Museum was just down Jackson Street, she could call there. She rolled her chair out to get the

Seattle phone book and banged into the crate. She rolled back under.

"Number four. Move statue." Absolutely. This had gone on too long. She'd call an off-campus moving company and have the bloody thing—oops, sorry, Virgin Mary—and have the thing moved out on her own, campus policy be damned.

"Number five. Was there a number five? Yes, something stupid and awful she had just been dragged into again but now couldn't remember. Three out of four, four out of five: for some reason memory always worked that way. Oh, yes, now she remembered. "Tell Rhodes no to any further Pickett involvement." Yeah, Morelli, right.

Suddenly Nigel squealed out in the hallway, "Welcome! We weren't expecting you so early! Your class isn't till the end of the hour!"

Teddy looked at her watch, wondering who deserved such an effusive welcome, and who might be teaching at noon.

"Dr. Czerny, good to see you."

President Rhodes! He was teaching here?

Rhodes continued, "Hope they don't miss me down at Rotary Club. Already racked up more fines than I can pay. Dr. Morelli, good to see you."

Dumbfounded, Teddy stood in the hallway. She didn't remember even leaving her office. "H-hi, Dr. Rhodes. Are you going to teach today?"

Nigel stirred uncomfortably, stepping between Teddy and Rhodes. Rhodes craned his neck around, nostrils flaring at Nigel's mothballs. "Well, I don't know if we can call what I do teaching anymore. I just try to keep them from falling asleep for an hour."

Teddy pressed, "You're taking the China classes?"

Nigel's eyes widened in alarm.

"That's right." President Rhodes sniffed and used his handkerchief. "They asked me to pinch-hit for a few days until they find a replacement."

"For Muffy Woo?"

Nigel's glasses fell on the floor, and he swooped down to pick them up. He came up walking, escorting the president to the faculty lounge.

Rhodes refused to budge. "Yes, I believe that was her name. Dr. Czerny, I just remembered some business I have with Dr. Morelli. Will you excuse us for a moment?"

Nigel stared, bug-eyed, then slipped into an office.

Teddy smiled blandly and took the plunge. "You know, I thought Muffy Woo was doing a great job, Dr. Rhodes. If she ever had a problem with harassment proceedings, I'm sure all that's behind her now." She opened her palms, pleading. "Her teaching references were good, too. I saw them."

President Rhodes looked away, adjusting the folder under his arm. "Well, you know, I can't really speak to any of that. All they told me was the young woman slated for the China job turned out not to be such a good fit with the department."

Teddy pressed her lips together, frustrated.

"Listen," said Rhodes. "What I wanted to talk to you about—well, actually there are two things. First of all, I want to apologize."

"Apologize?"

"Yes, my fault entirely. You see, until last night I didn't realize the grief I must be causing you. I was having dinner with the Pickett-Patchetts, and when Sally started talking about her research assistant in the history department, I said to myself, 'Oh, dear, what have I done to poor Dr. Morelli?' I have really put you through the wringer with these folks, haven't I?"

Teddy swallowed. "Yes."

"And I bet Mrs. Patchett's made your life hell. Sally doesn't have a mean bone in her body, but she can be a real can of worms."

"She is very . . . self-possessed."

"How about self-obsessed?" Rhodes smiled, trying to

coax a smile from Teddy. "Over the salmon bisque she starts talking about the biography you two were going to write and how much better it would sell if it was published under her name only." He glanced sideways. "That's what I'm supposed to do today—ask you if you'd consider publishing it under only her name."

Teddy tucked her hands in her tweed pockets.

"But don't worry. It's gotten out of hand, I know. I will tell the Patchetts that the writing project just wasn't something you had time for, and if Sally wants a panegyric on George Pickett, she'll just have to do it herself."

Teddy exhaled, a small explosion. "Thank you. That's quite a relief. And I'm very sorry it'll be costing the university so much money. Three point four million is an awful lot to lose, and I'm sure if I were in your shoes, I would have pursued it, too."

"Oh, no, no, no, no." Rhodes beamed. "That's the best part, which leads me right into my second question: The Pickett-Patchetts are still very much on board with the Pickett Scholars Endowment. They assured me they feel a great deal of affection for Rainwater and want to help us any way they can. We are going to introduce them Saturday afternoon at the Umbrella Club barbecue, and Sally wants to know if you'd consent to be the guest speaker, say a few words about the Chinook jargon you mentioned to her. Evidently her grandfather was quite fluent."

"I would imagine he was. He had to run his second marriage in Chinook."

"Well, sounds like fascinating stuff. I think it's very appropriate for the Umbrella Club. Umbrella will pay your stipend, of course. Dinner's always good, too."

"Where will this be?"

"Bow Lodge. It's down on Bow Hill Road."

"Saturday afternoon?"

"That's right. Leave here about two?"

"I think I could do that."

"Fine! Fine! And I'll tell Sally the writing project is off. You won't have to think about it anymore." He smiled. Teddy smiled. For some reason, she now had the advantage. Quickly—what could she use it for? "Dr. Rhodes, now that we're exchanging favors, may I ask you one?"

"Certainly, Professor, what is it?"

"I need to show you something." She led him down the hall to her office. Nigel popped, red-faced, out of the water fountain alcove where he had been hiding the whole time. They both ignored him. At Teddy's door, she stopped and gestured inside. Rhodes gawked at the nine-foot wooden crate. "What is *that*?"

"Our Lady of Guadalupe. It was supposed to go in a church out in the county. I need someone to move it out."

"For heaven's sake, let's call Maintenance."

"We have. They put me on their schedule, but they're being a little vague about when they might actually get here."

"No, no. Let me call someone for you right after my class." He scribbled a note on his manila folder.

But it wasn't his manila folder at all. It was one of Dr. Dedmarsh's. Nigel had wrested them from Muffy. Her neat printing, *Wah T'e Lu—Waterloo*, was penciled on the front.

Muffy, thought Teddy. Heartsick, she watched President Rhodes tuck his pen away. "Well," he said, "I need to go see if Dr. Czerny found me an empty office. I'll have Penny call you about Saturday with the particulars. And don't worry about transportation. We'll arrange that, too."

"Thank you. See you Saturday." She squeezed past the Virgin and sat down, unwrapping her bagel and cheese. Things were starting to work out. She took a big bite and looked up to see Muffy Woo in the doorway.

"Muffy!"

"Shhh." Muffy slipped in, closing the door.

Teddy chewed and swallowed, before she choked out a greeting. "How are you? You've been waiting in the stairwell, haven't you?"

"Not long. I don't want anybody to know I'm here. I came back to get my stuff, but there aren't any U-Hauls in this town. All they can rent me right now is a truck."

True. All the U-Hauls went back to Seattle on Monday mornings. "You can't use a truck."

"I can't use a truck." Muffy was wearing cheery red platform Keds and a tiny red cashmere sweater. Her face told a less cheery story. Her eyes were swollen, she looked as if she had spent the last three days underwater.

"Are you okay?"

Muffy shrugged. "I'm fine, I guess. Although I still don't understand why they pulled the position on me."

"I . . . uh." Teddy looked away, checking the location of her bagel. "I think they found out about the harassment charges you filed. They didn't think you'd be a good prospect."

"Harassment charges! I never filed harassment ch—! Teddy, I didn't. I'd die before I'd accuse anybody of harassment."

"They said you had a history of filing harassment charges, and it was better just to keep their distance."

"Oh, Teddy! Where could they possibly have heard that? What am I going to do?"

"Have you talked to Nigel?"

Muffy wrinkled her perfect forehead, tears of frustration welling in her half-moon eyes. "Not Nigel. He's taking orders from someone else. You can hear the words coming right out of his mouth, like some kind of parrot."

"Must be Dean Handy." Teddy sat down. "Did you tell your advisor?"

Muffy nodded. "He said he would call Nigel this morning and see if they could straighten things out. But I told him I didn't want the job anymore. I just wanted to get my stuff and leave."

"No! I think you should fight it."

"I think I should go home and finish my dissertation."

"I understand." Teddy sat down, embarrassed for Muffy, embarrassed for her school. "Do you still have my house key?"

Muffy displayed it on her key ring. "Should I keep it? I can't come back again until the weekend. I'll ask Aldo to move the racks out into the garage to get them out of your way."

"Aldo's back down on Chuckanut with his girlfriends."

"Girlfriends? Plural?"

"Twins."

Muffy giggled then sobered. "Who are they getting to take Dr. Dedmarsh's classes?"

"President Rhodes."

"President? Of the university?"

Teddy nodded. "He's an old China hand. He's going to guest-lecture for a few days until they find somebody else."

"Ooh, I know what happened! Nigel must have found out about the restraining order I filed against Dr. Dedmarsh. But how could they possibly get that confused with harassment charges?"

Teddy rolled back her chair smack into the Virgin. "You filed a restraining order against Dr. Dedmarsh?"

Muffy nodded. "Last winter. I wasn't going to tell you."

"What did he do?"

"After the ASA meeting in Denver, he started coming down to Seattle on Fridays to use the library—he *said*. He'd come by the department to see Waldron and Saks but always ended up dropping into the grad student bullpen to talk to me. He started taking up so much time I stopped coming in Fridays altogether, but then he found where I studied in the library and then, after that, where I lived. One day I came home, and he was just there, sitting at the dining room table, talking to my roommate. So I, like, walked out."

Stiff, urgent lines bracketed Muffy's cheeks. "Finally everybody started saying, 'Just tell him you don't want to see him anymore.' But it was, like, I'd tell him, and he'd refuse to hear what I was saying. He'd just keep asking questions and stuff, like trying to give me career advice. It was so weird.

"Finally, I moved back in with my parents. And then Dr. Dedmarsh started walking back and forth on the sidewalk across the street, so my dad had me file a restraining order." Muffy examined Teddy's face. "I have to ask you a question."

"Okay."

"You have to tell me honestly, not this fakey counseling stuff."

"Okay."

Muffy lifted her foot, holding up a funky, fat-soled Ked. "I know some guys can't handle my shoes. But do you think it's really wrong to wear them? Mostly I like them because I like being taller, but some of it really is about sex."

Teddy shrugged. "Sex is okay." She examined Muffy's perfect little face and sweetie-pie brown eyes. "Are you going back to Seattle now?"

Muffy jingled her keys. "Actually, I'm also supposed to do a favor for my dad first. Guess what's here?"

"What?"

"Remember the apothecary chest I told you was stolen from our pharmacy? It's here! Maybe. A Chinese antiquities dealer is advertising one on the Internet just like it, and I'm supposed to go check it out before I go home."

Teddy couldn't remember an Chinese antiques dealer in Bellingham. "Is he downtown?"

"No, it's an address near the college, 808 High Street."

Teddy knocked the pencil can off her desk. "You're kidding! Do you know the guy's name?"

Muffy read: " 'Scott O. Walper, Asian Antiquities: Specializing in Antique Weapons Appraisal.' "

12

"Muffy, 808 High Street is where Dr. Dedmarsh lived."

"Teddy! Should we tell the police?"

"Which part?"

"I don't know."

The two women read each other's eyes, and Teddy said, "What if Scotto doesn't let you see your chest?"

"I—I can't think this through. Teddy?"

"No, we'll be okay. All he's trying to do is sell an apothecary chest, as far as we know." Teddy glanced at her schedule. Nothing until committee at two. "I'm going with you."

"Good."

Minutes later they rolled down High Street in Muffy's sports van, Teddy explaining how Scotto the Tattoo Man and Scott O. Walper, antique weapons appraiser were probably one and the same. They parked in the church lot behind First Pres and crossed the street to the BOBs. "Dad said not to do anything if the chest is ours. I'm just supposed to look at it and walk out."

They trotted down the half-flight to the basement and knocked at the office door.

"Come in!"

Teddy hung back, letting Muffy push open the door.

"Hello."

Scotto sat behind the desk, wrapping sticky black string around the hilt of a short Asian sword he held between his thighs. The safe was open, just as it had been the first time Teddy was there. "What can I do for you?"

Muffy stepped gamely forward. "I'm interested in an old apothecary chest that you have for sale on the Internet."

Scotto looked them over. Then he recognized Teddy. "You were here last week when 107, uh . . ."

"That's right. Dr. Dedmarsh was in my department."

Scotto stared a moment. "I don't have the cabinet anymore. I sold it." He went back to wrapping string.

Muffy calmly readjusted her purse under her arm. "I'm sorry to hear that. My father was ready to pay up to fifty thousand dollars for it, if it was nice enough. He was going to use it to redecorate the restaurant."

Scotto reconsidered. "I might have one nearly identical in the next room. It's pretty expensive, though."

"I'd certainly like to see it."

Scotto carefully put his sword in the safe and made a show of spinning the lock. Then he led them through the hanging blue beads into his living room. On the wall above the TV was an incredible display of spears and pikes with odd-shaped blades and hooks. The mannequin in Japanese armor now sported a Burger King crown. Teddy walked over to inspect the armor—incredible stuff—thousands of thumb-sized metal plates laced together with red silk cord. And it wasn't actually antique, it was brand-spanking-new.

"Armor's not for sale," said Scotto. "I just got it for fun."

"Where's it made?" asked Teddy.

"Chinese. Taiwan. That's a *gusoku do-maru* from the Edo period. It's reproduction."

"*Gusoku do-maru*," repeated Teddy.

"Umm." Scotto disappeared into the bedroom, and the two women took in the javelins, swords, spears, and battle-axes mounted on the walls. How much of this was reproduction? Teddy went numb all over: on a shelf was a very old-looking carved polychrome Chinese lady. She was identical to the ones in the Tapaltos Island cave. Teddy stepped back, watching.

After a minute Scotto came out carrying a large polished black wood cabinet with thirty-six square drawers. It was the "tea caddy" that had been up in Dr. Dedmarsh's apartment. It was a beautiful piece of work. On both flanks were dreamlike carvings of mountain scenes with peaceful rivers at their base. On all eight corners elaborate brass cornerplates protected the points from wear. Muffy looked supremely disappointed.

"What do you think?" asked Scotto.

Muffy opened a drawer politely. "I thought you were going to show me something bigger."

"It's an extremely collectable piece. I get offers on it all the time."

Teddy opened a drawer, too. Dried pine needles littered the bottom. The whole cabinet smelled like acrid smoke. Innocently, she turned to Scotto. "How do you know if something isn't stolen?"

Scotto crossed his arms. "Oh, I deal strictly above board. I can give you references if you want. My banker, he buys from me."

Teddy glanced at his flattened forearm. "Your arm says Scotto but your ad says Scott."

He glanced at his blurry blue tattoo. "Actually, there's a space between the T and the O, you just can't see it. And there's a period after the O. Scott O."

"Oh, yes, I see."

"Merchant marine." His hair was showing dark roots. Time for the peroxide rinse. "Tattoo's the only thing I wish I hadn't gotten across the pond. My advice on tattoos is don't get anything printed in English in the Orient."

"Sounds like a good idea to me."

While Muffy made a pretense of examining the cabinet, Teddy walked around the room, trying to find objects that did not look like reproductions. She examined swords, handcuffs, brass knuckles, Rolls-Royce angels, all manner of cheap tools and pocket knives. Large size ammunition casings, Nazi memorabilia, machetes, Shang dynasty libation vessels, and India cloisonné vases. All the brass objects had the same greenish cast. Maybe from India. And now that she knew what she was looking at, she could see the bright spot on the wooden lady where the rock holding her underwater had left the paint intact.

Scotto stuffed his hands in his back pockets. "What kind of history you teach?"

Teddy and Muffy glanced at each another to see who should field the question. "Pacific Northwest" said Teddy, to let Muffy case the joint.

"Cool," said Scotto. "Did you read that book about the Gilman-Werner Sasquatch hoax? Evidently their famous sixteen-millimeter clip shows close-up that the Sasquatch suit is being held with a big metal clip."

Teddy curled her lip disapprovingly. "Real Sasquatch suits are made from high-quality bearskins. I have it on good authority."

"No kidding?" He stared, and said no more.

Muffy took a last desultory look around the room, then paced to the door. "Well, I'll tell my dad, see if he's interested in the cabinet. It's what? Three by four by . . . ?" It was clear she was just being polite.

"Two, maybe. I can give you a bargain on it," said Scotto.

"Yes, thank you, we'll think about it."

They walked back to the car, Teddy feeling she should not talk yet. They climbed in and slammed the doors, and Teddy practically burst. "That's the same cabinet that was up at Dr. Dedmarsh's! I thought it was a tea caddy. We need to call the police. And Scotto's a smuggler—or something. I saw statues identical to his yesterday. Someone was artificially aging them in a cave on Tapaltos Island."

Muffy buckled her seatbelt. "Dr. Dedmarsh had our chest?"

"That was yours. But you acted like it—"

Muffy turned in disbelief. "Teddy, I just about fell over when I saw it. I've got to tell my dad before Scotto sells it."

"Scott. Scott O. Walper. But what was Dr. Dedmarsh doing with it? Do you think he stole it?"

"I don't know." Nervously Muffy inserted the key. "I don't care. All I know is we've got to get it back for Grandpa." She looked at Teddy. "Teddy, I've got to hurry. Where do you want me to drop you?"

"Garden Street. Go to my house and use the phone. Are you going to call the police?"

"Yes. Yes. After I call my dad." Distractedly Muffy touched her purse. "And I can call on the way home. I've got his cell phone. Dad said if I find it I'm to be very careful and get back to Seattle immediately."

They sped up Garden Street, and Teddy hopped out of the van. "Let me know what happens."

"Sure." Muffy wanted to go.

"And I'm sorry things didn't work out here for you. It would have been lots of fun teaching with you."

Politely Muffy smiled. "I'm sorry, too." But her eyes were saying that she wanted nothing to do with Bellingham or Rainwater State ever again.

At two o'clock the Cold Beverage Contract Committee was treated to free cans of Koolie Cola and brass Koolie Cola paperweights similar in design to the discreet Koolie Cola plaques to be placed on all the weight room equipment Koolie would donate with its proposed 1.3-million-dollar student fitness center. After committee members had drunk their sodas and the Koolie Cola rep had left the room, the Topsie-Cola man came in and passed out brochures of the new digital scoreboard Topsie would install as a signing bonus if Topsie was awarded the campus cola contract for the next ten years.

Teddy tried to pay attention, listening to her supple-tongued colleagues coax extra goodies from the fizzy soda men who alternately addressed the group: racing shells, scanning microscopes, computers, couches in the library, a second scoreboard for the gym. But her heart wasn't in it, and her head was some place else. She kept thinking about Scotto, and he wasn't acting like a man who had poisoned his tenant. Why would he, anyway? Had there been a *Scotto* file at Dedmarsh's she had not seen?

The meeting lasted two hours, after which she went back to the office and started work on her burial caves report. But she still didn't called the police. She was waiting for Muffy.

At five o'clock she looked out the window to see that a Pacific front had moved in, complete with rainclouds and blue air. She packed and drove home, dropping her red canvas jacket at the cleaners. Eating stir-fry next to the telephone, Teddy waited anxiously for news from Muffy. But as darkness settled on the lake, it became apparent that Muffy would not call. Teddy wandered around the house fitfully, missing Muffy, trying to figure out what the Dedmarsh puzzle lacked.

The rain settled everyone into their work. On Tuesday Teddy finished the first draft of her burial cave report but had to put it aside when the Intellectual History class turned in their eight-page essays, "A Comparison of Enlightenment and Romantic Thought." Aurie telephoned from Seattle Tuesday night to remind her that he was on call for the weekend. He grumbled when he heard that she had to stay in Bellingham to attend a school function. And the boxed Virgin stayed exactly where she was.

On Wednesday Teddy spent most of the afternoon reading essays and putting together a talk on Chinook jargon for the Umbrella Club. And as afternoon arrived and it became clear that Our Lady was never leaving, Teddy scheduled Mount Baker Moving Company to come—all they needed was a destination or a hefty deposit for long-term storage. She had called Irene Dedmarsh several times and only got the answering machine.

It was Thursday morning when the weather unraveled, and so did the tangled knot that had tied up her thoughts about Dedmarsh. She was standing in the lounge, holding her first cup of negotiated department brew, ready to go back and begin her writing day. Stalling for a few more minutes, she stood at the bulletin board reading Paula Richman's postcards from India. Three had arrived together. Underneath the greetings from Mysore and Delhi, deep into the twenty-year-old mat of international postings, she spied an older card, newly familiar, a brilliant orange sunset behind a London bridge.

Unpinning the India cards, she took down the picture of the bridge and turned it over. Dedmarsh, from two summers ago: *"Greetings. Remodeling at the British Museum makes endeavor twice as difficult. Can recommend everyone wait until it's finished before coming to London. Best regards, Ira Dedmarsh."* Above, in six-point type, was the notation: *"Waterloo Bridge is the best place in London to watch the sun set over Westminster. From here, you can also see the last rays of sunlight bounce off the City spires."*

Waterloo. And Irene had had a small stack of them on her clothes dryer. Waterloo.

Teddy clutched her coffee mug and scurried to her office. Punching in the number of Mountainview Care Center, she asked for Irene. As she said the name, a freezing silence deadened the phone lines. Finally the receptionist answered, "I'm sorry, Mrs. Dedmarsh no longer works here."

Teddy breathed into the phone. "Could you tell me why she left?"

"I'm sorry. All I know is that she was asked to take

a leave of absence. May I refer you to our supervisor?"

Who would tell her the same thing. "No. No, thank you." Teddy was on her feet before she had hung up the phone. Locking the office, she trotted down to the faculty lot. Minutes later, she was driving out of the Bellingham basin, up onto the fertile Nooksack plain. The Canadian mountains sparkled cadmium white against the muted sky, and green hay fields rippled heavy warnings that they would soon fall over. The sewer work was closer to Irene.

Out in the strawberry fields Irene's car was in front of the closed garage. She was home. Teddy rolled up the long drive, got out, and knocked on the door. From the bedroom windows next to the front porch came hurried whispers in Spanish. Teddy waited. No one answered the door. She knocked again. And waited.

Finally Irene opened the door about ten inches, bracing it with her foot. "I'm sorry. I was sleeping." She was wearing a housecoat, and her hair was uncombed. Her face was putty-gray. "What can I do for you?"

"Irene. I didn't mean to disturb you, but I've been calling all week and couldn't get you, and then I called the Care Center and they said you weren't working there anymore."

"That's right. I'm taking a leave of absence."

"Are you all right?"

Irene flinched. "I'm fine. I have a lot of personal business to take care of. I'm going to sell the house, and somebody's already making an offer on that crazy cabin of Ira's out on Gilbert Island." She clutched her bathrobe so tightly her knuckles were white. "You still have the statue in your office. I need to get the return address from you so we can ship it back to Italy."

Teddy shifted her weight. "Yes, the statue, too. But what I came about is something else. When you gave me my deck shoes the other day, there was a little stack of postcards on your dryer. They were all the same scene, a bridge in London at sunset."

"Those were Ira's. I gave all that to the police."

"I believe they were of the Waterloo Bridge."

"Possibly, I couldn't tell you."

"And the police have them now?"

"That's what I just said." Irene looked at something behind the door, anxious to end the interview.

"Mrs. Dedmarsh, I know this is an odd question, but do you know why Ira had so many of the same scene?"

"He bought a bunch in London. Who knows? I never knew what Ira was thinking or what he needed from me or how to even reach him. Ira lived in his own twisted world." Irene exhaled anger then smiled blandly. "Is that all you need? I'd like to go back to bed."

"No, that's fine. Thank you very much."

"And I'll call you about the return address in Italy. Ortega, isn't it?"

"Ortisei?" called Teddy.

"Yes, that's right. I'll call you. Goodbye." Irene closed the door.

Teddy climbed into the driver's seat and turned the car around. Out on the road she took a deep breath and the image of the sweet, overweight Hispanic boy flashed in her brain. Carlos? That would explain a leave of absence, wouldn't it? And he was Irene's lover. Teddy clutched the steering wheel. Curiouser and curiouser.

At the crossroads she made a quick decision, swatting on the blinker to turn left, onto the Osnaburg Road and up to Mountainview Care Center. She parked in the lot and went inside to find no one behind the receptionist's desk. *Back momentarily.*

Silently Teddy walked down the hall to the nursing station, where again no one was present. In a few seconds a nurse came out of a patient's room. It was the nurse she had met the other day, Taggert, R.N. The nurse had steel gray hair and a very expensive chrome stethoscope.

"May I help you?"

"Mrs. Taggert, I'm trying to get some information

about my friend Irene Dedmarsh, but I've just been told she's been asked to take a leave of absence."

Stiffly Taggert answered, "That's correct."

"Should I call her here in a few days?"

"Try her at home. I can't imagine she'll be back."

"Ever?" asked Teddy.

"That's correct."

"Mrs. Taggert, I . . . what's the matter? What did she do? Is there some way we can help her?"

Taggert turned, waving to the freshly padlocked medication cabinet. "Not unless you know how to make the meds magically appear back on the shelf."

"The wh—? She was stealing medication?"

"No. Nobody ever said that. Meds were just disappearing on her shift when she was assigned to this end of the hall. And if you'll excuse me, I've already told you too much, we're not supposed to talk about it."

"Thank you. You've been very helpful." Teddy turned on her heel and trotted down the hall.

So there it was: Irene had been stealing heart medication, then slipping into Ira's apartment to sprinkle it on the food. Of course, of course she could do it. A heart patient's wife, Irene knew all about synergies and blood toxicities. She had lived with it for years. Teddy sighed. So now it was just a matter of waiting for the police to announce whatever they would announce. Anger made you do strange things, didn't it? It was frightening to think that anger could kill.

Or was it fear that drove Irene? Fear of poverty and of spending the rest of her life alone and ill-prepared?

Dutifully, Teddy drove to the office and closed the door. She punched words into the keyboard, birthing prose for the rest of the day. *She* would never get caught without a job in middle age, having to follow a man from place to place. On Friday she taught her morning classes, then spent the afternoon grading the Enlightenment/Romantic essays, finishing in the wee hours of Saturday morning. She slept late, waking to a blue sky and a very unrevealing Saturday morning *Tribune*. Teddy scanned the whole paper. What had happened to Irene? There was still no word of her arrest.

Teddy wandered around the condo, reading magazines and cleaning grout, then at noon stripped off the sweats she slept in and hopped into the shower. As soon as she stepped out, the doorbell rang; someone had arrived while she was in the shower and was waiting for her. She dashed downstairs in a bathrobe to find Herb Patchett at the door, his thick champagne hair gleaming in the sunlight like good sheepskin.

"Herb, hi. What can I do for you?"

"Sal and I have strict orders to make sure you get down to Umbrella Club this afternoon. Chop-chop."

Teddy narrowed the opening of the door. "But it's only noon. The Umbrella Club people are supposed to come for me at two."

"Sorry, that'd be us. We have a little business on the way we were hoping you would help us with. Sorry we're so early."

"But I'm not ready yet."

"Oh, no problem. Sally's reading in the car, and I can look around the property. This is a nice little setup here. Mind telling me how much you pay for dues?"

Suddenly angry, Teddy snapped, "I can't remember." She closed the door and stared at her bare feet on the oak. Oh, hell. There was nothing to do but get in the car with them, but this was the *last* time. She slipped on gabardine trousers and a turtleneck, tying a paisley scarf around her neck. Scrambling into her red canvas jacket, fresh from the cleaners, she took a deep breath and opened the door, hoping she looked pleasant.

She buckled herself into the backseat, and Sally turned around, eyes tawny with delight. "Theodore, I'm so glad you came! When Walter Rhodes told us the General Pickett biography was beyond your ability and that you wanted to beg off, I thought we'd never see you again."

Utterly miserable, Teddy looked out the window. Sally cocked her head sympathetically. "This isn't a good time for you, is it, Theodore, with your boyfriend dying and all? You'll have to come visit us down in La Jolla sometime when you feel better."

Teddy popped off the seat. "You're about the third person who's called him my boyfriend. The man who died on Monday was the chairman of my department, not my boyfriend."

Sally smiled knowingly. "That's all right. Walter Rhodes also said he was a very fine person. He also said that you're not too concerned with money and might be willing to barter what you have."

"What *do* I have?"

"Oh, never mind. We can talk about it when you're ready. Remember we have lots of resources."

Teddy lashed out, "I realize that. Are you counting the Kaiser Wilhelm portrait on the roof of your car last weekend? I was wondering if you've had a problem with the authorities?"

Herb swerved then caught himself. "Oh, no, no problem. The county got in touch with us. Turns out we had the sheriff a little worried. I told them we were having old Willie copied full-size at a photography studio and that we'd get it right back pronto. We paid some deposit fees, everything turned out fine."

"So it's going back?"

He narrowed his eyes at her in the rearview mirror. "Oh, absolutely. I'm taking it back this evening when I go see my new beach."

"You found some beachfront?"

"Perfect piece. Not quite on the market, but we'll work things out. As a matter of fact, we were hoping to take you out to see it after the festivities today. Love to get the opinion of a local."

"I don't think I—"

"Oh, don't worry, I was gonna ask Walter Rhodes to help us twist your arm. He seems to do a great job of getting what he needs from the employees." Herb grinned slyly in the mirror. "Am I right, or what?"

Primly Sally folded her hands in her lap. "I am *so* glad you're with us, Theodore. We told Water Rhodes we absolutely had to see you after what happened Wednesday."

Teddy stiffened. "What happened Wednesday?"

"Well, first of all, I wanted to tell you it was your way of thinking that opened my eyes about family history. It's like a miracle."

"What'd I say?"

"Well, when the elderly woman gave me her article about Grandpa George's sword disappearing during the funeral of the poor little Indian boy, I started thinking. If this really happened, and if someone really did steal the sword, then it should still be hanging around someplace. So Thursday morning Herb and I ran a full page ad in the Portland *Oregonian* offering a reward for the return of General Pickett's sword. Phone's been ringing off the hook. It's crazy, people calling in from all over the world. It's even on the Internet."

"How much are you offering?"

"A hundred thousand dollars."

Teddy's eyebrows lifted of their own accord. "At that price, I'd find one myself and to sell it to you."

"Ha-ha." Herb laughed genially. "That's right, exactly. The problem now is that we have to sort the crazies from whoever really has it. We were hoping you could be hired as a consultant, help us sort through this mess."

Teddy stared at a forest clear-cut above the highway. "I'm sorry. I don't know anything about Civil War swords."

"Oh, not the Civil War so much." Herb found her again in the rearview mirror. "That's pretty obvious from picture books. What we need is somebody who knows what the nineteenth century looks like."

Teddy blinked at his acuity. "Yes, the nineteenth century I see in my sleep."

"There you have it. You can tell us whether to throw this guy out the door or hand him a check for a hundred thousand dollars."

"What guy?"

"The guy we're meeting at the Alger Tavern. Turns out, he's right here in town, sounds like he actually has the genuine article. It's one of these exits coming up, isn't it?"

Teddy leaned forward. "I've never done it for money before."

"Don't worry, you'll be fine. We just don't want to look like the country kids we are, right, Sal? Always want to have the big guns on your side."

The Alger Tavern was at a crossroads a mile off the interstate. But it could have been forty years off the interstate, the way it looked. Loggers used it, as did all manner of working folks in the hills south of town.

They parked on the gravel out front and walked into the dark knotty pine room, letting their eyes adjust to the light. The place stank of cigarettes. In a corner booth sat Scotto. On the table before him was a long canvas-wrapped object. In the jukebox Tammy Wynette was still standing by her man. Scotto eyed Teddy fearsomely.

They walked over, and Scotto stood, clearly in pain.

"What's this?" asked Herb. "You all know each other?"

Scotto didn't answer, waiting for Teddy.

Coolly, Teddy turned to the Patchetts. "Our paths have crossed a bit in the past few weeks." She raised her eyebrows. "Mr. Walper has a wonderful old Chinese apothecary chest that a friend of mine was interested in." Innocently she turned to Scotto. "I haven't heard from Muffy Woo this week. Did she decide to buy the chest?"

Scotto crossed his arms. "Practically amazing news. You're not going to believe this, but the chest was stolen from her family pharmacy about three years ago. They have the pictures, insurance company sent up a rep. I was happy to cooperate. I'm strictly above board myself. Licensed and bonded."

Serenely Teddy slid into the booth. "So you didn't actually steal the chest from Dr. Dedmarsh's apartment after he died?"

"I what?"

"He what?"

"No!" Scotto stepped between them and the door. "I didn't do that." He pleaded with his eyes, to keep her on his side. "Dedmarsh was a customer, he was going to buy the chest from me, he was trying it out in his apartment to see if he wanted it. After he died, I went back and got it, so many people walking in and out of there. It was mine to begin with. I bought it at auction in Seattle."

Herb pulled a chair out for Sally. "Well, glad to hear that, my man. I make it a practice to never deal with frauds. And we were very excited when we heard about the provenance on your sword."

"Provenance, yes, sir." Scotto wedged himself into the booth. "Bet you've had imposters coming out the woodwork, eh?"

Herb and Sally smiled at each other. "Like you would not believe."

Sally settled in primly. "One dear little man tried to sell us something brand-spanking-new. It was a Civil War cavalry sword all right, but as Herb pointed out, he hadn't even bothered to try to get rid of the word "Toledo" stamped on the hilt. I thought it was Toledo, Ohio, but it's actually Toledo, Spain. Then for the next two days we were shown the exact same replica with all kinds of things done to it—acid-washed, lemon-washed, beat to hell with a brick."

"That'd be right." Scotto nodded. "Toledo makes the best replication these days. Although Taiwan makes some good ones, too." Serenely he undid the ties of the worn, tea-colored canvas wrap. He pulled back the canvas to show a scabbarded, very old nineteenth-century sword. There was no mistake about the patina of the scabbard—it was mottled black, the steel etched as randomly as algae puddles. With professional care Scotto pulled the sword from the scabbard and laid them side by side. The sword had a billowing hilt, stirrup-shaped, and a wickedly tapering blade upturned near the tip. The steel of the sword itself was old but shiny, its deep wear showing more polishing than actual use. Teddy immediately conjured the image of some poor orderly being given the daily task of cleaning an already bright blade—army make-work.

"Now tell her where you got it," said Herb.

Wide-eyed, Scotto stared Teddy in the face. "It has been in the possession of an old Portland family since 1889. They had it mounted on the wall of the library. Guy I got it from said his grandfather used to play cavalry with it when he was a boy."

"And how'd they get it?" prompted Sally.

Scotto turned to her earnestly. "The collector, my vendor's great-grandfather, bought it from a very unsavory character who lived in the same rooming house as Jimmie Pickett—corner of Sixth and Salmon Streets, downtown Portland. This guy reputedly liked his liquor, and when Jimmie Pickett died, he broke into Pickett's room during the funeral and stole the sword along with the general's letters and some pictures drawn by Jimmie Pickett. Jimmie Pickett was an artist. I don't know if you knew that."

"I did not," said Sally.

"I might be able to get a hold of his pictures for you if you're int—"

"I am *not*. May I pick it up?"

Scotto pulled several pairs of thin cotton gloves from his pocket and handed a pair to Sally. Tugging on the gloves, she picked up the sword by the handle and held it reverently to catch the light. Tears welled in her eyes. Teddy grabbed a pair of gloves and pulled them on quickly. "May I see after you're finished?"

Solemnly Sally took the blade in her hands and handed Teddy the hilt.

Teddy admired it in the golden light of the beer neon. It was an old sword. It was nineteenth-century American. The scabbard was oxidized, the hilt was oxidized, but the blade—always covered, rarely used—was not. That was exactly as it should be. Soft brass wire was wound around the handle to assure good grip. It was nicked randomly, worn, flattened in spots. Teddy held it up close, inspecting the maker's name stamped at the bottom of the blade: "Hartley & Schuyler." Who the heck were they?

"What kind of company was Hartley & Schuyler?"

"Oh, yes, ma'am. Very good."

"Schuyler sounds Dutch." She tried to remember an instance of Dutch settlement in the American South.

"Possibly, yes, ma'am. I could check that for you."

The Dutch were in New York. "Where were Hartley & Schuyler located, Mr. Walper?"

"I'm not certain, ma'am. I could check that for you."

The light went on in Herb Patchett's brain. He leaned forward. "General Pickett was in the Confederacy, you know."

Scotto leaned back. "Yes, okay, that's right. But you have to remember, the Confederate generals all graduated from West Point, and they all kept the same swords their whole lives. I can imagine this sword has seen a lot of action. Mexican War, out here in the Pig War, then of course Gettysburg."

"Gettysburg," breathed Sally.

No, thought Teddy, this sword has seen no action—just polishing. "So you're saying General Pickett had this sword since he graduated from West Point, he used it during the Pig War conflict, then in the Civil War?"

Scotto nodded, wide-eyed. "To my knowledge, that is correct."

Would a Southerner do that? Teddy imagined old

George Pickett secretly slipping away from his Union command at Bellingham to take a boat around South America to join the Confederacy. "Sally, I . . ." She turned instead to Scotto. "Excuse me, Mr. Walper, but Mrs. Pickett can tell you quite a bit about the unusual way General Pickett had to travel back to Richmond in 1860."

Sally understood instantly—and pounced. "That's right! Grandpa George couldn't have left Bellingham carrying his Union sword. To escape he disguised himself as Edward Eldridge, a local man from Bellingham. And this is much too big to hide."

Scotto's eyes went wild with panic. "Edward Eldridge?"

"Edward Eldridge."

"He, um . . ." Scotto was thinking hard. "Well, I bet Pickett sent the sword back separately. You know, packed it up and sent it to Richmond."

"Interesting idea." Teddy peeled off the gloves. "But you would think postal traffic would have been terminated between the western territories and the Confederacy, wouldn't you?" She nudged Herb with her shoulder to indicate she was ready to go. "Mr. Walper, we need to think about this for a while."

Herb stood and pulled Sally gently up by the hand.

Scotto held up the sword, appealing. "I swear this is a genuine American Civil War piece."

Herb leaned over. "I'm sure it is, my man. It's just not General Pickett's."

Scotto's brow furrowed thickly. His face looked like an expensive bulldog's. "But you can't do this. Are you impinging my reputation?"

Teddy stood close to Herb. "I know all about your reputation, Mr. Walper. I even know about your statues aging in the sea caves off Vancouver Island. In fact, I just realized that you almost killed me this weekend. You heard me say I was going out there at Dr. Dedmarsh's apartment the day he was killed. I'm going to call the police."

Scotto's face reddened. He scanned the tavern booths, searching for support. "I—I never tried to *kill* nobody. All I was trying to do was keep you and that ditzy boat blonde off my property. You guys should be happy I'm the one who found you and not the people I work with. My off-shore people aren't as nice as I am. You should be thankful."

"Why, you—" Herb leaned forward, muttering, "I've half a mind to call the police and tell them you're threatening women. And selling misrepresented property at the same time. My friend Walter Rhodes bet money that I'd end up dealing with a scumbag like you when I advertised for the sword. I'd love to drag you over to dinner right now and dump you out to show Rhodes what a real scumbag looks like."

"Oh, Walter Rhodes. I know about him. He's the president of the college. He's got more scumbag than you and I put together. Under a bottom drawer of the apothecary chest, I found the whole translation of what he was doing in Taiwan back then. Walter Rhodes. And Dedmarsh was ready to blab it to anybody who wanted to talk about it, too—all you had to do was ask him."

Teddy ripped furiously, "Dr. Dedmarsh was not blackmailing anybody. And even if he tried and failed, that still doesn't make what you're doing any less contemptible. In fact, I wouldn't be surprised if you killed Dr. Dedmarsh, I wouldn't be surprised at all."

Scotto stared, his face red with fear. No one spoke or moved. They all waited. After a tense moment Scotto grabbed the sword and its tea-colored canvas and padded swiftly out the back exit of the tavern.

Herb went over to peek out a high window into the back parking lot. "I don't see him." He came back to the booth. "Should we call the police?"

"No. I didn't mean that, it just came out," said Teddy. Irene had killed him.

"Are you certain? It certainly had a strong effect." Herb held out an arm to Sally. "Are you okay, Sal?"

"Just fine, Herbert. Thank you." Chin held high, Sally walked with great dignity to the door. Teddy followed. Outside on the gravel, the three of them checked cars in the parking lot, then took deep breaths in relief.

"Snickerdoo, I need a cigarette."

Herb presented Sally with a pack and watched anxiously as she lit up and dragged deeply, taking the cigarette down an inch. After three pulls the cigarette was gone and Herb held out a pack of mints. Sally took one, and they walked to the car. She settled into the front seat. On the road again, Sally reached over and righted Herb's hair, which was slipping off his head. "Well, that's better. Herbert, aren't you proud of me? I knew that sword couldn't be authentic. Grandpa George would never have carried a Union sword, never."

"I'll be damned if I'm going to give away a hundred thousand dollars for the wrong sword." He looked for Teddy in the rearview. "And what was this about blackmailing Walter Rhodes?"

"Nothing. Mr. Walper knows very little about nothing."

"He deals in stolen Asian antiques?"

"That and everything else." Teddy leaned forward to the front seat. "But you know," she said, "I have to tell you I'm worried about the two of you. If someone actually had Pickett's sword to sell, don't you think they would have already approached the Gettysburg Museum or the Richmond Civil War Museum?"

Sally smiled blandly. "That's why I like you, Theodore, you have such good ideas. We're going to take you out to a steak dinner tonight when we go see the new property. Herb, honey, we better step on it if we want to make it to the Umbrella Club."

The crossed the interstate and sped down the valley road, foothills thickly green on both sides. "This reminds me of West Virginia," said Sally. "Of course, I've only visited there." They came to a gravel driveway with captive helium balloons—blue and white—tied to a stone pillar. *Umbrella Club* read the sign.

"Here, Snickerdoo."

Herb looked over. "How you doing, Sal?"

"Fine, Herb."

Herb turned in. They followed the drive down to a rambling lodge on a quiet lake. Behind the lake the Chuckanut Hills rose straight up from the valley floor. They parked in an apple orchard, where just enough trees had been removed to provide parking. "Hurry, Theodore." Sally pressed the wrinkles in her slacks with warm hands. "We told Walter Rhodes we'd have you here fifteen minutes ago."

They walked into the lodge, and Teddy looked out across the valley at the immense green hills. When she looked back she saw that she was alone, the Pickett-Patchetts having been squired away by the Umbrella Club president. Across the room Walter Rhodes stood talking to a group of women in Italian knit pantsuits and high heels. He caught sight of Teddy and raised a hand but indicated with his eyes that he could not get away. Teddy smiled and went over to the bar, asking for a sparkling water. Why was there so much going on? What did she not understand? Waterloo. The apothecary chest. She propped herself on the edge of a bar stool and took out her Chinook note cards. And why the hell was she giving a speech in thirty minutes? Because Dedmarsh wasn't alive, that's why. Immature, bumbling, pathetic Ira Dedmarsh.

A woman came over, holding out her empty wine glass to the bartender. As he filled it, she turned to Teddy. "Hi, I'm Dee Bonilla. Bonilla Leasing and Manufacturing."

"I'm Teddy Morelli, in the history department. I'm the after dinner speaker."

"Oh, good. Whatcha going to talk about?"

"The Chinook trade jargon."

"The what?"

"It was a kind of hybrid language Northwesterners spoke last century, both Indian and white." The woman nodded knowingly. "I dropped a bundle last month at the Yakima Tribal Casino. My rule is a hundred dollars a day—that's it. That's how much you'd spend on a good meal and a movie anyway."

"I would imagine."

The woman moved away, and Teddy went out on the porch to see seafood being barbequed. She joined a group listening to the technical problems of a man who had built the working volcano for the Mirage Hotel in Vegas. Everyone generously offered after-the-fact engineering advice, including several Eastside software designers and a famous Seattle chocolatier. Then they were called to table. Herb and Sally were escorted far away to a table of architects, developers, and C. V. Jackson, the man who had built thirteen malls on the interstate. Teddy stood off uncertainly until Walter Rhodes beckoned her to his round table for six.

"Good," he said. "I need you close when I introduce your talk. You're going to talk for about fifteen minutes, right?" He gestured to a couple standing behind their chairs. "Dr. Morelli, this Jake and Maryanne Powers. Jake is with Boeing. Maryanne runs the Eastside social scene with a firm but velvet-gloved hand."

Maryanne Powers slapped him playfully on the arm. "Walter, stop it."

They shook hands, and Rhodes gestured to the next couple. "And this is Kingsley and Margot Mosse. Mosse Maritime Service."

"Oh, yes." Teddy put out a hand. "The tugboat family."

Kingsley Mosse brightened at being recognized.

"Dr. Morelli teaches in our history department."

"How do you do."

They all sat down to a salad of pine nuts and unusual

greens. Rhodes leaned over. "Did the Patchetts buy the sword?"

"No. It was a Union sword, as far as I could tell."

"I knew it! I hope you don't mind my sending them over. When they told me about the ad in the Portland *Oregonian*, I knew somebody had to put on the brakes." Rhodes smiled merrily. "Can't have them leaving good money all over town. Not till we've got ours."

"Well, I didn't mind going with them, but what I do mind is that Mrs. Patchett said you're the one telling everybody Dr. Dedmarsh was my boyfriend. It's making it awfully hard to face people when they talk about the murder."

"I said what?" Rhodes sniffed thoughtfully and stared off into middle space. "I can't even imagine what Sally misunderstood. That's not a topic I would ever discuss with the Pickett-Patchetts. Pass the salt, would you, please, Professor?"

Teddy passed the two shakers. "I don't think I would discuss anything about my personal life with Herb Patchett. He seems like he could find a way to use every fact he's ever learned in his wheeling and dealing."

"That's very observant of you, Professor Morelli. As a matter of fact, now that we've got a preliminary Pickett Scholars deal on paper, I should probably tell you that I don't think all the brouhaha about General Pickett is very important to Herb Patchett at all. We just have to act like it is."

He read the inquiry on Teddy's face. "You see, from what I've observed of Herb Patchett's way of operating, he simply likes to keep Sally out there attracting attention to herself so he can go do all that wheeling and dealing in the background. While we're all in a dither over Sally, who knows how much he's been buying and selling on the sly?"

"So the whole General Pickett thing"—Teddy swallowed. "You knew all the time it was just going to go away?"

"No, not go away. Not like that. Our job was to keep moving on it until Sally herself dropped out. I'm sorry the whole thing has been so difficult for you. I truly apologize. They really had me over a barrel." He used his napkin and sampled the beautiful red wine poured by a hovering waiter. "How could you tell the General Pickett sword was fake?"

"Couple of ways. It looked to be from a New York manufacturer, and we had reason to suspect the dealer in the first place. He deals in historical replicas. He's the man who manages Dr. Dedmarsh's apartment building."

"Apartment building?" Rhodes looked puzzled. "Oh, yes. I keep forgetting. I always think of Ira out there in the county with Irene."

A splendid lunch was served: grilled shrimp and salmon dripping lime marinade, sautéed vegetables, and peaches garnished with toasted hazelnuts. The garlic mashed potatoes were superb, and the luscious wines were from the Frateracelli Family Vineyards, two generations of whom were in the room. Talk through dinner was what had happened to everyone with their Y2K problems. Then Kingsley Mosse told the story of the homeless man who still paddles around Lake Union warning everyone about the affinity of the Antichrist for years with zeros. Across the table Maryanne Powers took a sip of wine and shuddered. "What is the Antichrist? It's such an ugly, vicious word."

"I think it's a pretty old idea, honey. As I remember, Martin Luther talked about the Antichrist."

Older than that, thought Teddy. But she was swallowing potatoes, so fellow historian Walter Rhodes picked up the ball. "It's a very old idea, Maryanne, certainly older than Martin Luther. As I recall, the first Antichrist was mentioned in the Bible. Character named Simon Magus, who thought he was godlike and tried to fly."

Everyone chewed and swallowed, nodding.

"As a matter of fact, Jake"—Rhodes turned to the

Boeing executive—"here's one to take back to work with you. I know about this nut here in town who thinks Boeing is the next Antichrist. Know why?"

"Oh, dear. I can already tell I don't want to get mixed up in this."

"He thinks you guys are full of bull. Boeing only *thinks* they can fly."

Teddy lifted her head, startled. Boeing? Antichrist? Where had she heard that before? She stopped chewing and went numb all over. President Rhodes *had* been to Dr. Dedmarsh's apartment, no matter how many times he denied it. Had he forgotten it was across the hall from Dedmarsh that he had seen the reference to Boeing, Simon Magus, the Antichrist? President Rhodes was a China scholar; Dr. Dedmarsh had been a China scholar, too. And what Scotto had just told her was true: Dedmarsh *was* blackmailing Rhodes; whatever Dedmarsh had set in the trap, blackmail on Rhodes had worked.

"Excuse me, please." She pushed back her chair and walked stiffly out of the room. When she was out the front door, she started jogging, then glanced down the wooded drive. No! Go back inside with the people! She turned to run back inside and smashed right into President Walter Rhodes. "Aagh!"

In one motion he stuffed a green dinner napkin in her mouth and picked her up around the waist, carrying her under his arm like a rag doll. Instantly he was off the driveway and into the apple orchard full of cars. The napkin was too deep. She gagged. He stuffed it farther in and she bit hard.

"Ouch, dammit!"

He pulled out his hand and swung her body around like Playing Statues in the orchard. Her head thunked against a tree—blinding brown. She stopped fighting. She waited for her vision to return. He dumped her on her back on the ground. Her eyes would work in a minute, just a minute. She worked her tongue and reached for the napkin, trying to get up. Rhodes dropped down on her chest like a schoolyard bully. Stuffing the napkin gingerly back in, he slapped her angrily when she tried to bite him. Clamping his big hand over her mouth, Rhodes held the sides of her jaw viselike, picking her up and dragging her backward through the apple trees. She screamed into the napkin. A high-pitched squeak came out. With clawing fingers she tried to tear his hand off her mouth. She pulled one of his fingers to her teeth and tried to bite. Angrily he clutched her jaw with both hands and clanged her forehead against an S.U.V. Her vision flashed white, she couldn't see. She kicked him.

"Little b—" With his knee he rammed her in the ass. Her tailbone hammered up into her skull. Her whole skeleton seemed to be separating from her skin. Something was terribly bruised or broken. Scared witless, she stopped fighting. Still clamping her jaw with his right hand, he picked her up again around the waist and carried her toward the president's plush maroon sedan. Good! He would not be able to open the trunk and still use both hands on her. She would scream, she would pull free. She went limp, waiting for her chance.

Magically, the car trunk popped open. The keyless remote keychain was in his left hand; it had been there the whole time. She twisted viciously, struggling. He held her cheekbones in a vise. Pain shot into her temples. She struggled, and he smashed her against the back bumper, then used her whole body to open the trunk the rest of the way. He slung her inside and climbed in on top of her. Sitting on her chest, he hunched forward, holding his hand over her jaw, her head between his thighs. It was the most astonishing thing that had ever happened to her.

13

Someone was bound to come. They couldn't all just stay in the dining room. She worked the napkin up with tongue and mouth. It had to come out of her throat.

With his hand, Rhodes leaned heavily on her upper jaw. He reached into his coat pocket, coming up with a turquoise spritzer bottle, the kind sold with travel accessories at the drug store. His body was so heavy her ribs were bending. She exhaled and his weight collapsed her chest. She couldn't fill it again. She squirmed to breathe.

"Hold still." With his knees he squeezed her head, positioning his finger on the spray tip.

"Uummph."

"Shut up." He pushed the tip of the spritzer up her nostril and squeezed. Nothing happened. He squeezed again. "And don't worry about the Umbrella Club. I just told them about your problem with panic attacks and depression since your boyfriend died." He squeezed the spritzer again. "I'm helping you call a cab, then I'll go back in and help folks enjoy the rest of the afternoon." Still nothing came out of the bottle.

She worked her mouth, making saliva, chewing the napkin into a sodden ball. She stared bug-eyed at the spray bottle, horrified at what it might contain.

"Well, damn it." Rhodes held the bottle up into the

air and squeezed the tiny mister. "Remind me to give this a trial run next time. And don't worry, you won't feel a thing. Just a little sedative called Versed. Most people take it IV, but we're gonna go nasal this time." He kept working the pump. Finally it spritzed a misty cloud into the air. "There we go."

Tightening his knees against her skull, he pressed harder on her mouth and sprayed Versed up her nose. She blew out her nostrils, he pumped. She blew out more. He inserted the spray tip directly into her nostril and pumped. She blew again. But she had to breathe in. She breathed. He pumped. Her sinuses stung with the liquid surprise, Versed trickled down her throat. She collected the drug in the back of her mouth and pressed it with her tongue onto the wet napkin. He sprayed and sprayed again. She had to breathe, she breathed. She was drowning! It was coming down her nose too fast. Panicky, she swallowed the liquid as fast as it trickled in. She sniffed in to get rid of it. He sprayed more. She tried to blow out, but he caught her each time she breathed in. Sniff and spray, sniff and spray. He must have emptied the whole bottle. He waited. She could see him staring, watching her. He waited more. But it didn't matter any longer, did it? She would be quiet now. She was his good little girl. Couldn't he see she was a good little girl?

They were moving. A road. She was in his trunk, cold. Had hours gone by? Her cheek was prickly against the carpet. Up above glistened the red jewel of his center brake light. White daylight streamed in from a row of vents inside the back window. Beside her face, a wet cloth—the green napkin. And the chain was cold. What chain?

She moved silently so he would not know she was awake. The chain was on her left wrist, like a handcuff. It *was* a handcuff, but her right hand was free. She tried to stretch her body. Damn. The handcuff was linked to her left ankle. She was hog-tied, one arm and one leg, like a steer at the rodeo.

She listened with her whole body. The road was quiet and paved. A pebbly asphalt, like a two-lane county road, but there was a wet forest smell coming in, not the farmland, with its sunny air and barnyard scents. Where were they? She waited, hoping for a town, an intersection, some people. They kept driving. Why wasn't her mouth gagged? She was going to yell at the first crowded intersection, didn't he know? Above her the sparkling red brake light had a cluster of black-taped wires dangling from it. She rolled onto her back and yanked the wires with her free hand. A round, clear light bulb came down. Maybe a policeman would stop them now. Or better yet . . .

She rolled back onto her side, facing the rear of the car. On the wall was the small plastic door to his tail lights. A policeman would really notice if these were out. The tail light door had a twist-off handle. She turned it, and the whole little door fell off. She caught it as it landed and stared at the clustered wires fed to various lights. A round white light. She yanked. A square red one. She yanked. A tiny orange circle—must be the blinker—she yanked again. Then a rectangular white one. All the lights on the left side. That should attract attention. She'd do the other side, too.

It was hard to move around, the way she was chained. She tried to sit up, head against her chest, but the car banked on a curve, and she fell over, bumping her head. She lay still, hoping he would misread the sound. Flopping over to her other side, she twisted in a semicircle, trying to position herself in front of the right tail light housing. Suddenly he braked, putting on the right blinker—it flashed behind the plastic door. He turned off onto crunchy gravel, and her heart sank. Gravel was remote, isolated. He braked. They were stopping!

Silently she spun around to her position on her right side, head in front of the left brake lights. The plastic housing was still off. She propped it up so he wouldn't see she had tampered with it.

He turned off the engine and sat silently in the driver's seat. Teddy listened, too. Birds. A crow. After a few minutes he opened the door and got out, crunching around to the back of the car. Teddy closed her eyes and went limp. The bright daylight almost made her flinch, but she drew calm behind her eyes, pretending she wasn't there. Relax and breathe. Relax and breathe.

Rhodes reached in past her and pulled something out of tissue paper—the sweet leather smell of new shoes. He weighed down the car as he leaned against the back bumper, changing out of his dress shoes, tossing them over Teddy into the far recesses of the trunk. Teddy peeked. Trees against the sky, the wet smell of forest. They were someplace very isolated.

He moved, and she closed her eyes. She felt his body over her, reaching past. She willed her eyes quiet behind her lids. He pulled out a canvas lump, which he buckled onto his body. Then a woolly shirt. He threw his sports coat past her. Then suddenly he picked her up around her waist and turned her over to her left side. Poking his head up under her belly, he grunted and lifted her onto his shoulders. Her back scraped the trunk lid as he tried to stand. He drew back carefully, then stood erect. She was on his shoulders in a fireman's carry, her arm and leg neatly bound together so he didn't even need to use his hands. He jostled her to move the weight around. "Umm." Then he slammed the trunk lid. With great woodsman's strides he started across the parking lot. Teddy opened her eyes.

They were in a damp forest clearing, a graveled trail-head, she had no idea where. He started up a wide beaten path, uphill. He was actually going to carry her? She slumped as heavily as possible to make dead weight.

"I know you're awake." He sniffed. "It doesn't matter. There's nobody within ten miles."

Eyes wide open, Teddy watched the moving patch of

earth and the side of his leg. She contemplated her next move. She was in a great deal of pain. The hamstrings in the back of her left leg were pulled too far forward, and he jabbed her solar plexus with his shoulder at every step. Finally she said, "Where are we?"

"On our way up to Alder Lake. Not that it matters."

She knew it. It was a pristine mountain pond not far from Bow Lodge, up on the east slope of Chuckanut Mountain. "You can't drown me. Bodies float, even if you tie them down."

He chuckled. "No, Professor, the overlook. Everyone already knows how depressed you've been over Ira Dedmarsh's death. What'll baffle them next month, when they find your body, is why you had Lanoxin in your pocket when you jumped off the cliff." He inhaled vigorously. "I love a mystery, don't you?"

She watched her small patch of earth. He was a practiced walker, using the muscles of his thighs and rear to do the work. His orange leather hiking boots were new and cheap. He would discard them as soon as he was done. She contemplated her options. She couldn't run chained like this. If she screamed, he would beat her to shut her up. Being heavy seemed like her best shot. He couldn't possibly make it up the mountain this way, he just couldn't. She slumped. In response he straightened his back and walked steadily uphill for twenty minutes. There had to be people up at the overlook. There just had to! Then her heart sank. No, he wouldn't have come here if there had been cars in the parking lot.

In a while they came to a footbridge over a sparkling stream. He grunted. He liked the place, with long views up and down the path. Leaning over, he dumped her on the ground and stood, working the kinks out of his neck. She strained against her bonds, scrambling into a sitting position. Craning her neck up, she watched the back of his green jacket. He pulled a water bottle out of his waist pack and squirted water into his mouth. She worked her way unsteadily onto her feet, left wrist still bound to her ankle, and galumphed a few pathetic steps—Quasimodo. "May I have some water?"

"No." He punched in the bottle's top. "I'm going to need it all."

She gestured to the stream. "What happens if I drink this?"

"Giardia. Suit yourself. You don't have anything to worry about." He zipped his waist pack emphatically. Crouched forward, Teddy dipped her right hand into a little pool. She sucked water from her hand, dipping over and over. She stole a glance up, then sucked some more.

"Get up, we need to go."

She slumped on the ground. "I can't. My chest is bruised where your shoulder's jabbing me. They'll find it."

"No, they won't." He pulled her up to her feet. "Nobody's going to notice another bruise after your fall." She was hunched over in an arch, unable to stand. He poked his head under her torso and lifted her up. A hundred and ten pounds was not enough. She hated him with a blue rage. She hated being small.

They walked still higher, then came to flat land, a boggy marsh. Yellow shafts of skunk cabbage bloomed in the black muck, and brown uncurling ferns dotted the fen like wildflowers. He came to a fork in the path and took the right fork. She let out an ear-piercing scream.

He didn't respond. Finally he said, "Do that again, and I'll tape your mouth."

She watched the dirt skim by. Why hadn't he taped her mouth in the first place? Because of the stickum on the tape. He didn't want any marks on her body. She screamed again, weakly.

"That's better," he said. "I was wondering if I was going to have to be a son of a bitch." He walked.

"You didn't need to kill him. Dedmarsh was harmless."

"On the contrary. Dedmarsh was entirely evil and very, very destructive. I'd needed to kill him three weeks after I arrived at Rainwater, when I started writing him checks for twenty-eight hundred dollars a month. That's how much it's been costing me to stay president here. I haven't liked it one bit. And I'd still be up in my office, writing those checks, if Dedmarsh hadn't had the great good sense to move out of his house two months ago. No way to get to him out there in the county with Irene. Too many nosy people around."

"But why'd you kill him? He didn't have anything on you."

"Stop playing the fool, Professor. You know perfectly well what's in that file."

"I don't! I swear I don't. He didn't even have one on you."

"Good try, but I knew you'd seen it the minute you said that over the phone."

"I haven't seen it! I don't know what it is. It's a secret, whatever it is."

He walked a few more strides. "What you need to understand about the excellent Ira Dedmarsh is that he just barely escaped jail himself a few times back there in Taiwan. He wasn't exactly God's gift to womankind himself. Here's a safety tip for you when you're traveling in Asia, Professor: don't think you can play by the same rules in a foreign country that the people there use themselves. Whole different set of rules for the Big-nose Foreigners."

"I don't know what you're talking about."

"Don't you?"

Desperately Teddy tried, "Jocelyn Woo knows, too. She knows even more than me."

"But we got rid of Jocelyn Woo, didn't we? Too bad we had to trash her career. And you, too—almost lost my lunch when you said he kept files on everybody but me. Nervy little bitch, make a good academic. But that's when I knew the two of you were lying. It was just a matter of time till you decided you could pull the same dumb nonsense as Dedmarsh. Then I pick up her teaching files Monday morning and she's already got it written right there—Waterloo, right on the cover." He gave a mock shudder. "You people have entirely too much free time. Certainly would have been a whole lot easier if you and your dyke friend had just died up there in the sea caves when Scott-Walper-Antiquities-Dealer took your boat."

Dyke friend? Willo? "You and Scott Walper! You're in this together!"

"Hardly," sneered Rhodes. "I went up to Vancouver Island last weekend to knock you off myself—couldn't get a clear shot at you out at Camp Pickett—but what do I find but Scott-Walper-Antiquities-Dealer following you around the Alberni Ditch like a lovesick whale. When I saw his smuggling operation and then what he was trying to do to keep you morons away, all I could do was stand back and cheer. Too bad he was so incompetent. I would have made sure the two of you never came off that island."

Rhodes's shoulder jabbed so far into her diaphragm it was as if she had been punched. She climbed up his shoulder a little for relief. He did not object to the cozier position. She asked, "How did you get Lanoxin into Dedmarsh's food?"

Rhodes walked on silently.

"I know you got a key from Walper's safe. It's broken."

"Very good, Professor. I had my own key made and put Mr. Walper's back."

"When did you get into the apartment? You hardly have any time."

Again he did not answer.

"The landlords meet Monday at noon," she said.

"So does Rotary Club. And you're right, you'd be astonished what you have to do to get a little time with a schedule like mine. Leave campus at eleven-thirty, show up at Rotary at twelve-fifteen. If it weren't for the back stairs at 808 High Street, I'd have been a goner for sure. Ever run into the nutcase across the hall? Tried to hand out religious tracts."

"They'll find out. They'll trace your Lanoxin. Jocelyn Woo knows. She worked in a pharmacy."

"I worked in a pharmacy, too, Professor, did you know that? Parents had a little drugstore in Pittsfield, Mass. Drug Mart wiped them clean out of business." He readjusted her weight. "Tell me, Professor, do you think it's worth it now? Would you do it again, knowing what happens when think you can blackmail and get away with it?"

Teddy squirmed forward. "But I didn't do anything! I don't even know what Waterloo is."

"Really? Think about it harder, you'll get his pun. You can't imagine the nightmares those London post-cards gave me when he didn't think the check was coming fast enough." He padded down the dark path, coming out into the bright light of Alder Lake. The path skirted the west shore, and Teddy watched his boot sink in the soft mud over and over. How could Rhodes possibly get away with this? He couldn't, someone would find him out. But that certainly wouldn't help her.

He followed the trail up and veered off west, coming out onto the windswept south side of the mountain. He followed the path, ridge-running around the bare sand-stone flank. Faraway rushing noises filled the air, and down below—far down below—Interstate 5 snaked through the green valley. Her head hit an outcropping of sandstone on the upper slope. "Ouch!"

"Sorry, there." At the next outcropping he twisted to avoid thumping her head. The path veered around a bend and out onto a wide sandstone ledge. Unceremoniously, he dumped her next to the cliff wall and staggered out to sit on a boulder. She had not realized he was so tired.

She scrambled to sit up. Directly below was Lake Samish, its suburban ring of emerald lawns and white roofs clear as day. Beside the lake was the interstate, some headlights already beaming yellow in the late afternoon. Out on the rock Rhodes panted and squirted water into his mouth. He did not take his eyes off her. "I think what we'll do to get the cuff marks off is unlock them and sit on you a while. Can't have marks on the body, can we?"

The key to the handcuffs was in his waist pack. Or his pocket. Down below, the highway sounded like faraway ocean. In one last effort she struggled up and hobbled away. On his feet instantly, he pushed her over again. "Scream on me. See what happens."

She screamed. He kicked her, but kicked into the handcuffs, which took the brunt. She slid across the sandstone ledge.

"Gonna do it again?" He hovered over her.

A large rock came rolling down from above. It hit the ledge, bounced, and tumbled down the hill. They both watched in amazement. Seconds later they heard it smash far below. Rhodes craned his neck to search the hillside above. Nothing moved.

Satisfied, Rhodes pulled a tiny set of cylindrical keys from his pocket. Clasping them tightly, he squatted, pressing both knees on her rib cage.

"Uuuh!" The air jolted out of her.

"I'm not that heavy."

Yes, he was. "I can't breathe."

"What a wuss. I would never have passed tenure on a wuss like you." He fingered the keys to get one in position.

A huge rock, big as a desk, tumbled down two feet away. "Jesus!" Rhodes stood and eyed the hillside fearfully. "Jesus!" Another rock followed. Rhodes dashed out of the way to avoid another tumbling rock. It landed behind Teddy and rolled onto her lower legs, pinning her to the ledge. In fetal position, she tried to cover her head. "Jesus! Someone's up there."

A horrible roar sounded on the hillside above—*aaargh*, deep and moaning, an animal in pain. Then grunting like she'd never heard, a pig in Dolby Sound. Rocks rolled down onto the ledge.

Pacing, Rhodes eyed the situation. He stared at her, her legs pinned to the ledge. Another boulder rested against her back. Half-heartedly, he tried to roll the rock off her calves, but would not squat down to actually do the work. Another boulder came crashing down several feet away. He glanced up, furious at whomever was above.

Another rock rolled down. He avoided it easily by stepping away. *Aaargh*, came the roar. Uncertain, Rhodes looked up and down the path. Quickly he tried to shove the boulder off Teddy again. Her legs had lost all feeling. Then Rhodes stood, looked up and down the path, and took off downhill. Teddy looked up to see his green shirt disappear around the cliff. She tried to prop herself up.

Seconds later there was a tramping down the hillside. Herb Patchett hopped down onto the ledge, Sally instantly followed.

"Theodore, my goodness!" Sally dropped to her knees, weakly trying to move the rocks. "Are you all right?"

14

"Herb, honey, help me get this rock off her legs."

Patchett dropped to his bottom and put both feet up on the TV-sized rock. "I'm sorry. I was trying . . . It's an old moonshiner's trick from West Virginia. I didn't know if he had a gun."

Sally darted an alarmed look at Herb and he explained, "I'm the one from West Virginia. Sal is pureblood Richmond." Herb rolled the rock off Teddy's legs, and they all looked at the damage. Deep purple grooves were imprinted in the soft muscles in her calves.

"Can you stand, Theodore?"

"No!" Suddenly furious—at the Patchetts, at the whole world—she lifted her handcuffed arm and leg. "And there's no way to get me off this mountain, either. And you're not going to leave me here."

"You're angry, Theodore. I would be, too. Herb, honey, go get the cell phone. I left my purse up in the bushes." Sally glanced down the path to make sure Walter Rhodes had not come back. "What an awful man. I couldn't believe what I was seeing! At the barbecue we watched him follow you out, and when he came back, we didn't believe a word about the taxi—I tried to call one this week to go sight-seeing, and they told me Bellingham taxis won't leave the city limits. So we thought, oh, these people are lovebirds, they're having a fight, why didn't they tell us? But after lunch, we came out, and you weren't in the van. And Herb knew you couldn't have walked back to town. So he started looking at the scuff marks in the parking lot, and he put it all together—he said you were in the trunk." Sally leaned forward conspiratorially. "Don't tell anybody, but Herb's daddy is the biggest moonshiner in Alderson, West Virginia. He knows his woods and his tracking."

Herb Patchett landed heavily on the sandstone ledge, skidding to a stop on his knees, holding out the cell phone to his wife. He examined Teddy wryly. "Sorry we didn't call for help sooner. At first we just didn't want to interfere. Even after I knew Rhodes had you in the trunk, when you were pulling out his tail lights, we still thought this might be some sort of game the two of you were playing."

Teddy growled.

"Herb, honey, do you know what? She doesn't have Grandpa's cavalry gloves after all. That was just the way Walter Rhodes made us keep an eye on her."

Teddy barked hoarsely, "President Rhodes told you I had General Pickett's cavalry gloves?"

The Pickett-Patchetts ignored her. Herb asked his wife, "But Sal, why'd he need us?"

"To know where he could always find her, honey. That's why he was so fussy about keeping track of our schedule."

"Well, I'll be damned. What a son of a bitch."

Sally brandished the cell phone in her perfectly manicured hand. "Theodore, do you have 911 here?"

"Yes," snapped Teddy.

"You're angry, aren't you, Theodore. I would be, too."

Late that night a police car dropped Teddy off and waited while she unlocked the door. She waved goodbye bravely as she entered. Then she closed the door and bawled. Call her mother, call Aurie—she needed somebody in the house. She stumbled over to the telephone and saw that her phone light was blinking. She pressed the button.

"Hello, Teddy? This is Muffy. I know this is entirely off the wall, but you said the president of the college was named Walter Roads, didn't you? Well, *lu* is 'road' in Chinese, and the visiting professor in Taiwan who tortured his housemaid was named Wah T'e Lu. Wa-ter Roads? Maybe he spells it with an 'h' but it's still a pretty good Chinese transliteration. I'd use it. Maybe you could play around with it for a while, see what you think. Only thing I could think of was maybe Dedmarsh was blackmailing President Roads about the housemaid and Roads decided to kill him. I don't know. Anyway, I'll be up Sunday afternoon for my clothes, if that's convenient. Call me back when you can. See ya." The phone chirped.

POSTSCRIPT

June 12

Teddy stood at the edge of the church parking lot watching Aldo maneuver the huge silver Land Yacht onto the empty basketball court. She smoothed her cotton sweater over her slacks, feeling terribly underdressed for the occasion.

Hispanic women in gorgeous finery paraded into the church. In pointed high heels and sexy seamed stockings, they bent down to hold the hands of doll-like little girls in fantastic party dresses complete with white lacy socks and black Mary Janes. Behind the women walked the men, sedately dark-suited, carrying shining little boys in white tuxedos. Joy hung bell-like over church; the pride was palpable.

Across the parking lot Aldo and the twins climbed down from the Land Yacht and locked the door. Aldo looked like he belonged here, dark-haired, brown-eyed, fresh haircut, wonderfully fit. He was wearing his red satin Arawak jacket and a black tie. The twins, like Teddy, were underdressed in neat slacks and sensible shoes. Teddy smiled as they approached. "When are you getting on the road?"

"Right after the service," said a twin. "We're leaving from here."

"Do you know where you're going yet?"

Marjorie (or Mae) slipped her arm around Aldo's and leaned cozily against him. "We wanted this guy to see Yosemite first. We couldn't believe he's never been there."

Aldo's brown eyes glowed like a puppy's. "Then we're going to Yellowstone, then to the Grand Canyon."

"No, Aldo. The Grand Canyon first, then Yellowstone."

"That's fine." Aldo nodded. "All those places, fine."

At the top of the steps was Irene Dedmarsh dressed in a rough linen alb. Around her neck was a long stole embroidered in primary colors. *"Buenos tardes,"* she greeted them. *"Buenas tardes, mis amigos."*

Teddy stepped up and smiled brightly. She noticed young Carlos hovering inside next to the holy water font. *"Buenas tardes,* Irene. How are you? I need to introduce some people." She stepped back to let in Aldo and the twins. "Irene, this is my Uncle Aldo Morelli, and these are his friends Marjorie and Mae."

"Oh, yes! The twins." Irene shook hands warmly. "I'm so glad to meet you. The Marthas Guild board of directors can't say enough about how the two of you have revitalized their group. I don't think they had any idea there were so many avenues for outreach in a simple nutrition-based ministry like theirs."

Marjorie (or Mae) still clutched Irene's hand. "Did your friend ever get into the Diabetes Program at the hospital?"

Irene gestured inside at Carlos. "Oh, yes. He's in, and they're paying for his Glucophage. We won't have to be stealing it off the shelves of nursing homes anymore."

"It's a shame when people get dropped through the cracks like that."

"Well Martha's Guild is going to make sure it doesn't happen again—to anybody. They're mortified that there was such a needful ministry here in their own town."

The twin plucked her hand away gently. "Well, I'm

so pleased the congregation is coming together. You've been a big part of that, you know."

"Good luck," said the other twin. "We'll be in touch when we get back from Yellowstone."

"Thank you," said Irene. "You're in my prayers." She turned to Teddy. "And thank *you* for being so understanding about my anger. I'm afraid I've been very destructive with it, I was even sending Carlos into town to spy on Ira in his apartment before he died. That was very, very wrong."

"I'm sure you were under a lot of stress," said Teddy.

"You're very kind to say that." Irene clasped her hands together to let them know they could go.

"Goodbye, Irene. Good luck."

"Thank you, dear."

Teddy, Aldo, and the twins entered the nave, where earnest teenagers in new jeans dutifully gave out programs. "*Gracias,*" said one of the twins, accepting a program. "*Gracias,*" mimicked Teddy.

The programs were formally printed on heavy cardstock, meant to be kept as souvenirs. Tears came to Teddy's eyes as she tried to read the program. And she didn't even know Spanish.

La dedicación del altar
a la Santisima Virgen de Guadalupe

se llevará a cabo en

la iglesia católica de los Santos Pedro y Pablo,
Lynden, Washington,

el sábado 12 de junio a las 6:00 de la tarde

La misa sagrada será ofrecida por

el Arzobispo Allen Burdett de la Arquidiócesis de Seattle
y
el Padre Woody Harmon

Plática por la Diaconisa Irene Dedmarsh

Favor di acompañernos después de la misa en el salón
de la iglesia con el "Guild of Martha."

Marjorie (or Mae) squeezed her arm. "They're nice women, aren't they?"

Discreetly Teddy wiped her eyes. "Who?"

"Martha's Guild. Mae and I are going to join when we get back. I think they always knew Gaudalupe should go on the side altar. They just wanted a reason to love her themselves."

"Do your friends in Mexico really pray to her for weight loss?" asked Teddy.

"Oh, sure, baby, no problem. They use her for everything."

EPILOGUE

July 12

Ms. Jocelyn Woo
Department of History
University of Washington
Seattle, WA

Dear Ms. Woo,

Rainwater State University is pleased you have accepted a Diversity Teaching Fellowship commencing on September 16 of this year. The Search Committee and others who interviewed you June 22 speak very highly of your promise as an instructor and researcher in the field of Asian Studies and Women's Cultural History.

The award of this fellowship includes the following for the coming school year: (1) salary of $33,000 plus benefits; (2) relocation expenses up to $500 for your move to Bellingham; (3) dissertation-related travel funding up to $4,000; (4) joint supervision of your activities by the Chair of the History Department and the Director of Women's Studies; and (5) the Provost's Office will furnish you with a computer. As required by the Internal Revenue Service, relocation benefits will be included in your taxable wages.

This agreement is for the upcoming school year and is renewable for a second year provided that satisfactory progress has been made toward the completion of your degree and that you have been satisfactorily evaluated by both Women's Studies and the History Department. Upon successful completion of your Ph.D, you will be strongly encouraged to apply for any appropriate faculty positions at Rainwater. However, the award of this Fellowship does not obligate either the University to create such a position or you to accept one.

If you accept the conditions of this letter of offer, please sign the enclosed copy and return it to my attention no later than August 10. After that date, this letter will no longer constitute a commitment to these conditions on our part unless extended by mutual agreement. Following receipt of your acceptance, we will proceed with preparation of the contract. We look forward to hearing from you.

Sincerely,

Arvil Handy
Dean of Arts and Science
Rainwater State University

NOTES AND ACKNOWLEDGMENTS

Readers will find no illustrations in William Prescott's classic *History of the Conquest of Mexico*. However, depictions of Spanish voyages of discovery are available in manuscript libraries throughout the West and were here added to Prescott's *History* for reasons of story economy. Inspiration for Uncle Aldo's trek up Puget Sound comes from Harvey Manning, *Walking the Beach to Bellingham* (Seattle, Madrona, 1986). Story inspiration also came from LaSalle Corbell Pickett's 1913 *Pickett and His Men*, (Lippincott, Philadelphia), a work of astonishing chutzpah.

Grateful thanks to Chinese historian Edward Kaplan and Pacific Northwest historian Christopher Friday, both of Western Washington University; Chinese Language and Literature professor Kate Tomlonovic; Spanish speakers Michael Teter and Dr. Nancy Van Deusen; Western literary scholar Roscoe Buckland; Bellingham Police Sergeant Dave Richards; marine services broker John Rich; Canadian Customs inspector Barry R. Joyal; San Juan Island centenarian and historian Etta Egeland (who never had a conversation with Sally Pickett-Patchett and whose fictional opinion about George Pickett's alcoholism is entirely my own); also to National Parks ranger and historian Michael Vouri for use of his article "Raiders from the North," *Columbia Magazine*, Fall, 1997; staff of the Washington State Archives, Bellingham; hydrologists Lynn Buckley and Rob Krebs; Bellingham pharmacist Paul Senuty; Seattle antique weapons specialist Morri Hart; Tveten RV Sales of Fife, WA; Wing Luke Asian Museum of Seattle; Ian Thompson, M.D.; veteran boaters Mel and Barbara Davidson; reference staffs of the Northwest Room of Seattle Public Library, Western Washington University Library, and Bellingham Public Library; reader Anna Mariz; agent Jane Chelius, and Avon Senior Editor Jennifer Sawyer Fisher.

And finally, a pair of General George Pickett's gloves can be seen in son Jimmie Pickett's trunk in the Washington State Historical Museum in Tacoma. General Pickett's sword, however, was indeed stolen from Jimmie's boarding house during his funeral in 1889 and has been missing ever since.